The Seven That Were Hanged
and other stories

LEONID ANDREYEV

The Seven That Were Hanged

and other stories

LEONID ANDREYEV

VINTAGE BOOKS

A DIVISION OF RANDOM HOUSE

New York

Contents

THE SEVEN THAT WERE HANGED
and other stories

THE SEVEN THAT WERE HANGED

I

"AT ONE O'CLOCK IN THE AFTERNOON,
YOUR EXCELLENCY!"

As the Minister was a very fat man, predisposed to apoplexy, and as it was necessary therefore to spare him every dangerous emotion, they took the minutest precautions in warning him that a serious attempt upon his life had been planned. When they saw that he received the news calmly, they gave him the details: the attempt was to be made the next day, at the moment when His Excellency was to leave the house to go to make his report. A few terrorists, armed with revolvers and bombs, whom a police spy had betrayed and who were now being watched by the police, were to meet near the steps at one o'clock in the afternoon, and await the Minister's exit. There the criminals would be arrested.

"Pardon me," interrupted the Minister in surprise. "How do they know that I am to go to present my report at one o'clock in the afternoon, when I learned it myself only two days ago?"

The commander of the body-guard made a vague gesture signifying ignorance.

"At one o'clock in the afternoon, Your Excellency!"

Astonished, and at the same time satisfied with the police who had managed the affair so well, the Minister shook his head; a disdainful smile appeared on his thick red lips; quickly he made all the necessary preparations to pass the night in another palace; in no way did he wish to embarrass the police. His wife and children also were removed from the dangerous premises.

As long as the lights gleamed in this new residence, and while his familiars bustled about him expressing their indignation, the Minister felt a sensation of agreeable excitement. It seemed to him that he had just received, or was about to receive, a great and unexpected reward. But the friends went away, and the lights were put out. The intermittent and fantastic glare of the arc lights in the street fell upon the ceiling and the walls, penetrating through the high windows, symbolizing the fragility of all bolts and walls, the vanity of all supervision. Then, in the silence and the solitude of a strange chamber, the dignitary was seized with an unspeakable terror.

He was afflicted with a kidney trouble. Every violent emotion caused his face, feet, and hands to swell, and made him appear heavier, more massive. Now, like a heap of bloated flesh that made the bed-springs bend, he suffered the anguish of the sick as he felt his face puff up and become almost something foreign to his body. His thought recurred obstinately to the cruel fate that his enemies were preparing for him. He evoked one after the other all the horrible attempts of recent date, in which bombs had been thrown against persons as noble as himself and bearing even higher titles, tearing their bodies into a thousand shreds, hurling their brains against foul brick walls, and knocking their teeth from their jaws. And, at these recollections, it seemed to him that his diseased body was another man's body suffering from the fiery shock of the explosion. He pictured to himself his arms detached from his shoulders, his teeth broken, his brain crushed. His legs, stretched out in the bed, grew numb and motionless, the feet pointing upward, like those of a dead man. He breathed noisily, coughing occasionally, to avoid all resemblance to a corpse: he moved about, that he might hear the sound of the metallic springs, the rustling of the silk coverlet. And, to prove that he was really alive, he exclaimed in a loud and clear voice:

"Brave fellows! Brave fellows!"

These words of praise were for the police, the gendarmes, the soldiers, all those who protected his life and had prevented the assassination. But in vain did he stir about, lavish his praise, and smile at the discomfiture of the terrorists; he could not yet believe that he was saved. It seemed to him that the death evoked for him by the anarchists, and which existed in their thought, was already there and would remain there, refusing to go away until the assassins should be seized, deprived of their bombs, and lodged safely in prison. There it stood, in the corner yonder, declining to leave, and unable to leave, like an obedient soldier placed on guard by an unknown will.

"At one o'clock in the afternoon, Your Excellency!" This phrase came back to him continually, uttered in all tones, now joyously and ironically, now irritably, now obstinately and stupidly. One would have said that a hundred phonographs had been placed in the chamber, and were crying one after the other, with the idiotic persistence of machines:

"At one o'clock in the afternoon, Your Excellency!"

And this "one o'clock in the afternoon" of the next day, which so short a time before was in no way to be distinguished from other hours, had taken on a menacing importance; it had stepped out of the clock dial, and was beginning to live a distinct life, stretching itself like an immense black curtain, to divide life into two parts. Before it and after it no other hour existed; it alone, presumptuous and obsessing, was entitled to a special life.

Grinding his teeth, the Minister raised himself in his bed to a sitting posture. It was positively impossible for him to sleep.

Pressing his bloated hands against his face, he pictured to himself with terrifying clearness how he would have risen on the morrow if he had been left in ignorance; he would have taken his coffee, and dressed. And neither he, nor the Swiss who would have helped him on with his fur coat, nor the valet who would have served his coffee, would have understood the uselessness of breakfasting and dressing, when a few moments later everything would be annihilated by the explosion. . . . The Swiss opens the door. . . . And it is he, this good and thoughtful Swiss, with the blue eyes, and the open countenance, and the numerous military decorations—it is he who opens the terrible door with his own hands. . . .

"Ah!" the Minister suddenly exclaimed aloud; slowly he removed his hands from his face. Gazing far before him into the darkness with a fixed and attentive look, he stretched out his hand to turn on the light. Then he arose, and in his bare feet walked around the strange chamber so unfamiliar to him; finding another light, he turned that on also. The room became bright and agreeable; there was only the disordered bed and the fallen coverlet to indicate a terror that had not yet completely disappeared.

Clad in a nightshirt, his beard in a tangle, a look of irritation on his face, the Minister resembled those old people who are tormented by asthma and insomnia. One would have said that the death prepared for him by others had stripped him bare, had torn him from the luxury with which he was surrounded. Without dressing he threw himself into an armchair, his eyes wandered to the ceiling.

"Imbeciles!" he cried in a contemptuous tone of conviction. "Imbeciles!" And he was speaking of the policemen whom but a few moments before he had called "brave fellows," and who, through excess of zeal, had told him all the details of the attack that had been planned.

Evidently, he thought with lucidity, I am afraid now because I have been warned and because I know. But, if I had been left in ignorance, I should have taken my coffee quietly. And then, evidently, this death . . . but am I then so afraid of death? I have a kidney trouble; some day I must die of it, and yet I am not afraid, because I don't know when. And these imbeciles say to me, "At one o'clock in the afternoon, Your Excellency!" They thought that I would be glad to know about it! Instead of that, death has placed himself in the corner yonder, and does not go away! He does not go away, because I have that fixed idea! To die is not so terrible; the terrible thing is to know that one is going to die. It would be quite impossible for a man to live if he knew the hour and day of his death with absolute certainty. And yet these idiots warn me, "At one o'clock in the afternoon, Your Excellency!"

Recently he had been ill, and the doctors had told

him that he was going to die and should make his final
arrangements. He had refused to believe them; and, in
fact, he did not die. Once, in his youth, he had decided
to put an end to his existence; he had loaded his revolver,
written some letters, and even fixed the hour of his
suicide; then, at the last moment, he had reconsidered.
And always, at the supreme moment, something unexpected may happen; consequently no man can know
when he will die.

"At one o'clock in the afternoon, Your Excellency!"
these amiable idiots had said to him. They had informed
him only because his death had been plotted; and yet he
was terrified simply to learn the hour when it might have
occurred. He admitted that they would kill him some day
or another, but it would not be the next day . . . it
would not be the next day, and he could sleep quietly,
like an immortal being. . . . The imbeciles! They did
not know what a gulf they had dug in saying, with stupid
amiability, "At one o'clock in the afternoon, Your Excellency!"

From the bitter anguish that shot through his heart,
the Minister understood that he would know neither sleep,
nor rest, nor joy, until this black and accursed hour, thus
detached from the course of time, had passed. It was
enough in itself to annihilate the light and enwrap the
man in the opaque darkness of fear. Now that he was
awake, the fear of death permeated his entire body,
filtered into his bones, exuded from every pore.

Already the Minister had ceased to think of the assassins of the morrow: they had disappeared, forgotten in
the multitude of inauspicious things that surrounded his
life. He feared the unexpected, the inevitable: an attack
of apoplexy, a laceration of the heart, the rupture of
a little artery suddenly made powerless to resist the flow

of blood and splitting like a glove on swollen hands.

His thick, short neck frightened him; he dared not look at his swollen fingers, full of some fatal fluid. And though, just before, in the darkness, he had been compelled to stir in order to avoid resemblance to a corpse, now, under this bright, cold, hostile, frightful light, it seemed to him horrible, impossible, to move even to light a cigarette or ring for a servant. His nerves were tense. With red and upturned eyes and burning head, he stifled.

Suddenly, in the darkness of the sleeping house, the electric bell just under the ceiling, among the dust and spiders' webs, became animate. Its little metallic tongue beat hurriedly against its sonorous edge. It stopped for a moment, and then began to ring again in a continuous and terrifying fashion.

People came running. Here and there lamps were lighted on the walls and chandeliers—too few of them for intense illumination, but enough to create shadows.

On every hand appeared these shadows: they arose in the corners and stretched out upon the ceiling, fastening upon all projections and running along the walls. It was difficult to understand where all these taciturn, monstrous, and innumerable shadows could have kept themselves before—mute souls of mute things.

A thick and trembling voice said something indistinguishable. Then they telephoned to the doctor: the Minister was ill. His Excellency's wife was summoned also.

II

SENTENCED TO BE HANGED

The predictions of the police were realized. Four terrorists, three men and one woman, carrying bombs, revolvers, and infernal machines, were taken in front of the steps of the residence; a fifth accomplice was arrested at her dwelling, where the implements had been manufactured and the conspiracy planned. A large quantity of dynamite and many weapons were found there. All five were very young: the eldest of the men was twenty-eight, the younger of the women nineteen. They were tried in the fortress where they had been imprisoned after their arrest; they were tried quickly and secretly, as was the custom at that merciless epoch.

Before the court all five were calm, but serious and thoughtful; their contempt for the judges was so great that they did not care to emphasize their fearlessness by a useless smile or a pretense of gaiety. They were just tranquil enough to protect their souls and the deep gloom of their agony from the malevolent gaze of strangers. Some questions they refused to answer, some they answered simply, briefly, precisely, as if they were speaking, not to judges, but to statisticians desirous of completing tables of figures. Three of them, one woman and two men, gave their real names; two refused to disclose their identity, which remained unknown to the court. In everything that happened they manifested that distant and attenuated curiosity peculiar to people seriously ill or possessed by a single all-powerful idea. They cast swift glances, seized upon an interesting word in its flight, and went back to their thoughts, resuming them at the exact point where they had dropped them.

The accused placed nearest the judges had given his name as Sergey Golovin, a former officer, son of a retired colonel. He was very young, with broad shoulders, and so robust that neither the prison nor the expectation of certain death had been able to dim the color of his cheeks or the expression of happy innocence in his blue eyes. Throughout the trial he twisted his thick blond beard, to which he had not yet become accustomed, and gazed steadily at the window, knitting his brows.

It was the latter part of winter, that period into which, among snowstorms and gray, cold days, the approaching spring projects sometimes, as a forerunner, a warm and luminous day, or even a single hour, so passionately young and sparkling that the sparrows in the street become mad with joy and men seem intoxicated. Now, through the upper window, still covered with the dust of the previous summer, a very odd and beautiful sky was to be seen; at the first glance it seemed a thick and milky gray; then, upon a second examination, it appeared to be covered with azure stains, of an ever-deepening blue, a blue pure and infinite. And because it did not strip itself suddenly, but modestly draped itself in the transparent veil of clouds, it became charming, like one's *fiancée*. Sergey Golovin looked at the sky, pulled at his mustache, winked now one and now the other of his eyes behind the long, heavy eyelashes, and reflected profoundly on nobody knows what. Once, even, his fingers moved rapidly, and an expression of naïve joy appeared upon his face; but he looked around him, and his joy was extinguished like a live coal upon which one steps. Almost instantaneously, almost without transition, the redness of his cheeks gave place to a corpse-like pallor; a fine hair painfully pulled out was pressed as in a vice between his bloodless finger ends. But the joy of life and of the spring was still stronger. A few minutes later the young face resumed its naïve expression and sought again the sky of spring.

Towards the sky also looked an unknown young girl, surnamed Musya. She was younger than Golovin, but seemed his elder because of the severity, the gravity, of her proud and loyal eyes. The delicate neck and slender arms alone revealed that intangible something which is youth itself, and which sounded so distinctly in the pure harmonious voice that resembled a costly instrument in perfect tune. Musya was very pale, of that passionate pallor peculiar to those who burn with an inner, radiant, and powerful fire. She scarcely stirred; from time to time only, with a gesture that was hardly visible, she felt for a deep trace in the third finger of her right hand—the trace of a ring recently removed. With calmness and indifference she looked at the sky; she looked at it simply because everything in this commonplace and dirty hall was hostile to her and seemed to scrutinize her face. This bit of blue sky was the only pure and true thing upon which she could look with confidence.

The judges pitied Sergey Golovin and hated Musya. Musya's neighbor, motionless also, with hands folded between his knees and something of affectation in his pose, was an unknown surnamed Werner. If one can bolt a face as one bolts a heavy door, the unknown had bolted his as if it were a door of iron. He gazed steadily at the floor, and it was impossible to tell whether he was calm or deeply moved, whether he was thinking of something or listening to the testimony of the policemen. He was rather short of stature; his features were fine and noble. He gave the impression of an immense and calm force, of a cold and audacious valor. The very politeness with which he uttered his clear and curt replies seemed dangerous on his lips. On the backs of the other prisoners the customary cloak seemed a ridiculous costume; on him it was not even noticeable, so foreign was the garment to the man. Although Werner had been armed only with a poor revolver, while the others carried bombs and infernal machines, the judges looked upon him as the leader, and treated him with a certain respect, with the same brevity which he employed toward them.

In his neighbor, Vasily Kashirin, a frightful moral struggle was going on between the intolerable terror of death and the desperate desire to subdue this fear and conceal it from the judges. Ever since the prisoners had been taken to court in the morning, he had been stifling under the hurried beating of his heart. Drops of sweat appeared continually on his brow; his hands were moist and cold; his damp and icy shirt, sticking to his body, hindered his movements. By a superhuman effort of the will, he kept his fingers from trembling, and maintained the firmness and moderation of his voice and the tranquillity of his gaze. He saw nothing around him; the sound of the voice that he heard seemed to reach him through a fog, and it was in a fog also that he stiffened himself in a desperate effort to answer firmly and aloud. But, as soon as he had spoken, he forgot the questions, as well as his own phrases; the silent and terrible struggle began again. And upon his person death was so in evidence that the judges turned their eyes away from him. It was as difficult to determine his age as that of a rotting corpse. According to his papers he was only twenty-three. Once or twice Werner touched him gently on the knee, and each time he answered briefly:

"It's nothing!"

His hardest moment was when he suddenly felt an irresistible desire to utter inarticulate cries, like a hunted beast. Then he gave Werner a slight push; without raising his eyes, the latter answered in a low voice:

"It's nothing, Vasya. It will soon be over!"

Consumed by anxiety, Tanya Kovalchuk, the fifth terrorist, sheltered her comrades with a maternal look. She was still very young; her cheeks seemed as highly colored as those of Sergey Golovin; and yet she seemed to be the mother of all the accused, so full of tender anxiety and infinite love were her looks, her smile, her fear. The progress of the trial did not interest her. She listened to her comrades simply to see if their voices trembled, if they were afraid, if they needed water.

But she could not look at Vasya; his anguish was too intense; she contented herself with cracking her plump fingers. At Musya and Werner she gazed with proud and respectful admiration, her face then wearing a grave and serious expression. As for Sergey Golovin, she continually tried to attract his attention by her smile. The dear comrade, he's looking at the sky. Look, look! she thought, as she observed the direction of his eyes. And Vasya? My God! My God! What can be done to comfort him? If I speak to him, perhaps it will make matters worse; suppose he should begin to weep?

Like a peaceful pool reflecting every wandering cloud, her amiable and clear countenance showed all the feelings and all the thoughts, however fleeting, of her four comrades. She forgot that she was on trial too and would be hanged; her indifference to this was absolute. It was in her dwelling that the bombs and dynamite had been found; strange as it may seem, she had received the police with pistol shots and had wounded one of them in the head.

The trial ended towards eight o'clock, just as the day was drawing to its close. Little by little, in the eyes of Sergey and Musya, the blue sky disappeared; without reddening, without smiling, it grew dim gently, as on a summer evening, becoming grayish and suddenly cold and wintry. Golovin heaved a sigh, stretched himself, and raised his eyes towards the window, where the chilly darkness of the night was already making itself manifest;

still pulling his beard, he began to examine the judges, the soldiers, and their weapons, exchanging a smile with Tanya Kovalchuk. As for Musya, when the sun had set completely, she did not lower her gaze to the ground, but directed it towards a corner, where a spider's web was swaying gently in the invisible current of warm air from the stove; and thus she remained until the sentence had been pronounced.

After the verdict, the condemned said their farewells to their lawyers, avoiding their disconcerted, pitying, and confused looks; then they grouped themselves for a moment near the door, and exchanged short phrases.

"It's nothing, Vasya! All will soon be over!" said Werner.

"But there's nothing the matter with me, brother!" answered Kashirin, in a strong, quiet, and almost joyous voice. In fact, his face had taken on a slight color, no longer resembling that of a corpse.

"The devil take them! They've hanged us all just the same!" swore Golovin naïvely.

"It was to have been expected," answered Werner, without agitation.

"Tomorrow the final judgment will be rendered, and they'll put us all in the same cell," said Tanya, to console her comrades. "We'll remain together until the execution."

Silently, and with a resolute air, Musya started off.

III

"I MUST NOT BE HANGED"

A fortnight before the affair of the terrorists, in the same court, but before other judges, Ivan Yanson, a peasant, had been tried and sentenced to be hanged.

Ivan Yanson had been hired as a farm hand by a
well-to-do farmer, and was distinguished in no way from
the other poor devils of his class. He was a native of
Wesenberg, in Esthonia; for some years he had been
advancing gradually towards the capital, passing from one
farm to another. He had very little knowledge of Russian.
As there were none of his countrymen living in the
neighborhood, and as his employer was a Russian, named
Lazaref, Yanson remained silent for almost two years. He
said hardly a word to either man or beast. He led the
horse to water and harnessed it without speaking to it,
walking about it lazily, with short hesitating steps. When
the horse began to run, Yanson did not say a word, but
beat it cruelly with his enormous whip. Drink transformed
his cold and wicked obstinacy into fury. The hissing of
the lash and the regular and painful sound of his wooden
shoes on the floor of the shed could be heard even at
the farmhouse. To punish him for torturing the horse, the
farmer at first beat Yanson, but, not succeeding in correcting him, he gave it up.

Once or twice a month Yanson got drunk, especially
when he took his master to the station. His employer
once on board the train, Yanson drove a short distance
away, and waited until the train had started. Then he
returned to the station, and got drunk at the buffet. He
went back to the farm on the gallop, a distance of seven
miles, beating the unfortunate beast unmercifully, giving
it its head, and singing and shouting incomprehensible
phrases in Esthonian. Sometimes silent, with set teeth,
impelled by a whirlwind of indescribable fury, suffering,
and enthusiasm, he was like a blind man in his mad
career; he did not see the passers-by, he did not insult
them, uphill and down he maintained his furious gait.

His master would have discharged him, but Yanson

did not demand high wages, and his comrades were no better than he.

One day he received a letter written in Esthonian; but, as he did not know how to read or write, and as no one about him knew this language, Yanson, with savage indifference, threw it into the muck heap, as if he did not understand that it brought him news from his native country. Probably needing a woman, he tried also to pay court to the girl employed on the farm. She repulsed his advances, for he was short and puny, and covered with hideous freckles; after that, he let her alone.

But, though he spoke little, Yanson listened continually. He listened to the desolate snow-covered fields, containing hillocks of frozen manure that resembled a series of little tombs heaped up by the snow; he listened to the bluish and limpid distance, the sonorous telegraph poles. He alone knew what the fields and telegraph poles were saying. He listened also to the conversation of men, the stories of murder, pillage, fire.

One night, in the village, the little church bell began to ring in a feeble and lamentable way; flames appeared. Malefactors from nobody knew where were pillaging the neighboring farm. They killed the owner and his wife, and set fire to the house. This caused a feeling of anxiety on the farm where Yanson lived: day and night the dogs were loose; the master kept a gun within reach of his bed. He wished also to give an old weapon to Yanson, but the latter, after examining it, shook his head and refused it. The farmer did not understand that Yanson had more confidence in the efficacy of his Finnish knife than in this rusty old machine.

"It would kill me myself!" he said.

"You're only an imbecile, Ivan!"

And one winter evening, when the other farm hand

had gone to the station, this same Ivan Yanson, who was afraid of a gun, committed robbery and murder, and made an attempt at rape. He did it with an astonishing simplicity. After shutting the servant in the kitchen, lazily, like a man almost dead with sleep, he approached his master from behind, and stabbed him several times in the back. The master fell unconscious; his wife began to cry and to run about the chamber. Showing his teeth, and holding his knife in his hand, Yanson began to ransack trunks and drawers. He found the money; then, as if he had just seen the master's wife for the first time, he threw himself upon her to rape her, without the slightest premeditation. But he happened to drop his knife; and, as the woman was the stronger, she not only resisted Yanson, but half strangled him. At this moment the farmer recovered his senses, and the servant broke in the kitchen door and came in. Yanson fled. They took him an hour later, as he was squatting in the corner of the shed and scratching matches, which continually went out. He was trying to set fire to the farm.

A few days later the farmer died. Yanson was tried and sentenced to death. In the court one would have said that he did not understand what was going on. Without curiosity he viewed the large, imposing hall and explored his nose with a shrunken finger that nothing disgusted. Only those who had seen him at church on Sunday could have guessed that he had done something in the way of making a toilet; he wore a knitted cravat of dirty red; in spots his hair was smooth and dark; in others it consisted of light, thin locks, like wisps of straw on an uncultivated and devastated field.

When the sentence of death by hanging was pronounced, Yanson suddenly showed emotion. He turned scarlet, and began to untie and tie his cravat, as if it were choking him. Then he waved his arms without knowing why, and declared to the presiding judge, who had read the sentence:

"She has said that I must be hanged."

" 'She'? Who?" asked the presiding judge, in a deep bass voice.

Yanson pointed with his finger, at the presiding judge, and, looking at him furtively, answered angrily:

"You!"

"Well?"

Again Yanson turned his eyes towards one of the judges, in whom he divined a friend, and repeated:

"She has said that I must be hanged. I must not be hanged."

"Take away the accused."

But Yanson still had time to repeat in a grave tone of conviction:

"I must not be hanged."

And with his outstretched finger and irritated face, to which he tried in vain to give an air of gravity, he seemed so stupid that the guard, in violation of orders, said to him in an undertone as he led him away:

"Well, you're a famous imbecile, you are!"

"I must not be hanged!" Yanson repeated obstinately.

They shut him up again in the cell in which he had passed a month, and to which he had become accustomed, as he had become accustomed to everything: to blows, to brandy, to the desolate and snow-covered country sown with rounded hillocks resembling tombs. It even gave him pleasure to see his bed again, and his grated window, and to eat what they gave him; he had taken nothing since morning. The disagreeable thing was what had happened in court, about which he knew not what to think. He had no idea at all of what death by hanging was like.

The guard said to him, in a tone of remonstrance:

"Well, brother, there you are, hanged!"

"And when will they hang me?" Yanson asked in a tone of incredulity.

The guard reflected. "Ah! wait, brother; you must have companions; they don't disturb themselves for a single individual, and especially for a little fellow like you."

"Then, when?" insisted Yanson.

He was not offended that they did not want to take the trouble to hang him all alone; he did not believe in this excuse, and thought they simply wanted to put off the execution, and then pardon him.

"When? When?" resumed the guard. "It's not a question of hanging a dog, which one takes behind a shed and dispatches with a single blow! Is that what you would like, imbecile?"

"Why, no, I would not like it!" said Yanson suddenly, with a joyous grimace. "It was she who said I must be hanged, but I, I do not want to be hanged!"

And, for the first time in his life perhaps, he began to laugh—a grinning and stupid laugh, but terribly gay. He seemed like a goose beginning to quack. The guard looked in astonishment at Yanson, and then knitted his brows: this stupid gaiety on the part of a man who was to be executed insulted the prison, the gallows itself, and made them ridiculous. And suddenly it seemed to the old guard, who had passed all his life in prison and considered the laws of the jail as those of nature, that the prison and all of life were a sort of madhouse in which he, the guard, was the chief madman.

"The Devil take you!" he said, spitting on the ground.

"Why do you show your teeth? This is no tea party!"

"And I, I do not want to be hanged! Ha! ha! ha!" Yanson went on laughing.

"Satan!" replied the guard, crossing himself.

All evening Yanson was calm, and even joyous. He repeated the phrase that he had uttered: "I must not be hanged," and so convincing, so irrefutable was it that he had no occasion for anxiety. He had long since forgotten his crime; sometimes he simply regretted that he had not succeeded in raping the woman. Soon he thought no more about the matter.

Every morning Yanson asked when he would be hanged, and every morning the guard answered him angrily:

"You have time enough." And he went out quickly, before Yanson began to laugh.

Thanks to this invariable exchange of words, Yanson persuaded himself that the execution would never take place; for whole days he lay upon his bed, dreaming vaguely of the desolate and snow-covered fields, of the buffet at the railway station, and also of things farther away and more luminous. He was well fed in prison, he took on flesh.

"She would love me now," he said to himself, thinking of his master's wife. "Now I am as big as her husband."

He had only one desire—to drink brandy and course madly over the roads with his horse at full gallop.

When the terrorists were arrested, the whole prison learned of it. One day, when Yanson put his customary question, the guard answered him abruptly, in an irritated voice:

"It will be soon. In a week, I think."

Yanson turned pale; the gaze of his glassy eyes became so thick that he seemed as if asleep.

"You are joking?" he asked.

"Formerly you couldn't await the time, today you say that I'm joking. No jokes are tolerated here. It's you who like jokes, but we don't tolerate them," the guard replied with dignity; then he went out.

When evening came, Yanson had grown thin. His skin, which had become smooth again for a few days, was contracted into a thousand little wrinkles. He took no notice of anything; his movements were made slowly, as if every toss of the head, every gesture of the arm, every step, were a difficult undertaking, that must first be deeply studied. During the night, Yanson lay on his camp bed, but his eyes did not close; they remained open until morning.

"Ah!" exclaimed the guard, on seeing him the next day.

With the satisfaction of the *savant* who has made a new and a successful experiment, he examined the condemned man attentively and without haste; now everything was proceeding in the usual fashion. Satan was covered with shame, the sanctity of the prison and of the gallows was reëstablished. Indulgent, and even full of sincere pity, the old man asked:

"Do you want to see someone?"

"Why?"

"To say good-bye, of course . . . to your mother, for instance, or to your brother."

"I must not be hanged," said Yanson in a low voice, casting a glance sidewise at the jailer. "I do not want to be hanged."

The guard looked at him, without saying a word.

Yanson was a little calmer in the evening. The day was so ordinary, the cloudy winter sky shone in so usual a fashion, so familiar was the sound of steps and conversations in the corridor, that he ceased to believe in the execution. Formerly the night had been to him simply the moment of darkness, the time for sleep. But now he was conscious of its mysterious and menacing essence. To disbelieve in death, one must see and hear the customary course of life: steps, voices, light. And now everything seemed extraordinary to him; this silence, these shades, that seemed to be already the shades of death; already he felt the approach of inevitable death; in bewilderment he climbed the first steps of the gibbet.

The day, the night, brought him alternations of hope and fear; and so things went until the evening when he felt, or understood, that the inevitable death would come three days later, at sunrise.

He had never thought of death; for him it had no shape. But now he felt plainly that it had entered his cell, and was groping about in search of him. To escape it, he began to run.

The room was so small that the corners seemed to push him back toward the center. He could not hide himself anywhere. Several times he struck the walls with his body; once he hurled himself against the door. He staggered and fell, with his face upon the ground; he felt the grasp of death upon him. Glued to the floor, his face touched the dirty black asphalt. Yanson screamed with terror until help came. When they had lifted him up, seated him on his bed, and sprinkled him with cold water, he did not dare open both eyes. He half opened one, perceived an empty and luminous corner of his cell, and began again to scream.

But the cold water had its effect. The guard, moreover, always the same old man, slapped Yanson several times on the head, in a fatherly fashion. This sensation of life drove out the thought of death. Yanson slept deeply the rest of the night. He lay on his back, with mouth open, snoring loud and long. Between his half-closed eyelids appeared a whitish, flat, and dead eye, without a pupil.

Then day, night, voices, steps, the cabbage soup, everything became for him one continuous horror that plunged him into a state of wild astonishment. His weak mind could not reconcile the monstrous contradiction between, on the one hand, the bright light and odor of the cabbage, and, on the other, the fact that two days later he must die. He thought of nothing; he did not even count the hour; he was simply the prey of a dumb terror in presence of this contradiction that bewildered his brain: today life, tomorrow death. He ate nothing, he slept no more; he sat timidly all night long on a stool, with his legs crossed under him, or else he walked up and down his cell, with furtive steps. He appeared to be in a state of openmouthed astonishment; before taking the most commonplace article into his hands he would examine it suspiciously.

The jailers ceased to pay attention to him. His was the ordinary condition of the condemned man, resembling, according to his jailer, who had not experienced it himself, that of an ox felled by a club.

"He's stunned; now he'll feel nothing more until the moment of death," said the guard, examining him with his experienced eye. "Ivan, do you hear? Hey there, Ivan!"

"I must not be hanged!" Yanson answered in a colorless voice; his lower jaw had dropped.

"If you had not killed, they would not hang you," reproachfully said the chief jailer, a highly important young man, wearing a decoration. "To steal, you have killed, and you don't want to be hanged!"

"I do not want to be hanged!" replied Yanson.

"Well, you don't have to want to; that's your affair. But, instead of talking nonsense, you would do better to dispose of your possessions. You surely must have something."

"He has nothing at all! A shirt and a pair of pantaloons! And a fur cap!"

Thus time passed until Thursday. And Thursday, at midnight, a large number of people entered Yanson's cell; a man with cloth epaulets said to him:

"Get ready! It's time to start."

Always with the same slowness and the same indolence Yanson dressed himself in all that he possessed, and tied his dirty shawl around his neck. While watching him dress, the man with the epaulets, who was smoking a cigarette, said to one of the assistants:

"How warm it is today! It's spring!"

Yanson's eyes closed; he was in a complete drowse. The guard shouted:

"Come, come! Make haste! You're going to sleep!"

Suddenly Yanson ceased to move.

"I must not be hanged," he said with indolence.

He began to walk submissively, shrugging his shoulders. In the courtyard the moist spring air had a sudden effect upon him: his nose began to run. It was thawing; close by, drops of water were falling with a joyous sound. While the gendarmes were getting into the unlighted vehicle, bending over and rattling their swords, Yanson lazily passed his finger under his running nose, or arranged his badly tied shawl.

IV

WE OF OREL

The court that had tried Yanson sentenced to death at the same session Michael Goloubetz, known as Michka the Gypsy, a peasant of the department of Orel, district of Eletz. The last crime of which they accused him, with evidence in support of the charge, was robbery, followed by the assassination of three persons. As for his past, it was unknown. There were vague indications to warrant the belief that the Gypsy had taken part in a whole series of other murders. With absolute sincerity and frankness he termed himself a brigand, and with his irony overwhelmed those who, to follow the fashion, pompously styled themselves "expropriators"; his last crime he described willingly in all its details. But, at the slightest reference to the past, he answered:

"Go and ask the wind that blows over the fields!"

And, if they persisted in questioning him, the Gypsy assumed a dignified and serious air.

"We of Orel are all hotheads, the fathers of all the robbers of the world," he said in a sedate and judicial tone.

They had nicknamed him Gypsy because of his physiognomy and his thieving habits. He was thin and strangely dark; yellow spots outlined themselves upon his cheekbones, which were as prominent as those of a Tartar. He had a way of rolling the whites of his eyes, that reminded one of a horse. His gaze was quick and keen, full of curiosity, terrifying. The things over which his swift glance passed seemed to lose something or other, and to become transformed by surrendering part of themselves to him. One hesitated to take a cigarette that he had looked at, as if it had already been in his mouth. His extraordinarily mobile nature made him seem now to coil and concentrate himself like a twisted handkerchief, now to scatter himself like a sheaf of sparks. He drank water almost by the pailful, like a horse.

When the judges questioned him, he raised his head quickly, and answered without hesitation, even with satisfaction:

"It is true!"

Sometimes, to lend emphasis, he rolled his "r's" vigorously.

Suddenly he jumped to his feet, and said to the presiding judge:

"Permit me to whistle?"

"Why?" the judge exclaimed in astonishment.

"The witnesses say that I gave the signal to my comrades; I'll show you how I did it. It's very interesting."

A little disconcerted, the judge granted the desired permission. The Gypsy quickly placed four fingers in his mouth, two of each hand; he rolled his eyes furiously. And the inanimate air of the courtroom was rent by a truly savage whistle. There was everything in the piercing sound, partly human, partly animal; the mortal anguish of the victim, and the savage joy of the assassin; a threat, a call, and the tragic solitude, the darkness, of a rainy autumn night.

The judge shook his hand; with docility the Gypsy stopped. Like an artist who has just played a difficult air with assured success, he sat down, wiped his wet fingers on his cloak, and looked at the spectators with a satisfied air.

"What a brigand!" exclaimed one of the judges, rubbing his ear.

But another, who had Tartar eyes like the Gypsy's,

was looking dreamily into the distance, over the brigand's head; he smiled, and replied:

"It was really interesting."

Without remorse the judges sentenced the Gypsy to death.

"It is just!" said the Gypsy, when the sentence had been pronounced. And, turning to a soldier of the guard, he added with an air of bravado, "Well, let's be off, imbecile! And keep a good hold of your gun, lest I snatch it from you!"

The soldier looked at him seriously and timidly; he exchanged a glance with his comrade, and tested his weapon to see if it was in working order. The other did the same. And all the way to the prison it seemed to the soldiers that they did not walk, but flew; they were so absorbed by the condemned man that they were unconscious of the route, of the weather, and of themselves.

Like Yanson, Michka the Gypsy remained seventeen days in prison before being executed. And the seventeen days passed as rapidly as a single day, filled with a single thought, that of flight, of liberty, of life. The turbulent and incoercible spirit of the Gypsy, stifled by the walls, the gratings, and the opaque window through which nothing could be seen, employed all its force in setting Michka's brain on fire. As in a vapor of intoxication, bright but incomplete images whirled, clashed, and mingled in his head; they passed with a blinding and irresistible rapidity, and they all tended to the same end: flight, liberty, life. For entire hours, with nostrils distended like those of a horse, the Gypsy sniffed the air; it seemed to him that he inhaled the odor of hemp and flame, of dense smoke. Or else he turned in his cell like a top, examining the walls, feeling them with his fingers, measuring them, piercing the ceiling with his gaze, sawing the bars in his mind. His agitation was a source of torture to the soldier who watched him through the window; several times he threatened to fire on him.

During the night the Gypsy slept deeply, almost without stirring, in an invariable but living immobility, like a temporarily inactive spring. But, as soon as he jumped to his feet, he began again to plan, to grope, to study. His hands were always dry and hot. Sometimes his heart suddenly congealed, as if they had placed in his breast a new block of ice which did not melt, and which caused a continuous shiver to run over his skin. At these times his naturally dark complexion became darker still, taking on the blue-black shade of bronze. Then a queer tic seized him; he constantly licked his lips, as if he had eaten a dish that was much too sweet; then, with a hiss, and with set teeth, he spat upon the ground the saliva that had thus accumulated in his mouth. He left his words unfinished; his thoughts ran so fast that his tongue could no longer keep up with them.

One day the chief of the guards entered his cell, accompanied by a soldier. He squinted at the spittle with which the ground was spattered, and said rudely:

"See how he has dirtied his cell!"

The Gypsy replied quickly:

"And you, you ugly mug, you have soiled the whole earth, and I haven't said a word to you. Why do you annoy me?"

With the same rudeness the chief of the guards offered him the post of hangman and began to laugh. The Gypsy showed his teeth, and began to laugh. "So they can find none! That's not bad! Go on then hanging people! Ah! Ah! There are necks and ropes, and nobody to do the hanging! My God, that's not bad."

"They will give your life as a reward!"

"I should say so: I could hardly play the hangman after I'm dead!"

"Well, what do you say, yes or no?"

"And how do they hang here? They probably choke people secretly."

"No, they hang them to music!" retorted the chief.

"Imbecile! Of course there must be music . . . like this. . . ."

And he began to sing a captivating air.

"You have gone completely mad, my friend!" said the guard. "Come, speak seriously, what is your decision?"

The Gypsy showed his teeth. "Are you in a hurry? Come back later, and I'll tell you!"

And to the chaos of unfinished images which overwhelmed the Gypsy was added a new idea: how agreeable it would be to be the headsman! He clearly pictured to himself the square black with people, and the scaffold on which he, the Gypsy, walks back and forth, in a red shirt, with axe in hand. The sun illuminates the heads, plays gaily on the axe blade; everything is so joyous, so sumptuous, that even he whose head is to be cut off smiles. Behind the crowd are to be seen the carts and the noses of the horses; the peasants have come to town for the occasion. Still farther away are the fields. The Gypsy licked his lips, and spat upon the ground. Suddenly it seemed to him that his fur cap had just been pulled down over his mouth; everything became dark; he gasped for breath; and his heart changed into a block of ice, while little shivers ran through his body.

Twice more the chief came back; the Gypsy, showing his teeth again, answered:

"What a hurry you're in! Come back another time!"

Finally, one day, the jailer cried to him, as he was passing by the window:

"You've lost your chance, my ill-favored raven. They've found another."

"The Devil take you! Go, be the hangman yourself!" replied the Gypsy. And he ceased to dream of the splendors of his trade.

But towards the end, the nearer drew the day of execution, the more intolerable became the impetuosity of the torn images. The Gypsy would have liked to wait, to halt, but the furious torrent carried him on, giving him no chance to get a hold on anything; for everything was in a whirl. And his sleep became agitated; he had new and shapeless visions, as badly squared as painted blocks, and even more impetuous than his thoughts had been. It was no longer a torrent, but a continual fall from an infinite height, a whirling flight through the whole world of colors. Formerly the Gypsy had worn only a mustache tolerably well cared for; in prison he had been obliged to grow his beard, which was short, black, and stubbly, giving him a crazy look. There were moments, in fact, when the Gypsy lost his mind. He turned about in his cell, entirely unconscious of his movements, continuing to feel for the rough and uneven walls. And he always drank great quantities of water, like a horse.

One evening, when they were lighting the lamps, the Gypsy dropped on all fours in the middle of his cell, and began to howl like a wolf. He did this very seriously, as if performing an indispensable and important act. He filled his lungs with air, and then expelled it slowly in a prolonged and trembling howl. With knit brows, he listened to himself attentively. The very trembling of the voice seemed a little affected; he did not shout indistinctly: he made each note in this wild beast's cry sound separately, full of unspeakable suffering and terror.

Suddenly he stopped, and remained silent for a few

minutes, without getting up. He began to whisper, as if speaking to the ground:

"Dear friends, good friends . . . dear friends . . . good friends . . . have pit . . . friends! My friends!"

He said a word, and listened to it. He jumped to his feet, and for a whole hour poured forth a steady stream of the worst curses.

"Go to the Devil, you scoundrels!" he screamed, rolling his bloodshot eyes. "If I must be hanged, hang me, instead of . . . ah, you blackguards!"

The soldier on guard, as white as chalk, wept with anguish and fear; he pounded the door with the muzzle of his gun, and cried in a lamentable voice:

"I'll shoot you! By God, do you hear? I'll shoot you!"

But he did not dare to fire; they never fire on prisoners sentenced to death, except in case of revolt. And the Gypsy ground his teeth, swore, and spat. His brain, placed on the narrow frontier that separates life from death, crumbled like a lump of dried clay.

When they came, during the night, to take him to the gallows, he regained a little of his animation. His cheeks took on some color; in his eyes the usual strategy, a little savage, sparkled again, and he asked of one of the functionaries:

"Who will hang us? The new one? Is he accustomed to it yet?"

"You needn't disturb yourself about that," answered the personage thus appealed to.

"What? Not disturb myself! It's not Your Highness that's going to be hanged, but I! At least don't spare the soap on the slipnoose; the State pays for it!"

"I beg you to hold your tongue!"

"This fellow, you see, consumes all the soap in the

prison; see how his face shines," continued the Gypsy, pointing to the chief of the guards.

"Silence!"

"Don't spare the soap!"

Suddenly he began to laugh, and his legs became numb. Yet, when he arrived in the courtyard, he could still cry:

"Say, there! you fellows yonder, come forward with my carriage!"

V

"KISS HIM AND BE SILENT"

The verdict against the five terrorists was pronounced in its final form and confirmed the same day. The condemned were not notified of the day of execution; but they foresaw that they would be hanged, according to custom, the same night, or, at the latest, the night following. When they were offered the opportunity of seeing their families the next day, they understood that the execution was fixed for Friday at daybreak.

Tanya Kovalchuk had no near relatives. She knew only of some distant relatives living in Little Russia, who probably knew nothing of the trial or the verdict. Musya and Werner, not having revealed their identity, did not insist on seeing any of their people. Only Sergey Golovin and Vasily Kashirin were to see their families. The thought of this approaching interview was frightful to both of them, but they could not make up their minds to refuse a final conversation, a last kiss.

Sergey Golovin thought sadly of this visit. He was fond of his father and mother; he had seen them very recently, and he was filled with terror at the thought of what was going to happen. The hanging itself, in all its monstrosity, in its disconcerting madness, outlined itself more readily in his imagination than these few short, incomprehensible minutes, that seemed apart from time, apart from life. What to do? What to say? The most simple and customary gestures—to shake hands, embrace, and say "How do you do, Father?"—seemed to him frightful in their monstrous, inhuman, insane insignificance.

After the verdict they did not put the condemned in the same cell, as Tanya expected them to do. All the morning, up to the time when he received his parents, Sergey Golovin walked back and forth in his cell, twisting his short beard, his features pitiably contracted. Sometimes he stopped suddenly, filled his lungs with air, and puffed like a swimmer who has remained too long under water. But, as he was in good health, and as his young life was solidly implanted within him, even in these minutes of atrocious suffering, the blood coursed under his skin, coloring his cheeks; his blue eyes preserved their usual brilliancy.

Everything went off better than Sergey expected; his father, Nicolas Sergiévitch Golovin, a retired colonel, was the first to enter the room where the visitors were received. Everything about him was white and of the same whiteness—face, hair, beard, hands. His old and well-brushed garment smelled of benzine; his epaulets seemed new. He entered with a firm and measured step, straightening himself up. Extending his dry, white hand, he said aloud, "How do you do, Sergey?"

Behind him came the mother, with short steps; she wore a strange smile. But she too shook hands with her son, and repeated aloud:

"How do you do, my little Sergey?"

She kissed him and sat down, without saying a word.

She did not throw herself upon her son, she did not begin to weep or cry, as Sergey expected her to do. She kissed him and sat down without speaking. With a trembling hand she even smoothed the wrinkles in her black silk gown.

Sergey did not know that the colonel had spent the entire previous night in rehearsing this interview. "We must lighten the last moments of our son's life, and not make them more painful for him," the colonel had decided; and he had carefully weighed each phrase, each gesture, of the morrow's visit. But sometimes, in the course of the rehearsal, he became confused, he forgot what he had prepared himself to say, and he wept bitterly, sunk in the corner of his sofa. The next morning he had explained to his wife what she was to do:

"Above all, kiss him and be silent," he repeated. "You'll be able to speak later, a little later; but, after kissing him, be silent. Don't speak immediately after kissing him, do you understand? Otherwise you'll say what you shouldn't."

"I understand, Nicholas Sergiévitch!" the mother answered, with tears.

"And don't weep! May God keep you from that! Don't weep! You'll kill him if you weep, Mother!"

"And why do you weep yourself?"

"Why shouldn't one weep here with the rest of you? You mustn't weep, do you hear?"

"All right, Nicolas Sergiévitch."

They got into a cab and started off, silent, bent, old; they were plunged in their thoughts amid the gay roar of the city; it was the carnival season, and the streets were filled with a noisy crowd.

They sat down. The colonel assumed a suitable attitude, his right hand thrust in the front of his frock coat. Sergey remained seated a moment; his look met his mother's wrinkled face; he rose suddenly.

"Sit down, my little Sergey!" begged the mother.

"Sit down, Sergey!" repeated the father.

They kept silence. The mother wore a strange smile.

"How many moves we've made in your behalf, Sergey! Your father . . ."

"It was useless, my little mother!"

The colonel said firmly, "We were in duty bound to do it that you might not think that your parents had abandoned you."

Again they became silent. They were afraid to utter a syllable, as if each word of the language had lost its proper meaning and now meant but one thing: death. Sergey looked at the neat little frock coat, which smelled of benzine, and thought: He has no orderly now; then he must have cleaned his coat himself. How is it that I've never seen him clean his coat? Probably he does it in the morning. Suddenly he asked, "And my sister? Is she well?"

"Ninotchka knows nothing!" the mother answered quickly.

But the colonel sternly interrupted her:

"What's the use of lying? She's read the newspaper . . . let Sergey know that . . . all . . . his own . . . have thought . . . and . . ."

Unable to continue, he stopped. Suddenly the mother's face contracted, her features became confused and wild. Her colorless eyes were madly distended; more and more she panted for breath.

"Se . . . Ser . . . Ser . . . Ser . . ." she repeated, without moving her lips; "Ser . . ."

"My little mother!"

The colonel took a step; trembling all over, without

knowing how frightful he was in his corpse-like pallor, in his desperate and forced firmness, he said to his wife:

"Be silent! Don't torture him! Don't torture him! Don't torture him! He must die! Don't torture him!"

Frightened, she was silent already, and he continued to repeat, with his trembling hands pressed against his breast:

"Don't torture him!"

Then he took a step backward, and again thrust his hand into the front of his frock coat; wearing an expression of forced calmness, he asked aloud, with pallid lips:

"When?"

"Tomorrow morning," Sergey answered.

The mother looked at the ground, biting her lips, as if she heard nothing. And she seemed to continue to bite her lips as she let fall these simple words: "Ninotchka told me to kiss you, my little Sergey!"

"Kiss her for me!" said the condemned man.

"Good! The Chvostofs send their salutations. . . ."

"Who are they? Ah! Yes. . . ."

The colonel interrupted him:

"Well, we must start. Rise, Mother, it's necessary!"

The two men lifted the swooning woman.

"Bid him farewell!" ordered the colonel. "Give him your blessing!"

She did everything that she was told. But, while giving her son a short kiss and making on his person the sign of the cross, she shook her head and repeated distractedly:

"No, it's not that! No, it's not that!"

"Adieu, Sergey!" said the father. They shook hands, and exchanged a short, but earnest, kiss.

"You . . ." Sergey began.

"Well?" the father asked spasmodically.

"No, not like that. No, no! What shall I say?" the

mother repeated, shaking her head. She had sat down
again, and was tottering.

"You . . ." Sergey resumed. Suddenly his face took on
a lamentable expression, and he grimaced like a child,
tears filling his eyes. Through their sparkling facets he
saw beside him the pale face of his father, who was
weeping also.

"Father, you're a strong man!"

"What do you say? What do you say?" said the bewildered colonel. Suddenly, as if completely broken, he
fell with his head on his son's shoulder. And the two
covered each other with ardent kisses, the father receiving them on his light hair, the prisoner on his cloak.

"And I?" a hoarse voice suddenly asked.

They looked: the mother was on her feet again, and
with her head thrown back, was watching them wrath-
fully, almost hatefully.

"What's the matter with you, Mother?" cried the colonel.

"And I?" she repeated, shaking her head with an
insane energy. "You embrace each other, and I? You're
men, are you not? And I? And I? . . ."

"Mother!" and Sergey threw himself into her arms.
The last words of the colonel were:

"My blessing for your death, Sergey! Die with courage,
like an officer!"

And they went away. . . . On returning to his cell,
Sergey lay upon his camp bed, with face turned towards
the wall that the soldiers might not see him, and wept a
long time.

Vasily Kashirin's mother came alone to visit him. The
father, a rich merchant, had refused to accompany her.
When the old woman entered, Vasily was walking in his

cell. In spite of the heat, he was trembling with cold. The conversation was short and painful.

"You shouldn't have come, Mother. Why should we two torment each other?"

"Why have you done this, Vasya? Why? Oh God!"

The old woman began to weep, drying her tears with her black silk neckerchief.

Accustomed as they were, his brothers and he, to treat their mother roughly, she being a simple woman who did not understand them, he stopped, and, in the midst of his shivering, said to her harshly:

"That's it, I knew how it would be. You understand nothing, Mama, nothing!"

"Very well, my son. What's the matter with you? Are you cold?"

"I'm cold," Vasily answered, and he began to walk again, now and then looking sidewise, with the same air of irritation, at the old woman.

"You're cold, my son. . . ."

"Ah! You speak of cold, but soon . . ." He made a gesture of desperation.

Again the mother began to sob:

"I said to your father: 'Go to see him, he's your son, your flesh; give him a last farewell.' He wouldn't."

"The Devil take him! He's not a father. All his life he's been a scoundrel. He remains one!"

"Yet, Vasya, he's your father. . . ." And the old woman shook her head reproachfully.

It was ridiculous and terrible. This paltry and useless conversation engaged them when face to face with death. While almost weeping, so sad was the situation, Vasily cried out, "Understand then, Mother. They're going to hang me, to hang me! Do you understand, yes or no?"

"And why did you kill?" she cried.

"My God! What are you saying? Even the beasts have feelings. Am I your son or not?"

He sat down and wept. His mother wept also; but, in their incapability of communicating in the same affection in order to face the terror of the approaching death, they wept cold tears that did not warm the heart.

"You ask me if I'm your mother? You heap reproaches on me; and yet I've turned completely white these last few days."

"All right, all right, forgive me. Good-bye! Embrace my brothers for me."

"Am I not your mother? Do I not suffer for you?"

At last she departed. She was weeping so much so that she could not see her way. And the farther she got from the prison, the more abundant became her tears. She retraced her steps, losing herself in this city in which she was born, in which she had grown up, in which she had grown old. She entered a little abandoned garden and sat down on a damp bench.

And suddenly she understood: tomorrow they would hang her son! She sprang to her feet and tried to shout and run, but suddenly her head turned and she sank to the earth. The path, white with frost, was wet and slippery; the old woman could not rise again. She rested her weight on her wrists and then fell back again. The black neckerchief slipped from her head, uncovering her dirty gray hair. It seemed to her that she was celebrating her son's wedding. Yes, they had just married him, and she had drunk a little wine; she was slightly intoxicated.

"I can't help myself! My God, I can't help myself!"

And, with swinging head, she said to herself that she had drunk too much, and was crawling around on the wet ground . . . but they gave her wine to drink, and wine again, and still more wine. And from her heart arose the laugh of the drunkard and the desire to abandon herself to a wild dance . . . but they kept on lifting cups to her lips, one after another, one after another.

VI

THE HOURS FLY

In the fortress where the condemned terrorists were confined, there was a steeple with an old clock. Every hour, every half hour, every quarter of an hour, this clock struck in a tone of infinite sadness, like the distant and plaintive cry of birds of passage. In the daytime this odd and desolate music was lost in the noise of the city, of the broad and animated street that passed the fortress. The tramways rumbled, the shoes of the horses rattled, the trembling automobiles sounded their hoarse horns far into the distance. As the carnival was approaching, the peasants of the suburbs had come to town to earn some money as cab drivers; the bells of the little Russian horses tinkled noisily. The conversations were gay and had a flavor of intoxication, real holiday conversations. The weather harmonized with the occasion; the spring had brought a thaw, and the road was wet with dirty puddles. The trees on the squares had suddenly darkened. A slightly warm wind was blowing from the sea in copious moist puffs—a light, fresh air that seemed to have started on a joyous flight towards the infinite.

By night the street was silent under the brilliancy of the large electric suns. The immense fortress with its smooth walls was plunged in darkness and silence; a barrier of calm and shadow separated it from the ever-living city. Then they heard the striking of the hours, the slow, sad

birth and death of a strange melody, foreign to the land.
Like big drops of transparent glass, the hours and the
minutes fell from an immeasurable height into a metallic
basin that was vibrating gently. Sometimes they were like
birds that passed.

Into the cells came, day and night, this single sound. It
penetrated through the roof, through the thick stone
walls; it alone broke the silence. Sometimes they forgot it,
or did not hear it. Sometimes they awaited it with despair;
they lived only by and for this sound, having learned to be
distrustful of silence. The prison was reserved for criminals of note; its special, rigorous regulations were as rigid
and sharp as the corners of the walls. If there is nobility in
cruelty, then the solemn, deaf, dead silence that caught
up every breath and every rustle was noble.

In this silence, penetrated by the desolate striking of
the flying minutes, three men and two women, separated
from the world, were awaiting the coming of the night, of
the dawn, and of the execution; and each was preparing
for it in his own fashion.

Throughout her life Tanya Kovalchuk had thought
only of others, and now also it was for the comrades that
she underwent suffering and torture. She pictured death to
herself only because it threatened Sergey Golovin, Musya,
and the others; but her thoughts did not dwell on the fact
that she too would be executed.

As if to reward herself for the artificial firmness that she
had shown before the judges, she wept for hours altogether. This is characteristic of old women who have suffered much. When it occurred to her that Sergey might be
unprovided with tobacco, or that Werner possibly was deprived of the tea of which he was so fond—and this at the
moment that they were about to die—she suffered perhaps as much as at the idea of the execution. The execu-

tion was something inevitable, even incidental, not worthy of consideration; but that an imprisoned man should be without tobacco on the very eve of his execution was an absolutely intolerable idea. Evoking the pleasant memories of their common life, she lamented over the interview between Sergey and his parents.

For Musya she felt a special pity. For a long time it had seemed to her, mistakenly, however, that Musya was in love with Werner; she had beautiful and luminous dreams for their future. Before her arrest Musya wore a silver ring on which were engraved a skull and crossbones surrounded with a crown of thorns. Often Tanya Kovalchuk had looked at this ring sorrowfully, viewing it as a symbol of renunciation; half serious, half joking, she had asked Musya to take it off.

"No, Tanya, I will not give it to you. You will soon have another on your finger!"

Her comrades always thought that she would soon be married, which much offended her. She wanted no husband. And, as she recalled these conversations with Musya and reflected that Musya was indeed sacrificed, Tanya, full of motherly pity, felt the tears choking her. Every time the clock struck, she lifted her face, covered with tears, and listened, wondering how this plaintive and persistent summons of death was being received in the other cells.

VII

THERE IS NO DEATH

And Musya was happy!

With arms folded behind her back, and dressed in a prisoner's gown that was too large for her and that made her look like a youth wearing a borrowed costume, she walked back and forth in her cell, at a regular pace, never wearying. She had tucked up the long sleeves of her gown, and her thin and emaciated arms, the arms of a child, emerged from the flaring breadths like flower stems from a coarse and unclean pitcher. The roughness of the stuff irritated the skin of her white and slender neck; sometimes, with her two hands, she exposed her throat, and felt cautiously for the spot where her skin was burning.

Musya walked with a long stride, and tried blushingly to justify to herself the fact that the finest of deaths, reserved hitherto for martyrs, had been assigned to her, so young, so humble, and who had done so little. It seemed to her that, in dying upon the scaffold, she was making a pretentious show that was in bad taste.

At her last interview with her lawyer she had asked him to procure poison for her, but immediately had given up the idea: would not people think that she was actuated by fear or by ostentation? Instead of dying modestly and unnoticed, would she not cause still further scandal? And she had added quickly:

"No, no, it's useless!"

Now her sole desire was to explain, to prove, that she was not a heroine, that it was not a frightful thing to die, and that no one need pity her or worry on her account.

Musya sought excuses, pretexts of such a nature as to exalt her sacrifice and give it a real value, as if it had actually been called in question.

"In fact," she said to herself, "I am young; I might have lived for a long time. But . . ."

Just as the gleam of a candle is effaced by the radiance of the rising sun, youth and life seem to her dull and somber beside the magnificent and luminous halo that is about to crown her modest person.

"Is it possible?" Musya asked herself, in great confusion. "Is it possible that I am worth anybody's tears?"

And she was seized with an unspeakable joy. There was no more doubt; she had been taken into the pale. She had a right to figure among the heroes who from all countries go to heaven through flames and executions. What serene peace, what infinite happiness! An immaterial being, she believed herself hovering in a divine light.

Of what else was Musya thinking? Of many things, since for her the thread of life was not severed by death, but continued to unroll in a calm and regular fashion. She was thinking of her comrades, of those who at a distance were filled with anguish at the idea of her approaching execution, of those who nearer at hand would go with her to the gallows. She was astonished that Vasily should be a prey to terror, he who had always been brave. On Tuesday morning, when they had prepared themselves to kill, and then to die themselves, Tanya Kovalchuk had trembled with emotion; they had been obliged to send her away, whereas Vasily joked and laughed and moved about amid the bombs, with so little caution that Werner had said to him severely:

"One should not play with death!"

Why, then, was Vasily afraid now? And this incomprehensible terror was so foreign to Musya's soul that she soon ceased to think about it and to inquire into its cause. Suddenly she felt a mad desire to see Sergey Golovin and laugh with him.

Perhaps too her thought was unwilling to dwell long on the same subject, resembling therein a light bird that hovers before infinite horizons, all space, the caressing and tender azure, being accessible to it. The hours continued to strike. Thoughts blended in this harmonious and distant symphony; fleeting images became a sort of music. It seemed to Musya that she was traveling on a broad and easy road in a quiet night; the carriage rode easily on its springs. All care had vanished; the tired body was dissolved in the darkness; joyous and weary, the thought peacefully created vivid images, and became intoxicated on their beauty. Musya recalled three comrades who had been hanged lately; their faces were illuminated and near, nearer than those of the living. . . . So in the morning one thinks gaily of the hospitable friends who will receive you in the evening with smiles on their lips.

At last Musya became weary from walking. She lay down cautiously on the camp bed and continued to dream, with half-closed eyes.

"Is this really death? My God, how beautiful it is! Or is it life? I don't know, I don't know! I'm going to see and hear."

From the first days of her imprisonment, she had been a prey to hallucinations. She had a very musical ear; her sense of hearing, sharpened by the silence, gathered in the slightest echoes of life; the footsteps of the sentinels in the corridor, the striking of the clock, the whispering of the wind over the zinc roof, the creaking of a lantern, all blended for her in a vast and mysterious symphony. At first the hallucinations frightened Musya, and she drove them away as morbid manifestations; then, perceiving that she was in good health and had no pathological symptoms, she ceased to resist.

But now she hears very plainly the sound of the military band. She opens her eyes in astonishment, and raises her head. Through the windows she sees the night; the clock strikes. Again! she thought, as she closed her eyes without disturbing herself. Again the music begins. Musya clearly distinguishes the steps of the soldiers as they turn the corner of the prison; a whole regiment is passing before her windows. The boots keep time to the music on the frozen ground; one! two! one! two! Sometimes a boot squeaks; a foot slips and then recovers itself. The music draws nearer; it is playing a noisy and stirring triumphal march which Musya does not know. There is probably some festival in the fortress.

The soldiers are under her windows, and the cell is filled with joyous, regular, and harmonious sounds. A big brass trumpet emits false notes: it is not in time; now it is in advance, now it lags behind in a ridiculous fashion. Musya pictures to herself a little soldier playing this trumpet assiduously, and she laughs.

The regiment has passed; the sound of the footsteps grows fainter and fainter; one! two! one! two! In the distance the music becomes gayer and more beautiful. Several times more the trumpet sounds out of time, with its metallic, sonorous, and gay voice, and then all is quiet. Again the clock in the steeple strikes the hours.

New forms come and lean over her, surrounding her with transparent clouds and lifting her to a great height, where birds of prey are hovering. At left and right, above and below, everywhere birds are crying like heralds; they call, they warn. They spread their wings, and immensity sustains them. And on their inflated breasts that split the air is reflected the sparkling azure. The beating of Musya's heart becomes more and more regular, her respiration more and more calm and peaceful. She sleeps; her face is pale; her features are drawn; there are dark rings around her eyes; on her lips is a smile. Tomorrow, when the sun rises, this intelligent and fine face will be deformed by a grimace in which no trace of the human will be left; the brain will be inundated with thick blood; the glassy eyes will protrude from their orbits. But today Musya sleeps quietly, and smiles in her immortality.

Musya sleeps.

And the prison continues to live its special, blind, vigilant life, a sort of perpetual anxiety. They walk. They whisper. A gun rings out. It seems as if someone cries out. Is this reality or hallucination?

The grating in the door lowers noiselessly. In the dark opening appears a sinister, bearded face. For a long time the widely opened eyes view with astonishment the sleeping Musya; then the face disappears as quietly as it came.

The bells in the steeple ring and sing interminably. One would say that the weary hours were climbing a high mountain towards midnight. The ascent grows more and more painful. They slip, fall back with a groan, and begin again to toil painfully towards the black summit.

There is a sound of footsteps. Whispering voices are heard. Already they are harnessing the horses to the somber, unlighted vehicle.

VIII

DEATH EXISTS, AND LIFE ALSO

Sergey Golovin never thought of death. It seemed to him something incidental and foreign. He was robust, endowed with that serenity in the joy of living which causes all evil thoughts, all thoughts fatal to life, to disappear rapidly, leaving the organism intact. Just as, with him, physical wounds healed quickly, so all injuries to his soul were immediately nullified. He brought into all his acts, into his pleasures and into his preparations for crime, the same happy and tranquil gravity: everything in life was gay, everything was important, worthy of being well done.

And he did everything well; he sailed a boat admirably, he was an excellent marksman. He was as faithful in friendship as in love, and had an unshakeable confidence in the "word of honor." His comrades declared laughingly that if one who had been proved a spy should swear to Sergey that he was not a spy, Sergey would believe him and shake hands with him. A single fault: he thought himself a good singer, whereas he sang atrociously false, even in the case of revolutionary hymns. He got angry when they laughed at him.

"Either you are all asses, or else I am an ass!" he said in a serious and offended tone. And, after a moment's reflection, the comrades declared in a tone quite as serious:

"It is you who are an ass. You show it in your voice!"

And, as is sometimes the case with worthy people, they loved him perhaps more for his eccentricities than for his virtues.

He thought so little of death, he feared it so little, that on the fatal morning, before leaving the dwelling of Tanya Kovalchuk, he alone had breakfasted with appetite, as usual. He had taken two glasses of tea and eaten a whole two-cent loaf. Then, looking with sadness at Werner's untouched bread, he said to him:

"Why don't you eat? Eat; it's necessary to get strength!"

"I'm not hungry."

"Well, I'll eat your bread! Shall I?"

"What an appetite you have, Sergey!"

By way of reply, Sergey, with his mouth full, began to sing in a false and hollow voice:

"A hostile wind is blowing o'er our heads."

After the arrest, Sergey had a moment of sadness; the plot had been badly planned. But he said to himself, "Now there's something else that must be done well: to die." And his gaiety returned. On his second day in the fortress he began gymnastic exercises, according to the extremely rational system of a German named Müller, which interested him much. He undressed himself completely; and, to the amazement of the anxious sentinel, he went carefully through the eighteen prescribed exercises.

As a propagandist of the Müller system, it gave him much satisfaction to see the soldier follow his movements. Although he knew that he would get no answer, he said to the eye that appeared at the grating:

"That's the kind of thing that does you good, brother; that gives you strength! That's what they ought to make you do in the regiment," he added in a gentle and persuasive voice so that he might not frighten the soldier, not suspecting that his guardian took him for a madman.

The fear of death progressively showed itself in him, seemingly by shocks: it seemed to him that someone was thumping him violently in the heart from below. Then the sensation disappeared, but came back a few hours later, each time more intense and prolonged. It was beginning already to take on the vague outlines of an unendurable anguish.

Is it possible that I'm afraid? Sergey thought in astonishment. "How stupid!"

It was not he who was afraid; it was his young, robust, and vigorous body, which neither the gymnastics of Müller nor the cold shower baths could deceive. The stronger and fresher he became after his cold-water ablutions, the more acute and unendurable was his sensation of temporary fear. And it was in the morning, after his deep sleep and physical exercises, that this atrocious fear, like something foreign, appeared—exactly at the moment when formerly he had been particularly conscious of his strength and his joy in living. He noticed this, and said to himself:

"You're stupid, my friend. In order that the body may die more easily, it should be weakened, not fortified."

From that time, he gave up his gymnastics and his massage. And, to explain this right-about-face, he cried to the soldier:

"Brother, the method is a good one. It's only for those who are going to be hanged that it's good for nothing."

In fact, he felt a sort of relief. He tried also to eat less in order to further weaken himself, but, in spite of the lack of air and exercise, his appetite remained excellent. Sergey could not resist it, and ate everything that they brought him. Then he resorted to a subterfuge; before sitting down at the table, he poured half of his soup into his bucket. And this method succeeded; a great weariness, a vague numbness, took possession of him.

"I'll teach you!" he said, threatening his body; and he sadly caressed his softening muscles.

But soon the body became accustomed to this régime, and the fear of death appeared again, not in so acute a form, but as a vague sensation of nausea, still harder to bear. It's because this lasts so long, Sergey thought. If only I could sleep all the time until the day of execution! He tried to sleep as much as possible. His first efforts were not altogether fruitless; then insomnia set in, accompanied with obsessing thoughts and, with these, a regret that he must part with life.

"Am I then afraid of it?" he asked himself, thinking of death. "It's the loss of life that I regret. Life is an admirable thing, whatever the pessimists may say. What would a pessimist say if they were to hang him? Ah! I regret to lose my life, I regret it much."

When he clearly understood that for him all was over, that he had before him only a few hours of empty waiting and then death, he had a queer feeling. It seemed to him that they had stripped him naked in an extraordinary fashion. Not only had they taken away his clothes, but also sun, air, sound and light, speech and the power of action. Death had not yet arrived, and yet life seemed already absent; he felt a strange sensation, sometimes incomprehensible, sometimes intelligible, but very subtle and mysterious.

"What is it then?" Sergey wondered, in his torment. "And I, where am I? I. . . . What I?"

He examined himself attentively, with interest, beginning with his loose slippers, such as the prisoners wore, and stopping with his belly, over which hung his ample cloak. He began to walk back and forth in his cell, with arms apart, and continued to look at himself as a woman does when trying on a gown that is too long. He tried to turn his head: it turned. And what seemed to him a little terrifying was he himself, Sergey Golovin, who soon would be no more!

Everything became strange.

He tried to walk, and it seemed queer to him to walk. He tried to sit down, and he was surprised that he could do so. He tried to drink water, and it seemed queer to him to drink, to swallow, to hold the goblet, to see his fingers, his trembling fingers. He began to cough, and thought:

How curious it is! I cough. What is the matter? Am I going mad? he asked himself. That would be the last straw, indeed!

He wiped his brow, and this gesture seemed to him equally surprising. Then he fixed himself in a motionless posture, without breathing—for entire hours, it seemed to him, extinguishing all thought, holding his breath, avoiding all motion; for every thought was madness, every gesture an aberration. Time disappeared as if transformed into space, into a transparent space in which there was no air, into an immense place containing everything—land

and life and men. And one could take in everything at a glance, to the very extremity, to the edge of the unknown gulf, to death. And it was not because he saw death that Sergey suffered, but because he saw life and death at the same time. A sacrilegious hand had lifted the curtain which from all eternity had hidden the mystery of life and the mystery of death; they had ceased to be mysterious, but they were no more comprehensible than truth written in a foreign language.

"And here we are back to Müller again!" he suddenly declared aloud, in a voice of deep conviction. He shook his head and began to laugh gaily, sincerely:

"Ah, my good Müller! My dear Müller! My worthy German! You are right, after all, Müller; as for me, brother Müller, I am only an ass!"

He quickly made the round of his cell; and, to the great astonishment of the soldier who was watching him through the grating, he entirely undressed and went through the eighteen exercises with scrupulous exactness. He bent and straightened up his young body, which had grown a little thin; he stooped, inhaling and exhaling the air; he raised himself on tiptoe, and moved his arms and legs.

"Yes, but, you know, Müller," reasoned Sergey, throwing out his chest, his ribs outlining themselves plainly under his thin, distended skin; "you know, Müller, there is still a nineteenth exercise—suspension by the neck in a fixed position. And that is called hanging. Do you understand, Müller? They take a living man, Sergey Golovin, for example, they wrap him up like a doll, and they hang him by the neck until he is dead. It is stupid, Müller, but that is the way it is; one must be resigned!"

He leaned on his right side, and repeated:

"One must be resigned, Müller!"

IX

THE HORRIBLE SOLITUDE

Under the same roof and to the same melodious chant of the different hours, separated from Sergey and from Musya by a few empty cells, but as isolated as if he alone had existed in the whole universe, the unhappy Vasily Kashirin was finishing his life in anguish and terror.

Covered with sweat, his shirt adhering to his body, his formerly curly hair now falling in straight locks, he went back and forth in his cell with the jerky and lamentable gait of one suffering atrociously with a toothache. He sat down for a moment and then began to run again; then he rested his forehead against the wall, stopped, and looked about as if in search of a remedy. He had so changed that one might think that he possessed two different faces, one of which, the younger, had gone nobody knows where, to give place to the second, a terrible face, that seemed to have come from darkness.

Fear had shown itself suddenly to him, and had seized upon his person as an exclusive and sovereign mistress. On the fatal morning, when he was marching to certain death, he had played with it; but that evening, confined in his cell, he had been carried away and lashed by a wave of mad terror. As long as he had gone freely forward to meet danger and death, as long as he had held his fate in his own hands, however terrible it might be, he had appeared tranquil and even joyous, the small amount of shameful and decrepit fear that he had felt having disappeared in a consciousness of infinite liberty, in the firm and audacious affirmation of his intrepid will, leaving no trace behind. With an infernal machine strapped around his waist, he had transformed himself into an instrument of death, he had borrowed from the dynamite its cruel reason and its flashing and homicidal power. In the street, among the busy people preoccupied with their affairs and quickly dodging the tramcars and the cabs, it seemed to him as if he came from another and an unknown world, where there was no such thing as death or fear.

Suddenly a brutal, bewildering change had taken place. Vasily no longer went where he wanted to go, but was led where others wanted him to go. He no longer chose his place; they placed him in a stone cage and locked him in, as if he were a thing. He could no longer choose between life and death; they led him to death, certainly and inevitably. He who had been for a moment the incarnation of will, of life, and of force, had become a lamentable specimen of impotence; he was nothing but an animal destined for the slaughter. Whatever he might say, they would not listen; if he started to cry out, they would stuff a rag in his mouth; and, if he even tried to walk, they would take him away and hang him. If he resisted, if he struggled, if he lay down on the ground, they would be stronger than he; they would pick him up, they would tie him, and thus they would carry him to the gallows. And his imagination gave to the men charged with this execution, men like himself, the new, extraordinary, and terrifying aspect of unthinking automata, whom nothing in the world could stop, and who seized a man, overpowered him, hanged him, pulled him by the feet, cut the rope, put the body in a coffin, carried it away, and buried it.

From the first day of his imprisonment, people and life had transformed themselves for him into an unspeakably frightful world filled with mechanical dolls. Almost mad with fear, he tried to fancy to himself that these people had tongues and spoke, but he did not succeed. Their mouths opened, something like a sound came from them:

then they separated with movements of their legs, and all was over. He was in the situation of a man who, left alone in a house at night, should see all things become animate, move, and assume over him an unlimited power; suddenly the wardrobe, the chair, the sofa, the writing table would sit in judgment upon him. He would cry out, call for help, beg, and rove from room to room; and the things would speak to each other in their own tongue; and then the wardrobe, the chair, the sofa, and the writing table would start to hang him, the other things looking on.

In the eyes of Vasily Kashirin, sentenced to be hanged, everything took on a puerile aspect; the cell, the grated door, the striking apparatus of the clock, the fortress with its carefully modeled ceilings, and, above, the mechanical doll equipped with a musket, who walked up and down in the corridor, and the other dolls who frightened him by looking through the grating, and without a word, handing him his food.

A man had disappeared from the world.

In court the presence of the comrades had brought Kashirin back to himself. Again for a moment he saw people; they were there, judging him, speaking the language of men, listening, and seeming to understand. But when he saw his mother, he felt clearly, with the terror of a man who is going mad and knows it, that this old woman in a black neckerchief was a simple, mechanical doll. He was astonished at not having suspected it before, and at having awaited this visit as something infinitely sorrowful in its distressing gentleness. While forcing himself to speak, he thought with a shudder:

My God! But it's a doll! A doll-mother! And yonder is a doll-soldier; at home there's a doll-father, and this is the doll Vasily Kashirin.

When the mother began to weep, Vasily again saw

something human in her, but this disappeared with the first words that she uttered. With curiosity and terror, he watched the tears flow from the doll's eyes.

When his fear became intolerable, Vasily Kashirin tried to pray. There remained with him only a bitter, detestable, and enervating rancor against all the religious principles upon which his youth had been nourished, in the house of his father, a prosperous merchant. He had no faith. But one day, in his childhood, he had heard some words that had made an impression upon him and that remained surrounded forever with a gentle poesy. These words were:

"Joy of all the afflicted!"

Sometimes, in painful moments, he whispered, without praying, without even accounting to himself for what he was doing: "Joy of all the afflicted!" And then he suddenly felt relieved; he had a desire to approach someone who was dear to him and complain gently:

"Our life! . . . but is it really a life? Say, my dear, is it really a life?"

And then suddenly he felt himself ridiculous; he would have liked to bare his breast and ask someone to beat it.

He had spoken to no one, not even to his best comrades, of his "Joy of all the afflicted!" He seemed to know nothing of it himself, so deeply hidden was it in his soul. And he evoked it rarely, with precaution.

Now that the fear of unfathomable mystery which was rising before him completely covered him, as the water covers the plants on the bank when the tide is rising, he had a desire to pray. He wanted to fall upon his knees, but was seized with shame before the sentinel; so, with hands clasped upon his breast, he murmured in a low voice:

"Joy of all the afflicted!"

And he repeated with anxiety, in a tone of supplication: "Joy of all the afflicted, descend into me, sustain me!" Something moved softly. It seemed to him that a sorrowful and gentle force hovered in the distance and then vanished, without illuminating the shades of the agony. In the steeple the hour struck. The soldier yawned long and repeatedly.

"Joy of all the afflicted! You are silent! And you will say nothing to Vasily Kashirin!"

He wore an imploring smile, and waited. But in his soul there was the same void as around him. Useless and tormenting thoughts came to him; again he saw the lighted candles, the priest in his robe, the holy image painted on the wall, his father bending and straightening up again, praying and kneeling, casting furtive glances at Vasily to see if he too was praying or was simply amusing himself. And Kashirin was in still deeper anguish than before.

Everything disappeared.

His consciousness went out like the dying embers that one scatters on the hearth; it froze, like the body of a man just dead in which the heart is still warm while the hands and feet are already cold.

Vasily had a moment of wild terror when they came into his cell to get him. He did not even suspect that the hour of the execution had arrived; he simply saw the people and took fright, almost like a child.

"I will not do it again! I will not do it again!" he whispered, without being heard; and his lips became icy as he recoiled slowly towards the rear of his cell, just as in childhood he had tried to escape the punishments of his father.

"You will have to go. . . ."

They talked, they walked around him. He closed his

eyes, staggered, and began to prepare himself painfully. Undoubtedly he had recovered consciousness; he suddenly asked a cigarette of one of the officials, who amiably extended his cigarette case.

X

THE WALLS CRUMBLE

The unknown, surnamed Werner, was a man fatigued by struggle. He had passionately loved life, the theatre, society, art, literature. Endowed with an excellent memory, he spoke several languages perfectly. He was fond of dress, and had excellent manners. Of the whole group of terrorists he was the only one who was able to appear in society without risk of recognition.

For a long time already, and without his comrades having noticed it, he had entertained a profound contempt for men. More of a mathematician than a poet, ecstasy and inspiration had remained, so far, things unknown to him; at times he would look upon himself as a madman seeking to square the circle in seas of human blood. The enemy, against which he daily struggled, could not inspire him with respect; it was nothing but a compact network of stupidities, treasons, falsehoods, base deceits. The thing that had finally destroyed in him forever, it seemed to him, the desire to live, was his execution of a police spy, in obedience to the order of his party. He had killed him tranquilly, but at the sight of this human countenance, inanimate, calm, but still false, pitiable in spite of everything, he suddenly lost his esteem for himself and his work. He considered himself as the most indifferent, the least interesting, of beings. Being a man of will, he did not leave his party; apparently he remained the same; but from that time, there was something cold and terrifying in his eyes. He said nothing to anyone.

He possessed also a very rare quality: he did not know fear. He pitied those of his comrades who had this feeling, especially Vasily Kashirin. But his pity was cold, almost official.

Werner understood that the execution was not simply death, but also something more. In any case, he was determined to meet it calmly, to live until the end as if nothing had happened or would happen. Only in this way could he express the profoundest contempt for the execution and preserve his liberty of mind. In the courtroom—his comrades, although knowing well his cold and haughty intrepidity, perhaps would not have believed it themselves—he thought not of life or of death: he played in his mind a difficult game of chess, giving it his deepest and quietest attention. An excellent player, he had begun this game on the very day of his imprisonment, and he kept it up continually. And the verdict that condemned him did not displace a single piece on the invisible board.

The idea that he probably would not finish the game did not stop Werner. On the morning of the last day, he began by correcting a plan that had failed the night before. With hands pressed between his knees, he sat motionless for a long time; then he arose, and began to walk, reflecting. He had a gait of his own; the upper part of his body inclined a little forwards, and he brought down his heels forcibly; even when the ground was dry, he left clear footprints behind him. He softly whistled a rather simple Italian melody, which helped him to reflect.

But now he was shrugging his shoulders and feeling his pulse. His heart beat fast, but tranquilly and regularly, with a sonorous force. Like a novice thrown into prison for the first time, he attentively examined the cell, the bolts, the chair screwed to the wall, and said to himself: Why do I have such a sensation of joy, of liberty? Yes, of liberty; I think of tomorrow's execution, and it seems to me that it does not exist. I look at the walls, and they seem to me not to exist either. And I feel as free as if instead of being in prison I had just come out of another cell in which I had been confined all my life.

Werner's hands began to tremble, a thing unknown to him. His thought became more and more vibrant. It seemed to him that tongues of fire were moving in his head, trying to escape from his brain to lighten the still obscure distance. Finally the flame darted forth, and the horizon was brilliantly illuminated.

The vague lassitude that had tortured Werner during the last two years had disappeared at the sight of death; his beautiful youth came back as he played. It was even something more than beautiful youth. With the astonishing clearness of mind that sometimes lifts man to the supreme heights of meditation, Werner suddenly saw both life and death; and the majesty of this new spectacle affected him. He seemed to be following a path as narrow as the edge of a blade, on the crest of the loftiest mountain. On one side he saw life, and on the other he saw death; and they were like two deep seas, sparkling and beautiful, melting into each other at the horizon in a single infinite extension.

"What is this, then? What a divine spectacle!" he said slowly.

He arose involuntarily and straightened up, as if in presence of the Supreme Being. And, annihilating the walls, annihilating space and time, by the force of his all penetrating look, he cast his eyes into the depths of the life that he had quitted.

And life took on a new aspect. He no longer tried, as of old, to translate into words what he was; moreover, in the whole range of human language, still so poor and miserly, he found no words adequate. The paltry, dirty, and evil things that suggested to him contempt and sometimes even disgust at the sight of men had completely disappeared, just as, to people rising in a balloon, the mud and filth of the narrow streets become invisible, and ugliness changes into beauty.

With an unconscious movement Werner walked towards the table and leaned upon it with his right arm. Haughty and authoritarian by nature, he had never been seen in a prouder, freer, and more imperious attitude; never had his face worn such a look, never had he so lifted up his head, for at no previous time had he been as free and powerful as now, in this prison, on the eve of execution, at the threshold of death.

In his illuminated eyes, men wore a new aspect, an unknown beauty and charm. He hovered above time, and never had this humanity, which only the night before was howling like a wild beast in the forests, appeared to him so young. What had heretofore seemed to him terrible, unpardonable, and base became suddenly touching and naïve, just as we cherish in the child the awkwardness of its behavior, the incoherent stammerings in which its unconscious genius glimmers, its laughable errors and blunders, its cruel bruises.

"My dear friend!"

Werner smiled suddenly, and his attitude lost its haughty and imposing force. Again he became the prisoner suffering in his narrow cell, weary of seeing a curious eye steadily fixed upon him through the door. He sat down, but not in his usual stiff position, and with a weak and gentle smile such as his face had never worn, looked at the walls and the gratings. And something happened which had never happened to him before: he wept.

"My dear comrades!" he whispered, shedding bitter tears. "My dear comrades!"

What mysterious path had he followed to pass from a feeling of unlimited and haughty liberty to this passionate and moving pity? He did not know. Did he really pity his comrades, or did his tears hide something more passionate, something really greater? His heart, which had suddenly revived and reblossomed, could not tell him. Werner wept, and whispered:

"My dear comrades! My dear comrades!"

And in this man who wept, and who smiled through his tears, no one—not the judges, nor his comrades, nor himself—would have recognized the cold and haughty Werner, skeptical and insolent.

XI

ON THE WAY TO THE GALLOWS

Before getting into the vehicles, all five of the condemned were gathered in a large, cold room with an arched ceiling, resembling an abandoned office or an unused reception room. They were permitted to talk with each other.

Only Tanya Kovalchuk took immediate advantage of the permission. The others pressed in silence hands as cold as ice or as hot as fire; dumb, trying to avoid each other's gaze, they formed a confused and distracted group. Now that they were reunited, they seemed to be ashamed of what they had felt individually in the solitude. They were afraid to look at each other, afraid to show the new, special, somewhat embarrassing thing that they felt or suspected in each other.

Nevertheless, they did look, and, after a smile or two, all found themselves at ease, as before; no change revealed itself, or, if something had happened, all had taken an equal share in it, so that nothing special was noticeable in any one of them. All talked and moved in a queer and jerky fashion, impulsively, either too slowly or too quickly. Sometimes one of them quickly repeated the same words, or else failed to finish a phrase that he had begun or thought he had already spoken. But they noticed nothing of all this. All blinkingly examined the familiar objects without recognizing them, like people who have suddenly taken off their glasses. They often turned around quickly, as if someone were calling them from the rear. But they did not notice this. The cheeks and ears of Musya and Tanya were burning. At first Sergey was a little pale; he soon recovered, and appeared as usual.

Vasily alone attracted attention. Even in such a group he was extraordinary and dreadful. Werner was moved, and said in a low voice to Musya, with deep anxiety:

"What's the matter with him, Musya? Is it possible that he has . . . ? Really, we must speak to him."

Vasily looked at Werner from a distance, as if he had not recognized him; then he lowered his eyes.

"But, Vasily, what's the matter with your hair? What's the matter with you? It's nothing, brother, it will soon be over! We must control ourselves! We really must!"

Vasily did not break the silence. But, when they had already concluded that he would say absolutely nothing, there came a hollow, tardy, terribly distant reply, such as the grave might give up after a long appeal:

"But there's nothing the matter with me. I'm in control of myself!"

He repeated:

"I'm in control of myself!"

Werner was delighted.

"Good, good! You're a brave fellow! All is well!"

But, when his eyes met the dark and heavy gaze of Vasily, he felt a momentary anguish, asking himself: "But whence does he look? whence does he speak?" In a tone of deep tenderness he said:

"Vasily, do you hear? I love you much!"

"And I too, I love you much!" replied a tongue that moved painfully.

Suddenly Musya seized Werner by the arm, and, expressing her astonishment forcibly, like an actress on the stage, she said:

"Werner, what's the matter with you? You said 'I love you'? You never said that to anyone before. And why is your face so sparkling and your voice so tender? What is it? What is it?"

And Werner, also in the manner of an actor dwelling upon his words, answered, as he pressed the young girl's hand:

"Yes, I love, now! Don't tell the others. I'm ashamed of it, but I love my brothers passionately!"

Their eyes met and burst into flame: everything about them became extinct, just as all other lights pale in the fugitive flash of the lightning.

"Yes!" said Musya. "Yes, Werner!"

"Yes!" he answered. "Yes, Musya, yes!"

They had understood something and ratified it forever. With sparkling eyes and quick steps Werner moved on again in the direction of Sergey.

"Sergey!"

But it was Tanya Kovalchuk who answered. Full of joy, almost weeping with maternal pride, she pulled Sergey violently by the sleeve.

"Just listen, Werner! I weep on his account. I torment myself, and he, he does gymnastics!"

"The Müller system?" Werner asked, with a smile. Sergey, somewhat confused, knit his brows.

"You do wrong to laugh, Werner! I have absolutely convinced myself . . ."

Everybody began to laugh. Gaining strength and firmness from their mutual communion, they gradually became again what they used to be; they did not notice it, and thought that they were always the same. Suddenly Werner stopped laughing; with perfect gravity he said to Sergey:

"You're right, Sergey! You're perfectly right!"

"Understand this then!" rejoined Sergey, satisfied. "Of course we . . ."

Just then they were asked to get into the vehicles. The officials even had the amiability to allow them to place themselves in their own fashion, in pairs. In general, they were very amiable with them, even too much so; were they trying to give evidence of a little humanity, or to show that they were not responsible for what was taking place and that everything was happening of itself? It is impossible to say, but all those taking part were pale.

"Go with him, Musya!" said Werner, directing the young girl towards Vasily, who stood motionless.

"I understand!" she answered, nodding her head. "And you?"

"I? Tanya will go with Sergey, you with Vasily. As for me, I shall be alone! What does it matter? I can stand it, you know!"

When they had reached the courtyard, the damp and

slightly warm air fell softly upon their faces and eyes, cut their breathing, and penetrated their shivering bodies, purifying them. It was hard to believe that this stimulant was simply the wind, a spring wind, gentle and moist.

The astonishing spring night had a flavor of melted snow, of infinite space; it made the stones resound. Brisk and busy little drops of water fell rapidly, one after another, making a sonorous song. But, if one of them delayed a little or fell too soon, the song changed into a joyous splash, an animated confusion. Then a big drop fell heavily, and again the spring-like song began, rhythmical and sonorous. Above the city, higher than the walls of the fortress, was the pale halo formed by the electric lights.

Sergey Golovin heaved a deep sigh, and then held his breath, as if regretting to expel from his lungs air so pure and fresh.

"Have we had this fine weather long?" Werner inquired. "It's spring!"

"Only since yesterday!" they answered politely and promptly. "There have been many cold days."

One after another the black vehicles came up, took in two persons, and went away in the darkness, towards the spot where a lantern was swinging in the gateway. Around each vehicle the gray outlines of soldiers were moving; their horses' shoes resounded loudly; often the beasts slipped on the wet snow.

When Werner bent to get into the vehicle, a gendarme said to him, in a vague way:

"There's another in there who *goes* with you!"

Werner was astonished. "Who *goes* where? Ah! Yes! Another one! Who is it?"

The soldier said nothing. In a dark corner something small and motionless, but alive, lay rolled up; an open eye shone under an oblique ray of the lantern. As he sat down, Werner brushed against a knee with his foot.

"Pardon me, comrade!"

There was no answer. Not until the vehicle had started did the man ask hesitatingly, in bad Russian:

"Who are you?"

"My name is Werner, sentenced to be hanged for an attempt upon the life of XX. And you?"

"I am Yanson . . . I must not be hanged."

In two hours they would be face to face with the great mystery as yet unsolved; in two hours they would leave life for death; both were going there, and yet they became acquainted. Life and death were marching simultaneously on two different planes, and to the very end, even in the most laughable and most stupid details, life remained life.

"What did you do, Yanson?"

"I stuck a knife into my boss. I stole money."

From the sound of his voice it seemed as if Yanson were asleep. Werner found his limp hand in the darkness, and pressed it. Yanson lazily withdrew it.

"You are afraid?" Werner asked.

"I do not want to be hanged."

They became silent. Again Werner found the Esthonian's hand, and pressed it tightly between his dry and burning palms. It remained motionless, but Yanson did not try again to release it.

They stifled in the cramped vehicle, whose musty smell mingled with the odors of the soldiers' uniforms, of the muck heap, and of wet leather. The breath of a young gendarme, redolent of garlic and bad tobacco, streamed continually into the face of Werner, who sat opposite. But the keen fresh air came in at the windows, and thanks to this the presence of spring was felt in the little moving box, even more plainly than outside. The vehicle turned now to the right, now to the left; sometimes it seemed to turn around and go back. There were moments when it appeared to the prisoners as if they had been going in a circle for hours. At first the bluish electric light came in between the heavy lowered curtains; then suddenly, after a turn, darkness set in; it was from this that the travelers gathered that they reached the suburbs and were approaching the station of S——. Sometimes, at a sudden turn, Werner's bent and living knee brushed in a friendly way against the bent and living knee of the gendarme, and it was hard to believe in the approaching execution.

"Where are we going?" Yanson asked suddenly. The continuous and prolonged shaking of the somber vehicle gave him vertigo and a little nausea.

Werner answered, and pressed the Esthonian's hand more tightly than before. He would have liked to say specially friendly and kind words to this little sleeping man, whom already he loved more than anyone in the world.

"Dear friend! I think that you're in an uncomfortable position! Draw nearer to me!"

At first Yanson said nothing, but after a moment he replied:

"Thank you! I am comfortable! And you, they are going to hang you too?"

"Yes!" Werner replied with an unlooked-for gaiety, almost laughing. He made a free-and-easy gesture, as if they were speaking of some futile and stupid prank that a band of affectionate practical jokers were trying to play upon them.

"You have a wife?" Yanson asked.

"No! A wife! I! No, I'm alone!"

"So am I! I am alone."

Werner too was beginning to feel the vertigo. At times it seemed to him that he was on his way to some festivity. A queer thing; almost all those who were going to the execution had the same feeling; though a prey to fear and anguish, they rejoiced vaguely in the extraordinary thing that was about to happen. Reality became intoxicated on madness, and death, coupling with life, gave birth to phantoms.

"Here we are at last!" Werner said, gay and curious, when the vehicle stopped; and he leaped lightly to the ground. Not so with Yanson, who resisted, without saying a word, very lazily it seemed, and who refused to descend. He clung to the handle of the door; the gendarme loosened his weak fingers, and grasped his arm. Ivan caught at the corner, at the door, at the high wheel, but yielded at every intervention of the gendarme. He adhered to things rather than gripped them. And it was not necessary to use much force to loosen his grasp. In short, they prevailed over him.

As always at night, the station was dark, deserted, and inanimate. The passenger trains had already passed, and for the train that was waiting on the track for the prisoners, there was no need of light or activity. Werner was seized with *ennui*. He was not afraid, he was not in distress, but he was bored; an immense, heavy, fatiguing *ennui* filled him with a desire to go away no matter where, lie down, and close his eyes. He stretched himself, and yawned repeatedly.

"If only they did these things more quickly!" he said wearily.

Yanson said nothing, and shuddered.

When the condemned passed over the deserted platform surrounded with soldiers, on their way to the poorly lighted railway carriages, Werner found himself placed beside Sergey Golovin. The latter designated something with his hand, and began to speak; his neighbor clearly understood only the word "lamp"; the rest of the phrase was lost in a weary and prolonged yawn.

"What did you say?" Werner asked, yawning also.

"The reflector . . . the lamp of the reflector is smoking," Sergey said.

Werner turned around. It was true; the glass shades were already black.

"Yes, it's smoking!"

Suddenly he thought: What does it matter to me whether the lamp is smoking, when . . . ? Sergey undoubtedly had the same idea. He threw a quick glance at Werner, and turned away his head. But both stopped yawning.

All walked without difficulty to the train; Yanson alone had to be led. At first he stiffened his legs, and glued the soles of his feet to the platform; then he bent his knees. The entire weight of his body fell upon the arms of the policemen; his legs dragged like those of a drunken man, and the toes of his boots ground against the wooden platform. With a thousand difficulties, but in silence, they lifted him into the railway carriage.

Even Vasily Kashirin walked without help; unconsciously he imitated the movements of his comrades. After mounting the steps of the carriage, he drew back; a policeman took him by the elbow to sustain him. Then Vasily began to tremble violently and uttered a piercing cry, pushing away the policeman:

"Aie!"

"Vasily, what's the matter with you?" Werner asked, rushing towards him.

Vasily kept silence, trembling violently. The policeman, vexed and even chagrined, explained:

"I wanted to sustain him, and he—he . . ."

"Come, Vasily, I'll sustain you," Werner said.

He tried to take his comrade's arm, but the latter rejected him, and cried louder than ever.

"Vasily, it's I, Werner!"

"I know! Don't touch me! I want to walk alone!" And, still trembling, he entered the carriage and sat down in a corner. Werner leaned towards Musya, and asked in a low voice, designating Vasily with his eyes:

"Well, how are things with him?"

"Badly!" Musya answered in a whisper. "He's already dead. Tell me, Werner, does death really exist?"

"I don't know, Musya; but I think not!" Werner answered in a serious and thoughtful tone.

"That's what I thought! And he? I suffered on his account during the whole ride; it seemed to me that I was traveling beside a dead man."

"I don't know, Musya. Perhaps death still exists for some. Later it will not exist at all. For me, for instance, death has existed, but now it exists no more."

The slightly pallid cheeks of Musya reddened.

"It has existed for you, Werner? For you?"

"Yes, but no more. As for you!"

They heard a sound at the door of the railway carriage; Michka the Gypsy entered spitting, breathing noisily, and making a racket with his boot heels. He glanced about him, and stopped short.

"There's no room left, officer!" he declared to the fatigued and irritated policeman. "See to it that I travel comfortably, otherwise I won't go with you! Rather hang me right here, to the lamppost! Oh, the scoundrels, what a carriage they've given me! Do you call this a carriage? The Devil's guts, yes, but not a carriage!"

But suddenly he lowered his head, stretched out his

neck, and advanced towards the other prisoners. From the frame of his bushy hair and beard his black eyes shot a savage, sharp, and rather crazy look.

"Oh, my God!" he cried; "so this is where we are! How do you do, sir!"

He sat down opposite Werner, holding out his hand; then, with a wink, he leaned over and swiftly passed his hand across his companion's neck:

"You too? Eh?"

"Yes!" Werner smiled.

"All?"

"All!"

"Oh! oh!" said the Gypsy, showing his teeth. He examined the other prisoners with a swift glance, which nevertheless dwelled longest on Musya and Yanson.

"On account of the Minister?"

"Yes. And you?"

"Oh, sir, my case is quite another story. I'm not so distinguished! I, sir, am a brigand, an assassin. That makes no difference, sir; move up a little to make room for me; it's not my fault that they have put me in your company! In the other world there will be room for all."

He took the measure of all the prisoners with a watchful, distrustful, and savage gaze. But they looked at him without a word, seriously and even with evident compassion. Again he showed his teeth, and slapped Werner several times on the knee.

"So that's how it is, sir! As they say in the song:

" 'Take care to make no sound,
  O forest of green oaks!' "

"Why do you call me sir, when all of us—"

"You're right!" the Gypsy acquiesced with satisfaction.

"Why should you be sir, since you're to be hanged beside me? There sits the real sir!"

He pointed his finger at the silent policeman.

"And your comrade yonder, he doesn't seem to be enjoying himself hugely!" he added, looking at Vasily. "Say there, are you afraid?"

"No!" answered a tongue that moved with difficulty.

"Well, then, don't be so disturbed; there's nothing to be ashamed of. It's only dogs that wag their tails and show their teeth when they're going to be hanged; you're a man. And this marionette, who is he? He certainly isn't one of your crowd?"

His eyes danced incessantly; constantly, with a hissing sound, he spat out his abundant and sweetish saliva. Yanson, doubled up motionless in a corner, slightly shook the ears of his bald fur cap, but said nothing. Werner answered for him:

"He killed his employer."

"My God!" the Gypsy exclaimed in astonishment. "How is it that they permit such birds as that to kill people?"

For a moment he looked stealthily at Musya; then suddenly he turned, and fixed his straight and piercing gaze upon her.

"Miss! Say there, Miss! what's the matter with you? Your cheeks are pink, and you're laughing! Look, she's really laughing! Look! Look!" And with his hooked fingers he seized Werner's knee.

Blushing and somewhat confused, Musya squarely returned the gaze of the attentive and savage eyes that questioned her. All kept silence.

The little cars bounced speedily along the narrow track. At every turn or grade crossing the whistle blew, the engineer being afraid of crushing somebody. Was it not atrocious to think that so much care and effort, in short, all human activity, was being expended in taking men to be hanged? The maddest thing in the world was being done with an air of simplicity and reasonableness. Cars were running; people were sitting in them as usual, traveling as people ordinarily travel. Then there would be a halt as usual: "Five minutes' stop."

And then would come death—eternity—the great mystery.

XII

THE ARRIVAL

The train advanced rapidly.

Sergey Golovin remembered to have spent the summer, some years before, in a little country house along this very line. He had often traveled the road by day and by night, and knew it well. Closing his eyes, he could fancy himself returning by the last train, after staying out late at night with friends.

"I shall arrive soon," he thought, straightening up: and his eyes met the dark, grated window. Around him nothing stirred. Only the Gypsy kept on spitting, and his eyes ran the length of the car, seeming to touch the doors and the soldiers.

"It's cold," Vasily Kashirin said between his thin lips, which seemed frozen.

Tanya Kovalchuk bestirred herself in a maternal fashion:

"Here's a very warm kerchief to wrap around your . . ."

"Neck?" Sergey asked, and he was frightened by his own question.

"What does it matter, Vasya? Take it."

"Wrap yourself up. You'll be warmer," Werner added. He turned to Yanson, and asked him tenderly:

"And aren't you cold, too?"

"Werner, perhaps he wants to smoke. Comrade, do you want to smoke?" Musya asked. "We have some tobacco."

"Yes, I want to."

"Give him a cigarette, Sergey," Werner said.

But Sergey was already holding out his cigarette case.

And all began to tenderly watch Yanson's clumsy fingers as they took the cigarette and struck the match, and the little curl of bluish smoke that issued from his mouth.

"Thank you," Yanson said. "It is good."

"How queer it is," Sergey said.

"How queer what is?" Werner asked.

"The cigarette," Sergey answered, unwilling to say all that he thought.

Yanson held the cigarette between his pale and living fingers. With astonishment he looked at it. And all fixed their gaze on this tiny bit of paper, on this little curl of smoke rising from the gray ashes.

The cigarette went out.

"It's out," Tanya said.

"Yes, it is out."

"The Devil take it!" Werner said, looking anxiously at Yanson, whose hand, holding the cigarette, hung as if dead. Suddenly the Gypsy turned, placed his face close to Werner's, and, looking into the whites of his eyes, whispered:

"Suppose, sir, we were to attack the soldiers of the convoy? What do you think about it?"

"No," Werner answered.

"Why? It's better to die fighting. I'll strike a blow, they'll strike back, and I'll die without noticing it."

"No, it's not necessary," Werner said. And he turned to Yanson:

"Why don't you smoke?"

Yanson's dried-up face wrinkled pitifully, as if someone had pulled the threads that moved the creases in his face. As in a nightmare, Yanson sobbed in a colorless voice, shedding no tears:

"I can't smoke. Ah! Ah! Ah! I must not be hanged. Ah! Ah! Ah!"

Everybody turned towards him. Tanya, weeping copiously, stroked his arms and readjusted his fur cap.

"My dear, my friend, don't cry, my friend! My poor friend!"

Suddenly the cars bumped into one another and began to slow up. The prisoners rose, but immediately sat down again.

"Here we are," Sergey said.

It was as if all the air had suddenly been pumped out of the car. It became difficult to breathe. Their swollen hearts became heavy in their breasts, rose to their throats, beat desperately, and their blood, in its terror, seemed to revolt. Their eyes looked at the trembling floor, their ears listened to the slowly turning wheels, which began to turn more slowly still, and gently stopped.

The train halted.

The prisoners were plunged into a strange stupor. They did not suffer. They seemed to live an unconscious life. Their corporeal being was absent; only its phantom moved about, voiceless but speaking, silent but walking. They went out. They arranged themselves in pairs, breathing in the fresh air of the woods. Like one in a dream, Yanson struggled awkwardly: they dragged him from the car.

"Are we to go on foot?" someone asked almost gaily.

"It isn't far," answered a careless voice.

Without a word they advanced into the forest, along a damp and muddy road. Their feet slipped and sank into the snow, and their hands sometimes clung involuntarily to those of their comrades. Breathing with difficulty, the soldiers marched in single file, on either side of the prisoners. An irritated voice complained:

"Couldn't they have cleared the road? It's difficult to advance."

A deferential voice answered:

"It was cleaned, Your Honor, but it's thawing. There's nothing to be done."

The prisoners began to recover their consciousness. Now they seemed to grasp the idea: "It is true, they could not clean the roads"; now it became obscured again, and there remained only the sense of smell, which perceived with singular keenness the strong and healthy odor of the forest; and now again all became very clear and comprehensible, the forest, and the night, and the road . . . and the certainty that very soon, in a minute, implacable death would lay its hands upon them. And little by little a whispering began:

"It's almost four o'clock."

"I told you so. We started too early."

"The sun rises at five."

"That's right, at five: we should have waited."

They halted in the twilight. Near by, behind the trees, whose huge shadows were waving on the ground, two lanterns swung silently. There the gallows had been erected.

"I've lost one of my rubbers," Sergey said.

"Well?" Werner asked, not understanding.

"I've lost it. I'm cold."

"Where's Vasily?"

"I don't know. There he is."

Vasily was standing close by them, gloomy and motionless.

"Where's Musya?"

"Here I am. Is that you, Werner?"

They looked at each other, their eyes avoiding the silent and terrible, significant swaying of the lanterns. At the left the thin forest seemed to be growing lighter. And beyond, something vast and gray and flat appeared, whence came a moist breeze.

"That's the sea," Sergey said, sucking in the damp air. "That's the sea."

Musya answered by a line from the song:

> *"My love as broad as is the sea."*

"What did you say, Musya?"

> *"The shores of life cannot contain*
> *My love as broad as is the sea."*

" 'My love as broad as is the sea,' " Sergey repeated pensively.

" 'My love as broad as is the sea,' " Werner echoed. And suddenly he exclaimed in astonishment:

"Musya, my little Musya, how young you still are!"

Just then, close to Werner's ear, sounded the breathless and passionate voice of the Gypsy:

"Sir, sir, look at the forest. My God! What is all that? And yonder! The lanterns! My God, is that the scaffold?"

Werner looked at him. The convulsed features of the unfortunate man were frightful to see.

"We must say our farewells," Tanya said.

"Wait! They still have to read the sentence. Where's Yanson?"

Yanson lay stretched in the snow, surrounded by people. A strong smell of ammonia filled the air around him.

"Well, doctor, will you soon be through?" someone asked impatiently.

"It's nothing. A fainting fit. Rub his ears with snow. He's better already. You can read."

The light of a dark lantern fell upon the paper and the ungloved, white hands. Both paper and hands trembled; the voice also.

"Gentlemen, perhaps it is better not to read. You all know the sentence."

"Don't read!" Werner answered for all; and the light immediately went out.

The condemned refused also the services of the priest. The Gypsy said: "No nonsense, Father; you will forgive me, they will hang me."

The broad, dark silhouette of the priest took a few steps backwards and disappeared. The day was breaking. The snow became whiter, the faces of the condemned darker, and the forest barer and sadder.

"Gentlemen, you will go in pairs, choosing your companion. But I beg you to make haste."

Werner pointed to Yanson, who now was standing again, sustained by two soldiers.

"I'll go with him. You, Sergey, take Vasily. You go first."

"All right."

"I'm going with you, Musya," Tanya said. "Come, let's kiss each other!"

Quickly they kissed all around. The Gypsy kissed forcibly; they felt his teeth. Yanson kissed gently and softly, with mouth half open. He did not seem to understand what he was doing. When Sergey and Kashirin had taken a few steps, the latter stopped suddenly, and in a loud

voice, which seemed strange and unfamiliar, shouted:
"Good-bye, comrades."

"Good-bye, comrade," they answered him.

The two started off again. All was quiet. The lanterns behind the trees became motionless. They expected to hear a cry, a voice, some sound or other, but there, as here, all was calm.

"Oh! My God!" someone exclaimed hoarsely.

They turned around: it was the Gypsy, crying desperately:

"They're going to hang us."

He struggled, clutching the air with his hands, and cried again:

"God! Am I to be hanged alone? My God!"

His convulsive hands gripped the hands of Werner, and he continued:

"Sir, my dear sir, my good sir. You'll come with me, won't you?"

Werner, his face drawn with sorrow, answered:

"I can't; I'm with Yanson."

"Oh! My God! then I shall be alone. Why? Why?"

Musya took a step towards him, and said softly:

"I'll go with you."

The Gypsy drew back, and fixed his big, swollen eyes upon her:

"Will you?"

"Yes."

"But you're so little! You're not afraid of me? No, I don't want you to. I will go alone."

"But I'm not afraid of you."

The Gypsy grinned.

"Don't you know that I'm a brigand? And you're willing to go with me? Think a moment. I won't be angry if you refuse."

Musya was silent. And in the faint light of the dawn her face seemed to take on a luminous and mystic pallor. Suddenly she advanced rapidly towards the Gypsy, and, taking his head in her hands, kissed him vigorously. He took her by the shoulders, put her away a little, and then kissed her loudly on her cheeks and eyes.

The soldier nearest them stopped, opened his hands, and let his gun fall. But he did not stoop to pick it up. He stood still for a moment, then turned suddenly, and began to walk into the forest.

"Where are you going?" his comrade shouted in a frightened voice. "Stay!"

But the other painfully endeavored to advance. Suddenly he clutched the air with his hands, and fell, face downward.

"Milksop, pick up your gun, or I'll pick it up for you," the Gypsy cried firmly. "You don't know your duty. Have you never seen a man die?"

Again the lantern swung. The turn of Werner and Yanson had come.

"Good-bye, sir!" the Gypsy said in a loud voice. "We shall meet again in the other world. When you see me there, don't turn away from me."

"Good-bye!"

"I must not be hanged," said Yanson again, in a faint voice.

But Werner grasped his hand, and Yanson took a few steps. Then he was seen to sink into the snow. They bent over him, lifted him up, and carried him, while he weakly struggled in the soldiers' arms.

And again the yellow lanterns became motionless.

"And I, Musya? Am I then to go alone?" Tanya said, sadly. "We've lived together, and now . . ."

"Tanya, my good Tanya!"

The Gypsy hotly interrupted, holding Musya as if he feared that they might tear her from him.

"Miss," he cried, "you're able to go alone. You have a pure soul. You can go alone where you like. But I can't. I'm a bandit. I can't go alone. 'Where are you going?' they'll say to me; 'you who have killed, you who have stolen?' For I've stolen horses, too, Miss. And with her I'll be as if I were with an innocent child. Do you understand?"

"Yes, I understand. Go on then! Let me kiss you once more, Musya."

"Kiss each other! Kiss each other!" the Gypsy said. "You're women. You must say good-bye to each other."

Then came the turn of Musya and the Gypsy. The woman walked carefully, her feet slipping, lifting her skirts by force of habit. Holding her with a strong hand, and feeling the ground with his foot, the man accompanied her to death. The lights became motionless. Around Tanya all was tranquil again, and solitary. The soldiers, gray in the dawn's pale light, were silent.

"I'm left alone," Tanya said. And she sighed. "Sergey is dead, Werner and Vasily are dead. And Musya is dying. I'm alone. Soldiers, my little soldiers, you see, I'm alone, alone. . . ."

The sun appeared above the sea. . . .

They placed the bodies in boxes, and started off with them. With elongated necks, bulging eyes, and blue tongues protruding from their mouths, the dead retraced the road by which, living, they had come.

And the snow was still soft, and the air of the forest was still pure and balmy.

On the white road lay the black rubber that Sergey had lost. . . .

Thus it was that men greeted the rising sun.

THE ABYSS

The day was coming to an end, but the young pair continued to walk and to talk, observing neither the time nor the
way. Before them, in the shadow of a hillock, there
loomed the dark mass of a small grove, and between the
branches of the trees, like the glowing of coals, the sun
blazed, igniting the air and transforming it into a flaming
golden dust. So near and so luminous the sun appeared
that everything seemed to vanish; it alone remained and it
painted the road with its own fiery tints. It hurt the eyes of
the strollers; they turned back, and all at once everything
within their vision was extinguished, became peaceful and
clear, and small and intimate. Somewhere afar, barely a
mile away, the red sunset seized the tall trunk of a fir, which
blazed among the green like a candle in a dark room; the
ruddy glow of the road stretched before them, and every
stone cast its long, black shadow; and the girl's hair, suf-

fused with the sun's rays, now shone with a golden-red
nimbus. A stray, thin hair, wandering from the rest, wav-
ered like a golden spider's thread in the air.

The newly fallen darkness did not break or change the
course of their talk. It continued as before, intimately and
quietly; it flowed along tranquilly on the same theme: on
strength, beauty, and the immortality of love. They were
both very young: the girl was no more than seventeen;
Nemovetsky was four years older. They wore students'
uniforms: she the modest brown dress of a pupil of a girls'
school, he the handsome attire of a technological student.
And, like their conversation, everything about them was
young, beautiful and pure. They had erect, flexible figures,
permeated, as it were, with the clean air and borne along
with a light, elastic gait; their fresh voices, sounding even the simplest words with a reflective tenderness,
were like a rivulet in a calm spring night, when the snow
had not yet wholly thawed from the dark meadows.

They walked on, turning the bend of the unfamiliar
road, and their lengthening shadows, with absurdly small
heads, now advanced separately, now merged into one
long, narrow strip, like the shadow of a poplar. But they
did not see the shadows, for they were too much absorbed
in their talk. While talking, the young man kept his eyes
fixed on the girl's handsome face, upon which the sunset
had seemed to leave a measure of its delicate tints. As for
her, she lowered her gaze on the footpath, brushed the
tiny pebbles to one side with her umbrella, and watched
now one foot, now the other as alternately, with a measured step, they emerged from under her dark dress.

The path was intersected by a ditch with edges of dust
showing the impress of feet. For an instant they paused.
Zinotchka raised her head, looked around her with a per-
plexed gaze, and asked:

"Do you know where we are? I've never been here before."

He made an attentive survey of their position. "Yes, I know. There, behind the hill, is the town. Give me your hand. I'll help you across."

He stretched out his hand, white and slender like a woman's, and which did not know hard work. Zinotchka felt gay. She felt like jumping over the ditch all by herself, running away and shouting "Catch me!" But she restrained herself, with decorous gratitude inclined her head, and timidly stretched out her hand, which still retained its childish plumpness. He had a desire to squeeze tightly this trembling little hand, but he also restrained himself, and with a half bow he deferentially took it in his and modestly turned away when the girl, in crossing, slightly showed her leg.

And once more they walked and talked, but their thoughts were full of the momentary contact of their hands. She still felt the dry heat of his palms and his strong fingers; she felt pleasure and shame, while he was conscious of the submissive softness of her tiny hand and saw the black silhouette of her foot and the small slipper which tenderly embraced it. There was something sharp, something perturbing in this unfading appearance of the narrow hem of white skirts and of the slender foot; with an unconscious effort of will he crushed this feeling. Then he felt more cheerful, and his heart so abundant, so generous in its mood that he wanted to sing, to stretch out his hands to the sky, and to shout "Run! I want to catch you!" —that ancient formula of primitive love among the woods and thundering waterfalls.

And from all these desires tears struggled to the throat.

The long, droll shadows vanished, and the dust of the footpath became gray and cold, but they did not observe this and went on chatting. Both of them had read many good books, and the radiant images of men and women who had loved, suffered, and perished for pure love were borne along before them. Their memories resurrected fragments of nearly forgotten verse, dressed in melodious harmony and the sweet sadness investing love.

"Do you remember where this comes from?" asked Nemovetsky, recalling: ". . . once more she is with me, she whom I love; from whom, having never spoken, I have hidden all my sadness, my tenderness, my love . . ."

"No," Zinotchka replied, and pensively repeated: "all my sadness, my tenderness, my love . . ."

"All my love," with an involuntary echo Nemovetsky responded.

Other memories returned to them. They remembered those girls, pure like the white lilies, who, attired in black nunnish garments, sat solitarily in the park, grieving among the dead leaves, yet happy in their grief. They also remembered the men, who, in the abundance of will and pride, yet suffered, and implored the love and the delicate compassion of women. The images thus evoked were sad, but the love which showed in this sadness was radiant and pure. As immense as the world, as bright as the sun, it arose fabulously beautiful before their eyes, and there was nothing mightier or more beautiful on the earth.

"Could you die for love?" Zinotchka asked as she looked at her childish hand.

"Yes, I could," Nemovetsky replied with conviction, and he glanced at her frankly. "And you?"

"Yes, I too." She grew pensive. "Why, it's happiness to die for one you love. I should want to."

Their eyes met. They were such clear, calm eyes, and there was much good in what they conveyed to the other. Their lips smiled.

Zinotchka paused. "Wait a moment," she said. "You have a thread on your coat." And trustfully she raised her hand to his shoulder and carefully, with two fingers, removed the thread. "There!" she said and, becoming serious, asked, "Why are you so thin and pale? You're studying too much, I fear. You mustn't overdo it, you know."

"You have blue eyes; they have bright points like sparks," he replied, examining her eyes.

"And yours are black. No, brown. They seem to glow. There is in them . . ."

Zinotchka did not finish her sentence, but turned away. Her face slowly flushed, her eyes became timid and confused, while her lips involuntarily smiled. Without waiting for Nemovetsky, who smiled with secret pleasure, she moved forward, but soon paused.

"Look, the sun has set!" she exclaimed with grieved astonishment.

"Yes, it has set," he responded with a new sadness.

The light was gone, the shadows died, everything became pale, dumb, lifeless. At that point of the horizon where earlier the glowing sun had blazed, there now, in silence, crept dark masses of cloud, which step by step consumed the light blue spaces. The clouds gathered, jostled one another, slowly and reticently changed the contours of awakened monsters; they unwillingly advanced, driven against their will by some terrible, implacable force. Tearing itself away from the rest, one tiny, luminous cloud drifted on alone, a frail fugitive.

Zinotchka's cheeks grew pale, her lips turned red; the pupils of her eyes imperceptibly broadened, darkening the eyes. She whispered, "I feel frightened. It's so quiet here. Have we lost our way?"

Nemovetsky contracted his heavy eyebrows and made a searching survey of the place.

Now that the sun was gone and the approaching night was breathing with fresh air, it seemed cold and uninviting. To all sides the gray field spread, with its scant grass, clay gullies, hillocks and holes. There were many of these holes; some were deep and sheer, others were small and overgrown with slippery grass; the silent dusk of night had already crept into them, and because there was evidence here of men's labors, the place appeared even more desolate. Here and there, like the coagulations of cold lilac mist, loomed groves and thickets which seemed to hearken to what the abandoned holes might have to say to them.

Nemovetsky crushed the heavy, uneasy feeling of perturbation which had arisen in him and said, "No, we have not lost our way. I know the road. First to the left, then through that tiny wood. Are you afraid?"

She bravely smiled and answered, "No. Not now. But we ought to be home soon and have some tea."

They increased their gait, but soon slowed down again. They did not glance aside, but felt the morose hostility of the dug-up field, which surrounded them with a thousand dim, motionless eyes, and this feeling bound them together and evoked memories of childhood. These memories were luminous, full of sunlight, of green foliage, of love and laughter. It was as if that had not been life at all, but an immense, melodious song, and they themselves had been in it as sounds, two slight notes: one clear and resonant, like ringing crystal, the other somewhat more dull yet more animated, like a small bell.

Signs of human life were beginning to appear. Two women were sitting at the edge of a clay hole. One sat with crossed legs and looked fixedly below. She raised her head with its kerchief, revealing tufts of entangled hair. Her bent back revealed a dirty blouse with its pattern of flowers as big as apples; its strings were undone and hung loosely. She did not look at the passers-by. The other woman half reclined near by, her head thrown backward. She had a coarse, broad face with a peasant's features, and under her eyes the projecting cheekbones showed two brick-red spots, resembling fresh scratches. She was even filthier than the first woman, and she bluntly stared at the passers-by. When they had passed, she began to sing in a thick, masculine voice:

> *For you alone, my adored one,*
> *Like a flower I did bloom . . .*

"Varka, do you hear?" She turned to her silent companion, and receiving no answer, broke into loud, coarse laughter.

Nemovetsky had known such women, who were filthy even when they were attired in costly, handsome dresses; he was used to them, and now they glided away from his glance and vanished, leaving no trace. But Zinotchka, who nearly brushed them with her modest brown dress, felt something hostile, pitiful and evil, which for a moment entered her soul. In a few minutes the impression was obliterated, like the shadow of a cloud running fast across the golden meadow; and when, going in the same direction, a barefoot man, accompanied by the same kind of filthy woman, passed by them, she saw them but gave them no thought.

And once more they walked on and talked, and behind them there moved, reluctantly, a dark cloud, which cast a transparent shadow. The darkness imperceptibly and stealthily thickened, so that it bore the impress of day, but day oppressed with illness and quietly dying. Now they talked about those terrible feelings and thoughts which visit man at night, when he cannot sleep, and neither sound nor speech give hindrance; when darkness, immense and multiple-eyed, that is life, closely presses to his very face.

"Can you imagine infinity?" Zinotchka asked, putting her plump hand to her forehead and tightly closing her eyes.

"No. Infinity? . . . No . . ." answered Nemovetsky, also shutting his eyes.

"I sometimes see it. I perceived it for the first time when I was yet quite little. Imagine a great many carts. There stands one cart, then another, a third, carts without end, an infinity of carts . . . It's terrible!" Zinotchka trembled.

"But why carts?" Nemovetsky smiled, though he felt uncomfortable.

"I don't know. But I did see carts. One, another—without end."

The darkness steathily thickened. The cloud had already passed over their heads and, being before them, was now able to look into their lowered, paling faces. The dark figures of ragged, sluttish women appeared oftener; it was as if the deep ground holes, dug for some unknown purpose, cast them up to the surface. Now solitary, now in twos or threes, they appeared, and their voices sounded loud and strangely desolate in the stilled air.

"Who are these women? Where do they all come from?" Zinotchka asked in a low, timorous voice.

Nemovetsky knew who these women were. He felt terrified at having fallen into this evil and dangerous neighborhood, but he answered calmly, "I don't know. It's nothing. Let's not talk about them. It won't be long now. We only have to pass through this little wood, and we shall reach the gate and town. It's a pity that we started out so late."

She thought his words absurd. How could he call it late, when they started out at four o'clock? She looked at him and smiled. But his eyebrows did not relax, and, in order to calm and comfort him, she suggested, "Let's walk faster. I want tea. And the wood's quite near now."

"Yes, let's walk faster."

When they entered the wood, and the silent trees joined in an arch above their heads, it became very dark but also very snug and quieting.

"Give me your hand," proposed Nemovetsky.

Irresolutely she gave him her hand, and the light contact seemed to lighten the darkness. Their hands were motionless and did not press each other. Zinotchka even slightly moved away from her companion. But their whole consciousness was concentrated in the perception of the tiny place of the body where the hands touched one another. And again the desire came to talk about the beauty and the mysterious power of love, but to talk without violating the silence, to talk by means not of words but of glances. And they thought that they ought to glance, and they wanted to, yet they didn't dare.

"And here are some more people!" said Zinotchka cheerfully.

In the glade, where there was more light, three men in silence sat near an empty bottle and expectantly looked at the newcomers. One of them, shaven like an actor, laughed and whistled in such a way as if to say, "Oho!"

Nemovetsky's heart fell and froze in a trepidation of

horror, but, as if pushed on from behind, he walked right near the sitting trio, beside whom ran the footpath. These men were waiting, and three pairs of eyes, motionless and terrifying, looked at the strollers. And, desirous of gaining the good will of these morose, ragged men, in whose silence he scented a threat, and of winning their sympathy for his helplessness, he asked, "Is this the way to the gate?"

They did not reply. The shaven one whistled something mocking and not quite definable, while the others remained silent and looked at them with a heavy, malignant intentness. They were drunk, and evil, and they were hungry for women and sensual diversion. One of the men, with a ruddy face, rose to his feet like a bear and sighed heavily. His companions quickly glanced at him, then once more fixed an intent gaze on Zinotchka.

"I feel terribly afraid," she whispered with lips alone.

He did not hear her words, but Nemovetsky understood her from the weight of the arm which leaned on him. And, trying to preserve a demeanor of calm, yet feeling the fated irrevocableness of what was about to happen, he advanced on his way with a measured firmness. Three pairs of eyes approached nearer, gleamed, and were left behind one's back. "It's better to run," Nemovetsky thought and answered himself, "No, it's better not to run."

"He's a dead 'un! You ain't afraid of him?" said the third of the sitting trio, a bald-headed fellow with a scant red beard. "And the little girl is a fine one. May God grant everyone such a one!"

The trio gave a forced laugh.

"Mister, wait! I want to have a word with you!" the tall man said in a thick bass voice and glanced at his comrades.

They rose.

Nemovetsky walked on, without turning around.

"You ought to stop when you're asked," said the red-haired man. "An' if you don't, you're likely to get something you ain't counting on!"

"D'you hear?" the tall man growled, and in two jumps caught up with the strollers.

A massive hand descended on Nemovetsky's shoulder and made him reel. He turned and met very close to his face the round, bulgy, terrible eyes of his assailant. They were so near that it was as if he were looking at them through a magnifying glass, and he clearly distinguished the small red veins on the whites and the yellowish matter on the lids. He let fall Zinotchka's numb hand and, thrusting his hand into his pocket, he murmured, "Do you want money? I'll give you some, with pleasure."

The bulgy eyes grew rounder and gleamed. And when Nemovetsky averted his gaze from them, the tall man stepped slightly back and, with a short blow, struck Nemovetsky's chin from below. Nemovetsky's head fell backward, his teeth clicked, his cap descended to his forehead and fell off; waving with his arms, he dropped to the ground. Silently, without a cry, Zinotchka turned and ran with all the speed of which she was capable. The man with the clean-shaven face gave a long-drawn shout, which sounded strangely: "A-a-ah! . . ."

And, still shouting, he gave pursuit.

Nemovetsky, reeling, jumped up, and before he could straighten himself he was again felled with a blow on the neck. There were two of them, and he was only one, frail and unused to physical combat. Nevertheless, he fought for a long time, scratched with his fingernails like an obstreperous woman, bit with his teeth, and sobbed with an unconscious despair. When he was too weak to do more, they lifted him and bore him away. He still resisted, but there was a din in his head; he ceased to understand what was being done with him and hung helplessly in the hands which bore him. The last thing he saw was a fragment of the red beard, which almost touched his mouth, and beyond it the darkness of the wood and the light-colored blouse of the running girl. She ran silently and fast, as she had run but a few days before when they were playing tag; and behind her, with short strides, overtaking her, ran the clean-shaven one. Then Nemovetsky felt an emptiness around him, his heart stopped short as he experienced the sensation of falling, then he struck the earth and lost all consciousness.

The tall man and the red-haired man, having thrown Nemovetsky into a ditch, stopped for a few moments to listen to what was happening at the bottom of the ditch. But their faces and their eyes were turned to one side, in the direction taken by Zinotchka. From there arose the high, stifled woman's cry, which quickly died. The tall man muttered angrily, "The pig!"

Then, making a straight line, breaking twigs on the way, like a bear, he began to run.

"And me! And me!" his red-haired comrade cried in a thin voice, running after him. He was weak and he panted; in the struggle his knee was hurt, and he felt badly because the idea about the girl had come to him first and he would get her last. He paused to rub his knee; then, putting a finger to his nose, he sneezed; and once more began to run and to cry his plaint:

"And me! And me!"

The dark cloud dissipated itself across the whole heavens, ushering in the calm, dark night. The darkness soon swallowed up the short figure of the red-haired man, but for some time there was audible the uneven fall of his feet, the rustle of the disturbed leaves, and the shrill, plaintive cry:

"And me! Brothers, and me!"

Earth got into Nemovetsky's mouth, and his teeth grated. On coming to himself, the first feeling he experienced was consciousness of the pungent, pleasant smell of the soil. His head felt dull, as if heavy lead had been poured into it; it was hard to turn it. His whole body ached, there was an intense pain in the shoulder, but no bones were broken. Nemovetsky sat up, and for a long time looked above him, neither thinking nor remembering. Directly over him a bush lowered its broad leaves, and between them was visible the now clear sky. The cloud had passed over, without dropping a single drop of rain, and leaving the air dry and exhilarating. High up, in the middle of the heavens, appeared the carven moon, with a transparent border. It was living its last nights, and its light was cold, dejected, and solitary. Small tufts of cloud rapidly passed over in the heights where, it was clear, the wind was strong; they did not obscure the moon, but cautiously passed it by. In the solitariness of the moon, in the timorousness of the high, bright clouds, in the blowing of the wind barely perceptible below, one felt the mysterious depth of night dominating over the earth.

Nemovetsky suddenly remembered everything that had happened, and he could not believe that it had happened. All that was so terrible and did not resemble truth. Could truth be so horrible? He, too, as he sat there in the night and looked up at the moon and the running clouds, appeared strange to himself and did not resemble reality. And he began to think that it was an ordinary albeit horrible nightmare. Those women, of whom they had met so many, had also become a part of this terrible and evil dream.

"It can't be!" he said with conviction, and weakly shook his heavy head. "It can't be!"

He stretched out his hand and began to look for his cap. His failure to find it made everything clear to him; and he understood that what had happened had not been a dream, but the horrible truth. Terror possessed him anew, as a few moments later he made violent exertions to scramble out of the ditch, again and again to fall back with handfuls of soil, only to clutch once more at the hanging shrubbery.

He scrambled out at last and began to run, thoughtlessly, without choosing a direction. For a long time he went on running, circling among the trees. With equal suddenness, thoughtlessly, he ran in another direction. The branches of the trees scratched his face, and again everything began to resemble a dream. And it seemed to Nemovetsky that something like this had happened to him before: darkness, invisible branches of trees, while he had run with closed eyes, thinking that all this was a dream. Nemovetsky paused, then sat down in an uncomfortable posture on the ground, without any elevation. And again he thought of his cap, and he said, "This is I. I ought to kill myself. Yes, I ought to kill myself, even if this is a dream."

He sprang to his feet, but remembered something and walked slowly, his confused brain trying to picture the place where they had been attacked. It was quite dark in the woods, but sometimes a stray ray of moonlight broke through and deceived him; it lighted up the white tree trunks, and the wood seemed as if it were full of motionless and mysteriously silent people. All this, too, seemed as if it had been, and it resembled a dream.

"Zinaida Nikolaevna!" Nemovetsky called, pronouncing the first word loudly, the second in a lower voice, as if with the loss of his voice he had also lost hope of any response.

And no one responded.

Then he found the footpath, and knew it at once. He reached the glade. Back where he had been, he fully understood that it all had actually happened. He ran about in his terror, and he cried:

"Zinaida Nikolaevna! It is I! I!"

No one answered his call. He turned in the direction where he thought the town lay, and uttered a prolonged shout:

"He-l-l-p!" . . .

And once more he ran about, whispering something while he swept the bushes, when before his eyes there appeared a dim, white spot, which resembled a spot of congealed faint light. It was the prostrate body of Zinotchka.

"Oh, God! What's this?" said Nemovetsky, with dry eyes, but in a voice that sobbed. He got down on his knees and came in contact with the girl lying there.

His hand fell on the bared body, which was so smooth and firm and cold but by no means dead. Trembling, he passed his hand over her.

"Darling, sweetheart, it is I," he whispered, seeking her face in the darkness.

Then he stretched out a hand in another direction, and again came in contact with the naked body, and no matter where he put his hand it touched this woman's body, which was so smooth and firm and seemed to grow warm under the contact of his hand. Sometimes he snatched his hand away quickly, and again he let it rest; and just as, all tattered and without his cap, he did not appear real to himself, so it was with this bared body: he could not associate it with Zinotchka. All that had passed here, all that men had done with this mute woman's body, appeared to him in all its loathsome reality, and found a strange, intensely eloquent response in his whole body. He stretched forward in a way that made his joints crackle, dully fixed his eyes on the white spot, and contracted his brows like a man thinking. Horror before what had happened congealed in him, and like a solid lay on his soul, something extraneous and impotent.

"Oh, God! What's this?" he repeated, but the sound of it rang untrue, like something deliberate.

He felt her heart: it beat faintly but evenly, and when he bent toward her face he became aware of its equally faint breathing. It was as if Zinotchka were not in a deep swoon, but simply sleeping. He quietly called to her:

"Zinotchka, it's I!"

But at once he felt that he would not like to see her awaken for a long time. He held his breath, quickly glanced round him, then he cautiously smoothed her cheek; first he kissed her closed eyes, then her lips, whose softness yielded under his strong kiss. Frightened lest she awaken, he drew back and remained in a frozen attitude. But the body was motionless and mute, and in its helplessness and easy access there was something pitiful and exasperating, not to be resisted and attracting one to itself. With infinite tenderness and stealthy, timid caution, Nemovetsky tried to cover her with the fragments of her dress, and this double consciousness of the material and the naked body was as sharp as a knife and as incomprehensible as madness. Here had been a banquet of wild beasts . . . he scented the burning passion diffused in the air, and dilated his nostrils.

"It's I! I!" he madly repeated, not understanding what surrounded him and still possessed of the memory of the white hem of the skirt, of the black silhouette of the foot and of the slipper which so tenderly embraced it. As he listened to Zinotchka's breathing, his eyes fixed on the spot where her face was, he moved a hand. He listened, and moved the hand again.

"What am I doing?" he cried out loudly in despair, and sprang back, terrified of himself.

For a single instant Zinotchka's face flashed before him and vanished. He tried to understand that this body was Zinotchka, with whom he had lately walked, and who had spoken of infinity; and he could not understand. He tried to feel the horror of what had happened, but the horror was too great for comprehension, and it did not appear.

"Zinaida Nikolaevna!" he shouted imploringly. "What does this mean? Zinaida Nikolaevna!"

But the tormented body remained mute, and, continuing his mad monologue, Nemovetsky descended on his knees. He implored, threatened, said that he would kill himself, and he grasped the prostrate body, pressing it to him . . . The now warmed body softly yielded to his exertions, obediently following his motions, and all this was so terrible, incomprehensible and savage that Nemovetsky once more jumped to his feet and abruptly shouted: "Help!"

But the sound was false, as if it were deliberate.

And once more he threw himself on the unresisting body, with kisses and tears, feeling the presence of some sort of abyss, a dark, terrible, drawing abyss. There was no Nemovetsky; Nemovetsky had remained somewhere behind, and he who had replaced him was now with passionate sternness mauling the hot, submissive body and was saying with the sly smile of a madman:

"Answer me! Or don't you want to? I love you! I love you!"

With the same sly smile he brought his dilated eyes to Zinotchka's very face and whispered:

"I love you! You don't want to speak, but you're smiling, I can see that. I love you! I love you! I love you!"

He more strongly pressed to him the soft, will-less body, whose lifeless submission awakened a savage passion. He wrung his hands, and hoarsely whispered:

"I love you! We'll tell no one, and no one will know. I'll marry you tomorrow, when you like. I love you. I'll kiss you, and you'll answer me—yes? Zinotchka . . ."

With some force he pressed his lips to hers, and felt conscious of his teeth's sharpness in her flesh; in the force and anguish of the kiss he lost the last sparks of reason. It seemed to him that the lips of the girl quivered. For a single instant flaming horror lighted up his mind, opening before him a black abyss.

And the black abyss swallowed him.

SILENCE

I

On a moonlit night in May, when the nightingales were singing, his wife came to Father Ignaty, who was sitting in his study. Her face was expressive of suffering, and the small lamp trembled in her hand. She came up to her husband, touched him on the shoulder, and said, sobbing, "Father, let's go to Verochka!"

Without turning his head, Father Ignaty frowned over his spectacles at his wife, and looked long and fixedly, until she made a motion of discomfort with her free hand, and sat down on a low divan.

"How pitiless you *both* are," she said slowly and with strong emphasis on the word "both," and her kindly puffed face was contorted with a look of pain and hardness, as though she wished to express by her looks how hard people were—her husband and her daughter.

Father Ignaty gave a laugh and stood up. Closing his

book, he took off his spectacles, put them into their case, and fell into a brown study. His big black beard, shot with silver threads, lay in a graceful curve upon his chest, and rose and fell slowly under his deep breathing.

"Well, then, we'll go!" he said.

Olga Stepanovna rose quickly and asked in a timid, ingratiating voice, "Only don't scold her, Father! You know what she is."

Vera's room was in a belvedere at the top of the house, and the narrow wooden stairs bent and groaned under the heavy steps of Father Ignaty. Tall and ponderous, he was obliged to stoop so as not to hit his head against the ceiling above, and he frowned fastidiously when his wife's white jacket touched his face. He knew that nothing would come of their conversation with Vera.

"What, is that you?" Vera asked, lifting one bare arm to her eyes. Her other arm rested on the top of the white summer counterpane, from which it was scarcely distinguishable—so white, transparent and cold was it.

"Verochka!" the mother began, but gave a sob and was silent.

"Vera!" the father said, endeavoring to soften his dry, hard voice. "Vera, tell us what's the matter with you?"

Vera was silent.

"Vera, are your mother and I undeserving of your confidence? Don't we love you? Have you anyone nearer to you than ourselves? Speak to us of your grief, and believe me, an old and experienced man, you'll feel the better for it. And, so shall we. Look at your old mother, how she's suffering."

"Verochka—!"

"And for me—" his voice trembled, as though something in it had broken in two "—and for me do you think it's easy? As though I didn't see that you were devoured by some grief—but what is it? And I, your father, am kept in ignorance. Is it right?"

Vera still kept silence. Father Ignaty stroked his beard with special precaution, as though he feared that his fingers would involuntarily begin to tear it, and continued:

"Against my wishes you went to St. Petersburg—did I curse you for your disobedience? Or did I refuse you money? Or do you say I wasn't kind? Well, why don't you speak? See the good your St. Petersburg has done you!"

Father Ignaty ceased speaking, and there rose before his mind's eye something big, granite-built, terrible, full of unknown dangers and of strange, callous people. And there, alone and weak, was his Vera, and there she had been ruined. An angry hatred of that terrible, incomprehensible city arose in Father Ignaty's soul, together with anger towards his daughter, who kept silent, so obstinately silent.

"St. Petersburg has nothing to do with it," Vera said crossly, and closed her eyes. "But there's nothing the matter with me. You'd better go to bed, it's late."

"Verochka!" her mother groaned. "My little daughter, confide in me!"

"Oh! Mama!" Vera said, impatiently interrupting her.

Father Ignaty sat down on a chair and began to laugh. "Well then, nothing's the matter after all?" he asked ironically.

"Father," Vera said in a sharp voice, raising herself up on her bed, "you know that I love you and Mama. But— I do feel so dull. All this will pass away. Really, you'd better go to bed. I want to sleep, too. Tomorrow, or sometime, we'll have a talk."

Father Ignaty rose abruptly, so that his chair bumped against the wall, and took his wife's arm. "Let's go!"

"Verochka—!"

"Let's go, I tell you," Father Ignaty cried. "If she's forgotten God, should we too? Why should we!"

He drew Olga Stepanovna away, almost by main force, and as they were descending the stairs, she, dragging her steps more slowly, said in an angry whisper, "Ugh! It's you who have made her so. It's from you she's got this manner. And you'll have to answer for it. Ah! how wretched I am."

And she began to cry and kept blinking her eyes, so much so that she could not see the steps, and letting her feet go down, as it were, into an abyss below, into which she wished to precipitate herself.

From that day forward, Father Ignaty ceased to talk to his daughter, and she seemed not to notice the change. As before, she would now lie in her room, now go about, frequently wiping her eyes with the palms of her hands, as though they were obstructed. And oppressed by the silence of these two people, the priest's wife, who was fond of jokes and laughter, became lost and timid, hardly knowing what to say or do.

Sometimes Vera went out for a walk. About a week after the conversation related above, she went out in the evening, as usual. They never again saw her alive, for that evening she threw herself under a train, which cut her in two.

Father Ignaty buried her himself. His wife was not present at the church because at the news of Vera's death she had had a stroke. She had lost the use of her feet and hands and tongue, and lay motionless in a semi-darkened room, while close by her the bells tolled in the belfry. She heard them all coming out of church, heard the choristers singing before their house, and tried to raise her hand to cross herself, but the hand would not obey her will. She wished to say "Good-bye, Vera," but her tongue, swollen and heavy, lay inert in her mouth. She lay so still that anyone who saw her would have thought that she was resting, or asleep. Only—her eyes were open.

There were many people in the church at the funeral, both acquaintances of Father Ignaty's and strangers. All present felt pity for Vera, who had died such a terrible death, and they tried to find signs of profound grief in Father Ignaty's movements and voice. They were not fond of Father Ignaty because he was rough and haughty in his manners, harsh and unforgiving with his penitents, while he himself was jealous and greedy, and availed himself of every chance to take more than his dues from a parishioner. They all wished to see him suffering, broken-down; they wished to see him acknowledge that he was doubly guilty of his daughter's death—as a harsh father, and as a bad priest, who could not protect his own flesh and blood from sin. So they all watched him with curiosity, but he, feeling their eyes directed on his broad, powerful back, endeavored to straighten it, and thought not so much of his dead daughter, as of not compromising his dignity.

"A well-seasoned priest," Karzenov the carpenter, to whom he still owed money for some frames, said with a nod in his direction.

And so, firm and upright, Father Ignaty went to the cemetery, and came back the same. And not till he reached the door of his wife's room did his back bend a little; but that might have been because the door was not high enough for his stature. Coming in from the light, he could only with difficulty distinguish his wife's face, and when he succeeded in so doing, he perceived that it was perfectly still and that there were no tears in her eyes. In them there was neither anger nor grief; they were dumb and painfully, obstinately silent, as was also her whole obese, feeble body, which was pressed against the bed rail.

"Well, what? How are you feeling?" Father Ignaty inquired.

But her lips were dumb, and her eyes were silent. Father Ignaty laid his hand on her forehead; it was cold and damp, and Olga Stepanovna gave no sign whatever that she had felt his touch. And when he removed his hands from her forehead, two deep, gray eyes looked at him without blinking; they seemed almost black on account of the dilation of the pupils, and in them was neither grief nor anger.

"Well, I'll go to my own room," said Father Ignaty, who had turned cold and frightened.

He went through the guestchamber, where everything was clean and orderly as ever, and the high-backed chairs stood swathed in white covers, like corpses in their shrouds. At one of the windows hung a wire cage, but it was empty, and the door was open.

"Nastasya!" Father Ignaty called, and his voice seemed rough to him, and he felt awkward about having called so loud in those quiet rooms, so soon after the funeral of their daughter. "Nastasya," he called more gently, "where's the canary?"

The cook, who had cried so much that her nose was swollen and as red as a beet, answered rudely, "Don't know. It flew away."

"Why did you let it go?" Father Ignaty said, angrily knitting his brows.

Nastasya burst out crying, and, wiping her eyes with the ends of a print kerchief she wore over her head, said through her tears, "The dear little soul of the young mistress. How could I keep it?"

And it seemed even to Father Ignaty that the happy little yellow canary, which used to sing always with its head thrown back, was really the soul of Vera, and that if it had not flown away, it would have been impossible to say that Vera was dead. And he became still more angry with the cook, and shouted, "Get along!" And when Nastasya did not at once make for the door, he added "Fool!"

II

From the day of the funeral, silence reigned in the little house. It was not stillness, for that is the mere absence of noise, but it was *silence,* which means that those who kept silence could, apparently, have spoken if they had pleased. So thought Father Ignaty when, entering his wife's chamber, he would meet an obstinate glance, so heavy that it was as though the whole air were turned to lead, and was pressing on his head and back. So he thought when he examined his daughter's music, on which her very voice was impressed; her books, and her portrait, a large one painted in colors, which she had brought with her from St. Petersburg. In examining her portrait, a certain order was evolved: first he would look at her neck, on which the light was thrown, and would imagine to himself a scratch on it, such as was on the neck of the dead Vera, and the origin of which he could not understand. And every time he meditated on the cause. If it had been the train which struck it, it would have shattered her whole head, and the head of the dead Vera was quite uninjured. Could it be that someone, when carrying home the corpse, had touched it with his foot; or was it done unintentionally with the nail?

But to think long about the details of her death was horrible to Father Ignaty, so he would pass on to the eyes of the portrait. They were black and beautiful, with long eyelashes, the thick shadow of which lay below, so that the whites seemed peculiarly bright, and the two eyes were as though enclosed in black mourning frames. The unknown artist, a man of talent, had given a strange expression to them: It was as though between the eyes, and that on which they rested, there was a thin, transparent film. It reminded one of the black top of a grand piano, on which the summer dust lay in a thin layer, almost imperceptible, but still dimming the brightness of the polished wood. And wherever Father Ignaty placed the portrait, the eyes continually followed him, not speaking, but silent; and the silence was so clear that it seemed possible to hear it. And by degrees Father Ignaty came to think that he did hear the silence.

Every morning after the Eucharist, Father Ignaty would go to the sitting room, would take in at a glance the empty cage, and all the well-known arrangement of the room, sit down in an armchair, close his eyes, and listen to the silence of the house. It was something strange. The cage was gently and tenderly silent; and grief and tears, and faraway dead laughter were felt in that silence. The silence of his wife, softened by the intervening walls, was obstinate, heavy as lead; and terrible, so terrible that Father Ignaty turned cold on the hottest day. Endless, cold as the grave, mysterious as death, was the silence of his daughter. It was as though the silence were a torture to itself, and as though it longed passionately to pass into speech, but that something strong and dull as a machine held it motionless, and stretched it like a wire. And then, somewhere in the far distance, the wire began to vibrate and emit a soft, timid, pitiful sound. Father Ignaty, with a mixture of joy and fear, would catch this incipient sound, and, pressing his hands on the arms of the chair, would stretch his head forwards and wait for the sound to reach him. But it would break off, and lapse into silence.

"Nonsense!" Father Ignaty would angrily exclaim, and

rise from the chair, tall and upright as ever. From the window was to be seen the market place, bathed in sunlight, paved with round, even stones, and across from it was the stone wall of a long, windowless storehouse. At the corner stood a cab like a statue in clay, and it was incomprehensible why it continued to stand there, when for whole hours together not a single passer-by was to be seen.

III

Out of the house Father Ignaty had much talking to do: with his ecclesiastical subordinates, and with his parishioners when he was performing his duties; and sometimes with acquaintances when he played with them at "Preference." But when he returned home he thought that he had been silent the entire day. This came of the fact that with none of these people could he speak of the question which was the chief and most important of all to him, which racked his thoughts every night: Why had Vera died?

Father Ignaty was unwilling to admit to himself that it was impossible now to solve this difficulty, and kept on thinking that it was still possible.

Every night—and they were all sleepless for him now— he would recall the moment when he and his wife had stood by Vera's bed at darkest midnight, and he had entreated her "Speak!" And when in his recollections he arrived at that word, even the rest of the scene presented itself to him as being different from what it had really been. His closed eyes preserved in their darkness a vivid, unblurred picture of that night; they distinctly saw Vera lifting herself up upon her bed and saying with a smile . . . But what did she say? And that unuttered word of hers, which would solve the whole question, seemed so near, that if he were to stretch his ear and still the beating of his heart, then, then he would hear it—and at the same time it was so infinitely, so desperately far.

Father Ignaty would rise from his bed, and, stretching forth his clasped hands in a gesture of supplication, entreat: "Vera!"

And silence was the answer he received.

One evening Father Ignaty went to Olga Stepanovna's room, where he had not been for about a week, and, sitting down near the head of her bed, he turned away from her doleful, obstinate gaze, and said, "Mother! I want to talk to you about Vera. Do you hear?"

Her eyes were silent, and Father Ignaty, raising his voice, began to speak in the loud and severe tones with which he addressed his penitents:

"I know you think that I was the cause of Vera's death. But consider, did I love her less than you? You judge strangely—I was strict, but did that prevent her from doing as she pleased? I made little of the respect due to a father; I meekly bowed my neck when she, with no fear of my curse, went away—there. And you—Mother— didn't you with tears entreat her to remain, until I ordered you to be silent? Am I responsible for her being born hard-hearted? Didn't I teach her of God, of humility, and of love?"

Father Ignaty gave a swift glance into his wife's eyes, and turned away.

"What could I do with her, if she wouldn't open her grief to me. Command? I commanded her. Entreat? I entreated. What? Do you think I ought to have gone down on my knees before the little chit of a girl, and wept, like an old woman! What she had got in her head, and where she got it, I don't know. Cruel, heartless daughter!"

Father Ignaty smote his knees with his fists.

"She was devoid of love—that's what it was! I know well enough what she called me—a tyrant. You she did love, didn't she? You who wept, and—humbled yourself?"

Father Ignaty laughed noiselessly.

"Lo—o—ved! That's it, to comfort you she chose such a death—a cruel, disgraceful death! She died on the ballast, in the dirt—like a d—d—og, to which someone gives a kick on the muzzle."

Father Ignaty's voice sounded low and hoarse.

"I'm ashamed! I'm ashamed to go out into the street! I'm ashamed to come out of the chancel! I'm ashamed before God. Cruel, unworthy daughter! One could curse you in your grave. . . ."

When Father Ignaty glanced again at his wife, she had fainted, and did not come to herself for some hours. And when she did come to herself her eyes were silent, and it was impossible to know whether or not she understood what Father Ignaty had said to her.

That same night—it was a moonlit night in July, still, warm, soundless—Father Ignaty crept on tiptoe, so that his wife and her nurse should not hear him, up the stairs to Vera's room. The window of the belvedere had not been opened since Vera's death, and the atmosphere was dry and hot, with a slight smell of scorching from the iron roof, which had become heated during the day. There was an uninhabited and deserted feeling about the apartment from which man had been absent so long, and in which the wood of the walls, the furniture and other objects gave out a faint smell of growing decay.

The moonlight fell in a bright stripe across the window and floor, and, reflected by the carefully washed white boards, it illumined the corners with a dim semilight, and the clean white bed with its two pillows, a big one and a little one, looked unearthly and ghostly. Father Ignaty opened the window, and the fresh air poured into the room in a broad stream, smelling of dust, of the neighboring river and the flowering lime, and bore on it a scarcely audible chorus, apparently, of people rowing a boat and singing as they rowed.

Stepping silently on his naked feet, like a white ghost, Father Ignaty approached the empty bed, and, bending his knees, fell face down on the pillows and embraced them—the place where Vera's face ought to have been.

He lay this way for a long time. The song became louder, and then gradually became inaudible; but he still lay there, with his long black hair dishevelled over his shoulders and on the bed.

The moon had moved on, and the room had become darker, when Father Ignaty raised his head, and, throwing into his voice all the force of a long-suppressed and long-unacknowledged love, listening to his words, as though not he, but Vera, were listening to them, exclaimed:

"Vera, my daughter! Do you understand what it means, daughter! Little daughter! My heart! My blood! My life! Your father, your poor old father, already gray and feeble."

His shoulders shook, and all his heavy frame was convulsed. With a shudder Father Ignaty whispered tenderly, as to a little child:

"Your poor old father asks you. Yes, Verochka, he entreats. He weeps. He who never was so wont. Your grief, my little daughter, your suffering, are my own. More than mine."

Father Ignaty shook his head.

"More, Verochka. What is death to me, an old man? But you . . . If only you had realized how tender, weak and timid you were! Do you remember how when you pricked your finger and the blood came, you began to cry? My little daughter! And you do indeed love me, love me dearly, I know. Every morning you kiss my hand. Speak, speak of what is grieving you—and I with these two hands will strangle your grief. They are still strong, Vera, these hands."

His locks shook.

"Speak!"

He fixed his eyes on the wall, and, stretching out his hands, cried:

"Speak."

But the chamber was silent, and from the far distance was borne in the sound of the long and short whistles of a locomotive.

Father Ignaty, rolling his distended eyes, as though there stood before him the frightful ghost of a mutilated corpse, slowly raised himself from his knees, and with uncertain movement lifted his hand, with the fingers separated and nervously stretched out, to his head. Going out by the door, Father Ignaty sharply whispered the word:

"Speak!"

And silence was the answer he received.

IV

The next day, after an early and solitary dinner, Father Ignaty went to the cemetery—for the first time since the death of his daughter. It was close, deserted, and still, as though the hot day were but an illumined night; but Father Ignaty, as his habit was, with an effort straightened his back, looked sternly from side to side, and thought that he was the same as heretofore. He did not regard the new, but terrible, weakness of his legs, nor that his long beard had grown completely white, as though bitten by a hard frost. The way to the cemetery led through the long, straight street, which sloped gently upwards, and at the end of which gleamed white the roof of the lych gate, which was like a black, ever-open mouth edged with gleaming teeth.

Vera's grave lay in the very depth of the cemetery, where the graveled pathways ended; and Father Ignaty had to wander for a long time on the narrow tracks, along a broken line of little mounds which protruded from the grass, forgotten and deserted by all. Here and there he came upon sloping monuments green with age, broken-down railings, and great, heavy stones cast upon the ground and pressing it with a sort of grim, senile malignity.

Vera's grave was next to one of these stones. It was covered with new sods, already turning yellow, while all around it was green. A rowan tree was intertwined with a maple, and a widely spreading clump of hazel stretched its pliant branches with rough-furred leaves over the grave. Sitting down on the neighboring tomb, and sighing repeatedly, Father Ignaty looked around, cast a glance at the cloudless desert sky, in which the red-hot disc of the sun hung suspended in perfect immobility—and only then did he become conscious of that profound stillness, like nothing else in the world, which holds sway over a cemetery, when there is not a breath of wind to rustle the dead leaves. And once more the thought came to Father Ignaty, that this was not stillness, but silence. It overflowed to the very brick walls of the cemetery, climbed heavily over them, and submerged the city. And its end was only there—in those gray, stubbornly, obstinately silent eyes.

Father Ignaty shrugged his shoulders, which were becoming cold, and let his eyes fall on Vera's grave. He gazed long at the short little seared stalks of grass, which had been torn from the ground somewhere in the wide wind-swept fields and had failed to take root in the new soil; and he could not realize that there, under that grass, a few feet from him, lay Vera. And this nearness seemed incomprehensible, and imbued his soul with a confusion and strange alarm. She, of whom he was accustomed to think as having forever disappeared in the dark depth of infinity, was here, close—and it was difficult to understand that nevertheless she was not, and never would be, again. And it seemed to Father Ignaty that if he spoke some word, which he almost felt upon his lips, or if he made some movement, Vera would come forth from the tomb, and stand up as tall and beautiful as ever. And that not only would she arise, but that all the dead, who could be felt, so awesome in their solemn, cold silence, would rise too.

Father Ignaty took off his black, wide-brimmed hat, smoothed his wavy locks, and said in a whisper:

"Vera!"

He became uneasy lest he should be heard by some stranger, and stood upon the tomb and looked over the crosses. But there was no one near, and he repeated aloud:

"Vera!"

It was Father Ignaty's old voice, dry and exacting, and it was strange that a demand made with such force remained without answer.

"Vera!"

Loud and persistently the voice called, and when it was silent for a moment it seemed as though somewhere below, a vague answer resounded. And Father Ignaty looked around once more, removed his hair from his ears, and laid them on the rough, prickly sod.

"Vera! Speak!"

And Father Ignaty felt with horror that something cold as the tomb penetrated his ear and froze the brain, and that Vera spoke—but what she said was ever the same long silence. It became ever more and more alarming and terrible, and, when Father Ignaty with an effort dragged his head from the ground, pale as that of a corpse, it seemed to him that the whole air trembled and vibrated with a resonant silence, as though a wild storm had arisen on that terrible sea. The silence choked him: it kept rolling backwards and forwards through his head in icy waves, and stirred his hair; it broke against his bosom, which groaned beneath the shocks. Trembling all over, casting from side to side quick, nervous glances, he slowly raised himself, and strove with torturing efforts to straighten his back and to restore the proud carriage to his trembling body. And in this he succeeded. With slow deliberation he shook the dust from his knees, put on his hat, made the sign of the cross three times over the grave, and went with even, firm gait, and yet did not recognize the well-known cemetery, and lost his way.

"Lost my way!" he laughed, and stood still at the branching paths.

He stood still for a moment, and then, without thinking, turned to the left because it was impossible to stand still and wait. The silence pursued him. It rose from the green graves; the grim, gray crosses breathed it; it came forth in thin, suffocating streams from every pore of the ground, which was sated with corpses. Father Ignaty's steps became quicker and quicker. Dazed, he went around the same paths again and again, he leaped the graves, stumbled against the railings, grasped the prickly tin wreaths, and the soft stuff tore to pieces in his hands. Only one thought, that of getting out, was left in his head.

He rushed from side to side, and at last ran noiselessly, a tall figure, almost unrecognizable in his streaming cassock, with his hair floating on the air. Anyone who had met this wild figure of a man running, leaping, waving his arms would have been more frightened than at the sight of a corpse risen from the grave—if he had recognized his mad, distorted face, and heard the dull rattle that escaped from his open mouth.

At full run Father Ignaty jumped out upon the little square, at the end of which stood the low white mortuary chapel. In the porch, on a little bench, there dozed an old man who looked like a pilgrim from afar, and near him two old beggar women were flying at one another, quarreling and scolding.

When Father Ignaty reached home, it was already getting dark, and the lamp was lit in Olga Stepanovna's room. Without change of clothes or removing his hat, torn and dusty, he came hurriedly to his wife and fell on his knees.

"Mother—Olga—pity me!" he sobbed; "I'm going out of my mind."

He beat his head against the edge of the table, and sobbed tumultuously, painfully, as a man does who never weeps. He lifted his head, confident that in a moment a miracle would be performed, and that his wife would speak, and pity him.

"Dear!" With his whole big body he stretched out towards his wife, and met the look of the gray eyes. In them there was neither compassion nor anger. Maybe his wife forgave and pitied him, but in those eyes there was neither pity nor forgiveness. They were dumb and silent.

* * *

And the whole desolate house was silent.

THE LIE

"You lie! I know you lie!"

"What are you shouting for? Is it necessary that every-one should hear us?"

And here again she lied, for I had not shouted, but spoken in the quietest voice, holding her hand and speaking quite gently while that venomous word "lie" hissed like a little serpent.

"I love you," she continued, "and you ought to believe me. Doesn't this convince you?"

And she kissed me. But when I was about to take hold of her hand and press it, she was already gone. She left the semidark corridor, and I followed her once more to the place where a gay party was just coming to an end. How did I know where it was? She had told me that I might go there, and I went there and watched the dancing all the night through. No one came near me, or spoke to me; I was a stranger to all and sat in the corner near the band.

Pointed straight at me was the mouth of a great brass instrument, through which someone hidden in the depths of it kept bellowing, and every minute or so would give a rude staccato laugh: "Ho! ho! ho!"

From time to time a scented white cloud would come close to me. It was she. I did not know how she managed to caress me without being observed, but for one short little second her shoulder would press mine, and for one short little second I would lower my eyes and see a white neck in the opening of a white dress. And when I raised my eyes I saw a profile as white, severe, and truthful as that of a pensive angel on the tomb of the long-forgotten dead. And I saw her eyes. They were large, wide open, beautiful, and calm. From their blue-white setting the pupils shone black, and the more I looked at them the blacker they seemed, and the more unfathomable their depths. Maybe because I looked at them for so short a time my heart failed to make the slightest impression, but certainly never did I understand so profoundly and terribly the meaning of Infinity, nor ever realized it with such force. I felt in fear and pain that my very life was passing out in a slender ray into her eyes, until I became a stranger to myself—desolated, speechless, almost dead. Then she would leave me, taking my life with her, and dance again with a certain tall, haughty, but handsome partner of hers. I studied his every characteristic—the shape of his shoes, the width of his rather high shoulders, the rhythmic sway of one of his locks, which separated itself from the rest, while with his indifferent, unseeing glance he, as it were, crushed me against the wall, and I felt myself as flat and lifeless to look at as the wall itself.

When they began to extinguish the lights, I went up to her and said, "It's time to go. I'll accompany you."

But she expressed surprise. "But certainly I'm going with him," and she pointed to the tall, handsome man, who was not looking at us. She led me out into an empty room and kissed me.

"You lie," I said very softly.

"We'll meet again tomorrow. You must come," was her answer.

When I drove home, the green frosty dawn was looking out from behind the high roofs. In the whole street there were only we two, the sleigh driver and I. He sat with bent head and wrapped-up face, and I sat behind him, wrapped up to the very eyes. The sleigh driver had his thoughts, and I had mine, and there behind the thick walls thousands of people were sleeping, and they had their own dreams and thoughts. I thought of her and of how she lied. I thought of death, and it seemed to me that those dimly lightened walls had already looked upon my death, and that was why they were so cold and upright. I do not know what the thoughts of the sleigh driver may have been, neither do I know of what those hidden by the walls were dreaming. But then, neither did they know my thoughts and reveries.

And so we drove on through the long and straight streets, and the dawn rose from behind the roofs, and all around was motionless and white. A cold, scented cloud came close to me, and straight into my ear someone unseen laughed:

"Ho! ho! ho!"

II

She had lied. She did not come, and I waited for her in vain. The gray, uniform, frozen semidarkness descended from the lightless sky, and I was not conscious of when

the twilight passed into evening, and when the evening
passed into night—to me it was all one long night. I kept
walking backwards and forwards with the same even,
measured steps of hope deferred. I did not come close to
the tall house, where my beloved dwelt, nor to its glazed
door, which shone yellow at the end of the iron covered
way, but I walked on the opposite side of the street with
the same measured strides—backwards and forwards,
backwards and forwards. In going forwards, I did not take
my eye off the glazed door, and when I turned back I
stopped frequently and turned my head around, and then
the snow with its sharp needles pricked my face. And so
long were those sharp, cold needles that they penetrated to
my very heart and pierced it with grief and anger at my
useless waiting. The cold wind blew uninterruptedly from
the bright north to the dark south and whistled playfully
on the icy roofs, and rebounding, cut my face with sharp,
little snowflakes and softly tapped the glasses of the empty
lanterns, in which the lonely yellow flame, shivering with
cold, bent to the draught. And I felt sorry for the lonely
flame, which lived only by night, and I thought to myself,
When I go away all life will end in this street, and only
the snowflakes will fly through the empty space; but still
the yellow flame will continue to shiver and bend in loneliness and cold.

I waited for her, but she did not come. And it seemed
to me that the lonely flame and I were like one another,
only that my lamp was not empty, for in that void, which
I kept measuring with my strides, people did sometimes
appear. Big and dark, they grew up unheard behind my
back; they passed me and, like ghosts, suddenly disappeared around the corner of the white building. Then
again they would come out from around the corner,
come up alongside me and then gradually melt away

in the great distance, obscured by the silently falling snow. Muffled up, formless, silent, they were so like to one another and to myself that it seemed as if scores of people were walking backwards and forwards and waiting, as I was, shivering and silent, and were thinking their own enigmatic, sad thoughts.

I waited for her, but she did not come. I do not know why I did not cry out and weep for pain. I do not know why I laughed and was glad and crooked my fingers like claws, as though I held in them that little, venomous thing which kept hissing like a snake: a lie! It wriggled in my hands and bit my heart, and my head reeled with its poison. Everything was a lie! The boundary line between the future and the present, the present and the past, vanished. The boundary line between the time when I did not yet exist, and the time when I began to be, vanished, and I thought that I must have always been alive, or else never have lived at all. And always, before I lived and when I began to live, she had ruled over me, and I felt it strange that she should have a name and a body and that her existence should have a beginning and an end. She had no name, she was always the one who lies, who makes eternally to wait, and never comes. And I do not know why, but I laughed, and the sharp needles pierced my heart, and right into my ear someone unseen laughed:

"Ho! ho! ho!"

Opening my eyes, I looked at the lighted windows of the lofty house, and in their blue and red language they quietly said to me:

You are deceived by her. At this very moment, while you are wandering, waiting, and suffering, she, all bright, lovely, and treacherous, is there, listening to the whispers of that tall, handsome man, who despises you. If you were to break in there and kill her, you would be doing a good deed, for you would slay a lie.

I gripped the knife tighter in my hand and answered laughingly, "Yes, I'll kill her."

But the windows gazed at me mournfully, and added sadly:

You will never kill her. Never! because the weapon you hold in your hand is as much a lie as are her kisses.

The silent shadows of my fellow watchers had disappeared long ago, and I was left alone in the cold void, I—and the lonely tongues of fire, shivering with cold and despair. The clock in the neighboring church tower began to strike, and its dismal, metallic sound trembled and wept, flying away into the void and being lost in the maze of silently whirling snowflakes. I began to count the strokes and went into a fit of laughter. The clock struck fifteen! The belfry was old, and so too was the clock, and although it indicated the right time, it struck spasmodically, sometimes so often that the gray, ancient bell ringer had to clamber up and stop the convulsive strokes of the hammer with his hand. For whom did those senilely tremulous, melancholy sounds, which were embraced and throttled by the frosty darkness, tell a lie? So pitiable and inept was that useless lie.

With the last, lying sounds of the clock the glazed door slammed, and a tall man made his way down the steps. I saw only his back, but I recognized it since I had seen it, proud and contemptuous, only last evening. I recognized his walk, and it was lighter and more confident than it was last evening: thus had I often left that door. He walked as those do, whom the lying lips of a woman have just kissed.

III

I threatened and entreated, grinding my teeth: "Tell me the truth!"

But with a face cold as snow, while from beneath her brows, lifted in surprise, her dark, inscrutable eyes shone passionless and mysterious as ever, she assured me: "But I'm not lying to you."

She knew that I could not prove her lie, and that all my heavy, massive structure of torturing thought would crumble at one word from her, even one lying word. I waited for it, and it came forth from her lips, sparkling with the colors of truth on the surface, but dark in its innermost depths: "I love you! Aren't I all yours?"

We were far from the town, and the snow-clad plain looked in at the dark windows. Upon it was darkness, and around it was darkness, gross, motionless, silent, but the plain shone with its own latent coruscation, like the face of a corpse in the dark. In the overheated room only one candle was burning, and on its reddening flame there appeared the white reflection of the death-like plain.

"However sad the truth may be, I want to know it. Maybe I'll die when I know it, but death rather than ignorance of the truth. In your kisses and embraces I feel a lie. In your eyes I see it. Tell me the truth and I'll leave you forever," I said.

But she was silent. Her coldly searching look penetrated my innermost depths, and drawing out my soul, regarded it with strange curiosity.

And I cried, "Answer, or I'll kill you!"

"Yes, do!" she quietly replied; "sometimes life is so wearisome. But the truth is not to be extracted by threat."

And then I knelt before her. Clasping her hand, I wept and prayed for pity and the truth.

"Poor fellow!" she said, putting her hand on my head. "Poor fellow!"

"Pity me," I prayed; "I want so much to know the truth."

And as I looked at her pure forehead, I thought that truth must be there behind that slender barrier. And I madly wished to smash the skull to get at the truth. There too, behind a white bosom, beat a heart, and I madly wished to tear her bosom with my nails, to see just for once an unveiled human heart. And the pointed, motionless flame of the expiring candle burned yellow— and the walls grew dark and seemed farther apart—and it felt so sad, so lonely, so eery.

"Poor fellow!" she said. "Poor fellow!"

And the yellow flame of the candle shivered spasmodically, burned low and became blue. Then it went out, and darkness enveloped us. I could not see her face, nor her eyes, for her arms embraced my head—and I no longer felt the lie. Closing my eyes, I neither thought nor lived, but only absorbed the touch of her hands, and it seemed to me true. And in the darkness she whispered in a strangely fearsome voice:

"Put your arms around me—I'm afraid."

Again there was silence, and again the gentle whisper fraught with fear!

"You desire the truth—but do I know it myself? And oh! don't I wish I did? Take care of me; oh! I'm so frightened!"

I opened my eyes. The paling darkness of the room

fled in fear from the lofty windows, and gathering near the walls, hid itself in the corners. But through the windows something huge, deadly white silently looked in. It seemed as though someone's dead eyes were searching for us and enveloping us in their icy gaze. Presently we pressed close together, while she whispered, "Oh! I'm so frightened!"

IV

I killed her. I killed her, and when she lay in a flat, lifeless heap by the window, beyond which shone the dead-white plain, I put my foot on her corpse and burst into a fit of laughter. It was not the laugh of a madman; oh, no! I laughed because my bosom heaved lightly and evenly, and within it, all was cheerful, peaceful, and void, because from my heart the worm which had been gnawing it had fallen. And bending down, I looked into her dead eyes. Great, greedy of the light, they remained open, and were like the eyes of a wax doll—so round and dull were they, as though covered with mica. I was able to touch them with my fingers, open and shut them, and I was not afraid, because in those black, inscrutable pupils there lived no longer that demon of lying and doubt, which so long, so greedily, had sucked my blood.

When they arrested me I laughed. And this seemed terrible and wild to those who seized me. Some of them turned away from me in disgust and went aside; others advanced threateningly straight towards me, with condemnation on their lips, but when my bright, cheerful glance met their eyes, their faces blanched and their feet became rooted to the ground.

"Mad!" they said, and it seemed to me that they

found comfort in the word because it helped to solve the enigma of how I could love and yet kill the beloved —and laugh. Only one of them, a man of full habit and sanguine temperament, called me by another name, which I felt as a blow, and which extinguished the light in my eyes.

"Poor man!" he said in compassion, devoid of anger, for he was stout and cheerful. "Poor fellow!"

"Don't!" I cried. "Don't call me that!"

I do not know why I threw myself upon him. Indeed, I had no desire to kill him, or even to touch him; but all these cowed people, who looked on me as a madman and a villain, were all the more frightened and cried out, so that it seemed to me again quite ludicrous.

When they were leading me out of the room where the corpse lay, I repeated loudly and persistently, looking at the stout, cheerful man:

"I am happy, happy!"

And that was the truth.

V

Once, when I was a child, I saw in a menagerie a panther, which struck my imagination and for long held my thoughts captive. It was not like the other wild beasts, which dozed without thought or angrily gazed at the visitors. It walked from corner to corner, in one and the same line, with mathematical precision, each time turning on exactly the same spot, each time grazing with its tawny side one and the same metal bar of the cage. Its sharp, ravenous head was bent down, and its eyes looked straight before it, never once turning aside. For whole days a noisily chattering crowd trooped before its cage, but it kept up its tramp and never once turned an eye on the spectators. A few of the crowd laughed, but the majority looked seriously, even sadly, at that living picture of heavy, hopeless brooding, and went away with a sigh. And as they retired, they looked back at her once more—a doubting, inquiring glance—and sighed, as though there was something in common between their own lot, free as they were, and that of the unhappy, eager, wild beast. And when later on I was grown up, and people or books spoke to me of eternity, I called to mind the panther, and it seemed to me that I knew eternity and its pains.

Such a panther did I become in my stone cage. I walked and thought. I walked in one line from corner to corner, right across the floor of my cage, and along one short line traveled my thoughts, so heavy that it seemed that my shoulders carried not a head, but a whole world. But it consisted of only one word, but what an immense, what a torturing, what an ominous word it was.

"Lie!"—that was the word.

Once more it crept forth hissing from all the corners and twined itself about my soul; but it had ceased to be a little snake, it had developed into a great, glittering, fierce serpent. It bit me and stifled me in its iron coils, and when I began to cry out with pain, as though my whole bosom were swarming with reptiles, I could only utter that abominable, hissing, serpent-like sound: "Lie!"

And as I walked and thought, the gray level asphalt of the floor changed before my eyes into a gray, transparent abyss. My feet ceased to feel the touch of the floor, and I seemed to be soaring at a limitless height above the fog and mist. And when my bosom gave

forth its hissing groan, thence—from below—from under
that rarefying, but still impenetrable shroud, there slowly
issued a terrible echo, so slow and dull—as though it
were passing through a thousand years. And every now
and then, as the fog lifted, the sound became less loud,
and I understood that there—below—it was still whistling
like a wind, that tears down the trees, while it reached
my ears in a short, ominous whisper:

"Lie!"

This mean whisper worked me up into a rage, and I
stamped on the floor and cried:

"There is no lie! I killed the lie."

Then I purposely turned aside, for I knew what it
would reply. And it did reply slowly from the depths of
the bottomless abyss:

"Lie!"

The fact is, as you perceive, that I had made a grievous
mistake. I had killed the woman, but made the lie
immortal. Kill not a woman till you have, by prayer, by
fire, and torture, torn from her soul the truth!

So I thought, and continued my endless tramp from
corner to corner of the cell.

VI

Dark and terrible is the place to which she had carried
the truth and the lie—and I am going there. At the very
throne of Satan I shall overtake her, and, falling on my
knees, will weep; and cry:

"Tell me the truth!"

But God! This is also a lie. There, there is darkness,
there is the void of ages and of infinity, and there she is
not—she is nowhere. But the lie remains, it is immortal.
I feel it in every atom of the air, and when I breathe, it

enters my bosom with a hissing and then rends it—yes, rends!

Oh! what madness it is—to be man and to seek the truth! What pain!

Help! Help!

LAZARUS

I

When Lazarus rose from the grave, after three days and nights in the mysterious thraldom of death, and returned alive to his home, it was a long time before anyone noticed the evil peculiarities in him that were later to make his very name terrible. His friends and relatives were jubilant that he had come back to life. They surrounded him with tenderness, they were lavish of their eager attentions, spending the greatest care upon his food and drink and the new garments they made for him. They clad him gorgeously in the glowing colors of hope and laughter, and when, arrayed like a bridegroom, he sat at the table with them again, ate again, and drank again, they wept fondly and summoned the neighbors to look upon the man miraculously raised from the dead.

The neighbors came and were moved with joy. Strangers arrived from distant cities and villages to worship the miracle. They burst into stormy exclamations, and buzzed around the house of Mary and Martha, like so many bees.

That which was new in Lazarus' face and gestures they explained naturally, as the traces of his severe illness and the shock he had passed through. It was evident that the disintegration of the body had been halted by a miraculous power, but that the restoration had not been complete; that death had left upon his face and body the effect of an artist's unfinished sketch seen through a thin glass. On his temples, under his eyes, and in the hollow of his cheek lay a thick, earthy blue. His fingers were blue, too, and, under his nails, which had grown long in the grave, the blue had turned livid. Here and there on his lips and body, the skin, blistered in the grave, had burst open and left reddish glistening cracks, as if covered with a thin, glassy slime. And he had grown exceedingly stout. His body was horribly bloated and suggested the fetid, damp smell of putrefaction. But the cadaverous, heavy odor that clung to his burial garments, and, as it seemed, to his very body, soon wore off, and after some time the blue of his hands and face softened, and the reddish cracks of his skin smoothed out, though they never disappeared completely. Such was the aspect of Lazarus in his second life. It looked natural only to those who had seen him buried.

Not merely Lazarus' face, but his very character, it seemed, had changed; though it astonished no one and did not attract the attention it deserved. Before his death Lazarus had been cheerful and careless, a lover of laughter and harmless jest. It was because of his good humor, pleasant and equable, his freedom from meanness and gloom, that he had been so beloved by the Master. Now he was grave and silent; neither he himself jested nor did he laugh at the jests of others; and the words he occasionally spoke were simple, ordinary and necessary words —words as much devoid of sense and depth as are the sounds with which an animal expresses pain and pleasure, thirst and hunger. Such words a man may speak all his life, and no one would ever know the sorrows and joys that dwelt within him.

Thus it was that Lazarus sat at the festive table among his friends and relatives—his face the face of a corpse over which, for three days, death had reigned in darkness; his garments gorgeous and festive, glittering with gold, bloody red and purple; his mien heavy and silent. He was horribly changed and strange, but as yet undiscovered. In high waves, now mild, now stormy, the festivities went on around him. Warm glances of love caressed his face, still cold with the touch of the grave; and a friend's warm hand patted his bluish, heavy hand. And the music played joyous tunes mingled of the sounds of the tympanum, the pipe, the zither and the dulcimer. It was as if bees were humming, locusts buzzing and birds singing over the happy home of Mary and Martha.

II

Someone recklessly lifted the veil. By one breath of an uttered word he destroyed the serene charm, and uncovered the truth in its ugly nakedness. No thought was clearly defined in his mind when he smilingly asked, "Why don't you tell us, Lazarus, what was There?" And all became silent, struck with the question. Only now did it seem to occur to them that for three days Lazarus had been dead; and they looked with curiosity, awaiting an answer. But Lazarus remained silent.

"You won't tell us?" the inquirer wondered. "Is it so terrible There?" Again his thought lagged behind his words. Had it preceded them, he would not have asked the question, for, at the very moment he uttered it, his heart sank with a dread fear.

All grew restless; they awaited the words of Lazarus anxiously. But he was silent, cold and severe, and his eyes were cast down. And now, as if for the first time, they perceived the horrible bluishness of his face and the loathsome corpulence of his body. On the table, as if forgotten by Lazarus, lay his livid blue hand, and all eyes were riveted upon it, as though expecting the desired answer from that hand. The musicians still played; then silence fell upon them, too, and the gay sounds died down, as scattered coals are extinguished by water. The pipe became mute, and the ringing tympanum and the murmuring dulcimer; and as though a chord were broken, as though song itself were dying, the zither echoed a trembling, broken sound. Then all was quiet.

"You won't?" the inquirer repeated, unable to restrain his babbling tongue. Silence reigned, and the livid blue hand lay motionless. It moved slightly, and the company sighed with relief and raised their eyes. Lazarus, risen from the dead, was looking straight at them, embracing all with one glance, heavy and terrible.

This was on the third day after Lazarus had arisen from the grave. Since then, many had felt that his gaze was the gaze of destruction, but neither those who had been forever crushed by it, nor those who in the prime of life (mysterious even as death) had found the will to resist his glance, could ever explain the terror that lay immovable in the depths of his black pupils. He looked

quiet and simple. One felt that he had no intention to
hide anything, but also no intention to tell anything. His
look was cold, as of one who is entirely indifferent to all
that is alive. And many careless people who pressed
around him, and did not notice him, later learned with
wonder and fear the name of this stout, quiet man who
brushed against them with his sumptuous, gaudy garments. The sun did not stop shining when he looked,
neither did the fountain cease playing, and the eastern
sky remained cloudless and blue as always; but the man
who fell under his inscrutable gaze could no longer feel
the sun, nor hear the fountain, nor recognize his native
sky. Sometimes he would cry bitterly, sometimes tear his
hair in despair and madly call for help; but generally it
happened that the men thus stricken by the gaze of
Lazarus began to fade away listlessly and quietly and
pass into a slow death lasting many long years. They
died in the presence of everybody, colorless, haggard and
gloomy, like trees withering on rocky ground. Those who
screamed in madness sometimes came back to life; but the
others, never.

"So you won't tell us, Lazarus, what you saw There?"
the inquirer repeated for the third time. But now his
voice was dull, and a dead, gray weariness had appeared
in his eyes. The faces of all present were also covered
by the same dead, gray weariness, like a mist. The guests
stared at one another stupidly, not knowing why they
had come together or why they sat around this rich table.
They stopped talking, and vaguely felt it was time to
leave; but they could not overcome the lassitude that
spread through their muscles. So they continued to sit
there, each one isolated, like little dim lights scattered
in the darkness of night.

The musicians were paid to play, and they again took

up the instruments, and again played gay or mournful airs. But it was music made to order, always the same tunes, and the guests listened wonderingly. Why was this music necessary, they thought, why was it necessary and what good did it do for people to pull at strings and blow their cheeks into thin pipes, and produce varied and strange-sounding noises?

"How badly they play!" someone said.

The musicians were insulted and left. Then the guests departed one by one, for it was nearing night. And when the quiet darkness enveloped them, and it became easier to breathe, the image of Lazarus suddenly arose in stern splendor before each one. There he stood, with the blue face of a corpse and the raiment of a bridegroom, sumptuous and resplendent, in his eyes that cold stare in the depths of which lurked *The Horrible!* They stood still as if turned into stone. The darkness surrounded them, and in the midst of this darkness flamed up the horrible apparition, the supernatural vision, of the one who for three days had lain under the measureless power of death. Three days he had been dead. Thrice had the sun risen and set—and he had lain dead. The children had played, the water had murmured as it streamed over the rocks, the hot dust had clouded the highway—and he had been dead. And now he was among them again, touched them, looked at them— *looked at them!* And through the black rings of his pupils, as through dark glasses, the unfathomable *There* gazed upon humanity.

III

No one took care of Lazarus, and no friends or kindred remained with him. Only the great desert, enfolding the

Holy City, came close to the threshold of his abode. It entered his home, and lay down on his couch like a spouse, and put out all the fires. No one cared for Lazarus. One after the other went away, even his sisters, Mary and Martha. For a long while Martha did not want to leave him, for she did not know who would nurse him or take care of him; and she cried and prayed. But one night, when the wind was roaming about the desert, and the rustling cypress trees were bending over the roof, she dressed herself quietly, and quietly went away. Lazarus probably heard how the door was slammed—it had not shut properly, and the wind kept knocking it continually against the post—but he did not rise, did not go out, did not try to find out the reason. And the whole night until the morning the cypress trees hissed over his head, and the door swung to and fro, allowing the cold, greedily prowling desert to enter his dwelling. Everybody shunned him as though he were a leper. They wanted to put a bell on his neck to avoid meeting him. But someone, turning pale, remarked it would be terrible if at night, under the windows, one should happen to hear Lazarus' bell, and all grew pale and assented.

Since he did nothing for himself, he would probably have starved had not his neighbors, in trepidation, saved some food for him. Children brought it to him. They did not fear him, neither did they laugh at him in the innocent cruelty in which children often laugh at unfortunates. They were indifferent to him, and Lazarus showed the same indifference to them. He showed no desire to thank them for their services; he did not try to pat the dark hands and look into the simple, shining, little eyes. Abandoned to the ravages of time and the desert, his house was falling to ruins, and his hungry, bleating goats had long been scattered among his neighbors. His wedding garments had grown old. He wore them without changing them, as he had donned them on that happy day when the musicians played. He did not see the difference between old and new, between torn and whole. The brilliant colors were burnt and faded; the vicious dogs of the city and the sharp thorns of the desert had rent the fine clothes to shreds.

During the day, when the sun beat down mercilessly upon all living things, and even the scorpions, convulsed with a mad desire to sting, hid under the stones, he sat motionless in the burning rays, lifting high his blue face and shaggy, wild beard.

While yet the people were unafraid to speak to him, someone had asked him, "Poor Lazarus! Do you find it pleasant to sit so, and look at the sun?" And he answered, "Yes, it is pleasant."

The thought suggested itself to people that the cold of the three days in the grave had been so intense, its darkness so deep, that there was not in all the earth enough heat or light to warm Lazarus and lighten the gloom of his eyes; and inquirers turned away with a sigh.

And when the setting sun, flat and purple-red, descended to earth, Lazarus went into the desert and walked straight towards it, as though intending to reach it. Always he walked directly towards the sun, and those who tried to follow him and find out what he did at night in the desert had indelibly imprinted upon their mind's vision the black silhouette of a tall, stout man against the red background of an immense disk. The horrors of the night drove them away, and so they never found out what Lazarus did in the desert; but the image of the black form against the red was burned forever into their brains. Like an animal with a cinder in its eye, which furiously rubs its muzzle against its paws, they foolishly rubbed their eyes; but the impression left by Lazarus was ineffaceable, forgotten only in death.

There were people living far away who never saw Lazarus and only heard of him. With an audacious curiosity which is stronger than fear and feeds on fear, with a secret sneer in their hearts, some of them came to him one day as he basked in the sun, and entered into conversation with him. At that time his appearance had changed for the better and was not so frightful. At first the visitors snapped their fingers and thought disapprovingly of the foolish inhabitants of the Holy City. But when the short talk came to an end and they went home, their expression was such that the inhabitants of the Holy City at once knew their errand and said, "Here go some more madmen at whom Lazarus has looked." The speakers raised their hands in silent pity.

Other visitors came, among them brave warriors in clinking armor, who knew not fear, and happy youths, who made merry with laughter and song. Busy merchants, jingling their coins, ran in for a while, and proud attendants at the Temple placed their staffs at Lazarus' door. But no one returned the same as he came. A frightful shadow fell upon their souls, and gave a new appearance to the old, familiar world.

Those who felt any desire to speak, after they had been stricken by the gaze of Lazarus, described the change that had come over them somewhat like this:

All objects seen by the eye and palpable to the hand became empty, light and transparent, as though they were light shadows in the darkness; and this darkness enveloped the whole universe. It was dispelled neither by the sun, nor by the moon, nor by the stars,

but embraced the earth like a mother, and clothed it
in a boundless, black veil.

Into all bodies it penetrated, even into iron and
stone; and the particles of the body lost their unity
and became lonely. Even to the heart of the particles
it penetrated, and the particles of the particles became
lonely.

The vast emptiness which surrounds the universe
was not filled with things seen, with sun or moon or
stars; it stretched boundless, penetrating everywhere,
disuniting everything, body from body, particle from
particle.

In emptiness the trees spread their roots, themselves
empty; in emptiness rose phantom temples; palaces
and houses—all empty; and in the emptiness moved
restless Man, himself empty and light, like a shadow.

There was no more a sense of time; the beginning
of all things and their end merged into one. In the
very moment when a building was being erected and
one could hear the builders striking with their hammers,
one seemed already to see its ruins, and then emptiness where the ruins were.

A man was just born, and funeral candles were already lighted at his head, and then were extinguished;
and soon there was emptiness where before had been the
man and the candles.

And surrounded by Darkness and Empty Waste, Man
trembled hopelessly before the dread of the Infinite.

So spoke those who had a desire to speak. But much
more could probably have been told by those who did
not want to talk, and who died in silence.

IV

At that time there lived in Rome a celebrated sculptor by the name of Aurelius. Out of clay, marble and bronze he created forms of gods and men of such beauty that this beauty was proclaimed immortal. But he himself was not satisfied, and said there was a supreme beauty that he had never succeeded in expressing in marble or bronze. "I have not yet gathered the radiance of the moon," he said; "I have not yet caught the glare of the sun. There is no soul in my marble, there is no life in my beautiful bronze." And when by moonlight he would slowly wander along the roads, crossing the black shadows of the cypress trees, his white tunic flashing in the moonlight, those he met used to laugh good-naturedly and say, "Is it moonlight that you're gathering, Aurelius? Why didn't you bring some baskets along?"

And he, too, would laugh and point to his eyes and say, "Here are the baskets in which I gather the light of the moon and the radiance of the sun."

And that was the truth. In his eyes shone moon and sun. But he could not transmit the radiance to marble. Therein lay the greatest tragedy of his life. He was a descendant of an ancient race of patricians, had a good wife and children, and except in this one respect, lacked nothing.

When the dark rumor about Lazarus reached him, he consulted his wife and friends and decided to make the long voyage to Judea, in order that he might look upon the man miraculously raised from the dead. He felt lonely in those days and hoped on the way to renew his jaded energies. What they told him about Lazarus did not frighten him. He had meditated much upon death. He did not like it, nor did he like those who tried to harmonize it with life. On this side, beautiful life; on the other, mysterious death, he reasoned, and no better lot could befall a man than to live—to enjoy life and the beauty of living. And he already had conceived a desire to convince Lazarus of the truth of this view and to return his soul to life even as his body had been returned. This task did not appear impossible, for the reports about Lazarus, fearsome and strange as they were, did not tell the whole truth about him, but only carried a vague warning against something awful.

Lazarus was getting up from a stone to follow in the path of the setting sun on the evening when the rich Roman, accompanied by an armed slave, approached him, and in a ringing voice called to him: "Lazarus!"

Lazarus saw a proud and beautiful face, made radiant by fame, and white garments and precious jewels shining in the sunlight. The ruddy rays of the sun lent to the head and face a likeness to dimly shining bronze—that was what Lazarus saw. He sank back to his seat obediently, and wearily lowered his eyes.

"It is true you are not beautiful, my poor Lazarus," the Roman said quietly, playing with his gold chain. "You are even frightful, my poor friend; and death was not lazy the day when you so carelessly fell into its arms. But you are as fat as a barrel, and 'Fat people are not bad,' as the great Cæsar said. I do not understand why people are so afraid of you. You will permit me to stay with you overnight? It is already late, and I have no abode."

Nobody had ever asked Lazarus to be allowed to pass the night with him.

"I have no bed," he said.

"I am somewhat of a warrior and can sleep sitting," the Roman replied. "We shall make a light."

"I have no light."

"Then we shall converse in the darkness, like two friends. I suppose you have some wine?"

"I have no wine."

The Roman laughed. "Now I understand why you are so gloomy and why you do not like your second life. No wine? Well, we shall do without. You know there are words that go to one's head even as Falernian wine."

With a motion of his head he dismissed the slave, and they were alone. And again the sculptor spoke, but it seemed as though the sinking sun had penetrated into his words. They faded, pale and empty, as if trembling on weak feet, as if slipping and falling, drunk with the wine of anguish and despair. And black chasms appeared between the two men—like remote hints of vast emptiness and vast darkness.

"Now I am your guest and you will not ill-treat me, Lazarus!" said the Roman. "Hospitality is binding even upon those who have been three days dead. Three days, I am told, you were in the grave. It must have been cold there . . . and it is from there that you have brought this bad habit of doing without light and wine. I like a light. It gets dark so quickly here. Your eyebrows and forehead have an interesting line: even as the ruins of castles' covered with the ashes of an earthquake. But why in such strange, ugly clothes? I have seen the bridegrooms of your country, they wear clothes like that—such ridiculous clothes—such awful garments. . . . Are you a bridegroom?"

Already the sun had disappeared. A gigantic black shadow was approaching fast from the west, as if prodigious bare feet were rustling over the sand. And the chill breezes stole up behind.

"In the darkness you seem even bigger, Lazarus, as though you had grown stouter in these few minutes. Do you feed on darkness, perchance? . . . And I would like a light . . . just a small light . . . just a small light. And I am cold. The nights here are so barbarously cold. . . . If it were not so dark, I should say you were looking at me, Lazarus. Yes, it seems, you are looking. You are looking. *You are looking at me!* . . . I feel it . . . now you are smiling."

The night had come, and a heavy blackness filled the air.

"How good it will be when the sun rises again to-morrow. . . . You know, I am a great sculptor . . . so my friends call me. I create, yes, they say I create, but for that daylight is necessary. I give life to cold marble. I melt the ringing bronze in the fire, in a bright, hot fire. Why did you touch me with your hand?"

"Come," Lazarus said, "you are my guest." And they went into the house. And the shadows of the long evening fell on the earth. . . .

The slave at last grew tired waiting for his master, and when the sun stood high he came to the house. And he saw, directly under its burning rays, Lazarus and his master sitting close together. They looked straight up and were silent.

The slave wept and cried aloud, "Master, what ails you, Master!"

The same day Aurelius left for Rome. The whole way he was thoughtful and silent, attentively examining everything, the people, the ship, and the sea, as though endeavoring to recall something. On the sea a great storm overtook them, and all the while Aurelius remained on deck and gazed eagerly at the approaching and falling waves. When he reached home his family were shocked at the terrible change in his demeanor, but he calmed them with the words, "I have found it!"

In the dusty clothes which he had worn during the entire journey and had not changed, he began his work, and the marble ringingly responded to the resounding blows of the hammer. Long and eagerly he worked, admitting no one. At last, one morning, he announced that the work was ready, and gave instructions that all his friends, and the severe critics and judges of art, be called together. Then he donned gorgeous garments, shining with gold, glowing with the purple of the byssin.

"Here is what I have created," he said thoughtfully.

His friends looked, and immediately the shadow of deep sorrow covered their faces. It was a thing monstrous, possessing none of the forms familiar to the eye, yet not devoid of a hint of some new unknown form. On a thin, tortuous little branch, or rather an ugly likeness of one, lay crooked, strange, unsightly, shapeless heaps of something turned outside in, or something turned inside out—wild fragments which seemed to be feebly trying to get away from themselves. And, accidentally, they noticed under one of the wild projections a wonderfully sculptured butterfly, with transparent wings, trembling as though with a weak longing to fly.

"Why that wonderful butterfly, Aurelius?" someone timidly asked.

"I do not know," the sculptor answered.

The truth had to be told, and one of his friends, the one who loved Aurelius best, said, "This is ugly, my poor friend. It must be destroyed. Give me the hammer." And with two blows he destroyed the monstrous mass, leaving only the wonderfully sculptured butterfly.

After that, Aurelius created nothing. He looked with

absolute indifference at marble and at bronze and at his own divine creations, in which dwelt immortal beauty. In the hope of breathing into him once again the old flame of inspiration, with the idea of awakening his dead soul, his friends led him to see the beautiful creations of others, but he remained indifferent and no smile warmed his closed lips. And only after they spoke to him much and long of beauty, he would reply wearily, "But all this is—a lie."

And in the daytime, when the sun was shining, he would go into his rich and beautifully laid-out garden, and finding a place where there was no shadow, would expose his bare head and his dull eyes to the glitter and burning heat of the sun. Red and white butterflies fluttered around; down into the marble cistern ran splashing water from the crooked mouth of a blissfully drunken Satyr; but he sat motionless, like a pale shadow of that other one who, in a far land, at the very gates of the stony desert, also sat motionless under the fiery sun.

V

And it came about finally that Lazarus was summoned to Rome by the great Augustus.

They dressed him in gorgeous garments as though it had been ordained that he was to remain a bridegroom to an unknown bride until the very day of his death. It was as if an old coffin, rotten and falling apart, were regilded over and over, and gay tassels were hung on it. And solemnly they conducted him in gala attire, as though in truth it were a bridal procession, the runners loudly sounding the trumpet that the way be made for the ambassadors of the Emperor. But the roads along which he passed were deserted. His entire native land cursed the execrable name of Lazarus, the man miraculously brought to life, and the people scattered at the mere report of his horrible approach. The trumpeters blew lonely blasts, and only the desert answered with a dying echo.

Then they carried him across the sea on the saddest and most gorgeous ship that was ever mirrored in the azure waves of the Mediterranean. There were many people aboard, but the ship was silent and still as a coffin, and the water seemed to moan as it parted before the short, curved prow. Lazarus sat lonely, baring his head to the sun and listening in silence to the splashing of the waters. Further away the seamen and the ambassadors gathered like a crowd of distressed shadows. If a thunderstorm had happened to burst upon them at that time, or the wind had overwhelmed the red sails, the ship would probably have perished, for none of those who were on her had strength or desire enough to fight for life. With supreme effort some went to the side of the ship and eagerly gazed at the blue, transparent abyss. Perhaps they imagined they saw a naiad flashing a pink shoulder through the waves, or an insanely joyous and drunken centaur galloping by, splashing up the water with his hoofs. But the sea was deserted and mute, and so was the watery abyss.

Listlessly Lazarus set foot on the streets of the Eternal City, as though all its riches, all the majesty of its gigantic edifices, all the luster and beauty and music of refined life, were simply the echo of the wind in the desert, or the misty images of hot, running sand. Chariots whirled by; the crowd of strong, beautiful, haughty men passed on, builders of the Eternal City and proud partakers of its life; songs rang out; fountains laughed; pearly laughter of women filled the air, while the drunkard philosophized and the sober ones smilingly listened; horseshoes rattled on the pavement. And surrounded on all sides by glad sounds, a fat, heavy man moved like a cold spot of silence through the center of the city, sowing in his path grief, anger and vague, carking distress. Who dared to be sad in Rome? frowning citizens indignantly demanded; and in two days the swift-tongued Rome knew of Lazarus, the man miraculously raised from the grave, and timidly evaded him.

There were many brave men ready to try their strength, and at their senseless call Lazarus came obediently. The Emperor was so engrossed with state affairs that he delayed receiving the visitor, and for seven days Lazarus moved among the people.

A jovial drunkard met him, with a smile on his red lips. "Drink, Lazarus, drink!" he cried. "Wouldn't Augustus laugh to see you drink!" And naked, besotted women laughed, and decked the blue hands of Lazarus with rose leaves. But the drunkard looked into the eyes of Lazarus—and his joy ended forever. Thereafter he was always drunk. He drank no more, but was drunk all the time, shadowed by fearful dreams, instead of the joyous reveries that wine gives. Fearful dreams became the food of his broken spirit. Fearful dreams held him day and night in the mists of monstrous fantasy, and death itself was no more fearful than the apparition of its fierce precursor.

Lazarus came to a youth and his lass who loved each other and were beautiful in their love. Proudly and strongly holding in his arms his beloved one, the youth said, with gentle pity, "Look at us, Lazarus, and rejoice with us. Is there anything stronger than love?"

And Lazarus looked at them. And their whole life they continued to love one another, but their love became mournful and gloomy, even as those cypress trees over the tombs that feed their roots on the putrescence of the grave and strive in vain in the quiet evening hour to touch the sky with their pointed tops. Hurled by fathomless life forces into each other's arms, they mingled their kisses with tears, their joy with pain, and only succeeded in realizing the more vividly a sense of their slavery to the silent Nothing. Forever united, forever parted, they flashed like sparks, and, like sparks, went out in boundless darkness.

Lazarus came to a proud sage, and the sage said to him, "I already know all the horrors that you may tell me, Lazarus. With what else can you terrify me?"

Only a few moments passed, before the sage realized that the knowledge of the horrible is not the horrible, and that the sight of death is not death. And he felt that in the eyes of the Infinite, wisdom and folly are the same, for the Infinite knows them not. And the boundaries between knowledge and ignorance, between truth and falsehood, between top and bottom, faded, and his shapeless thought was suspended in emptiness. Then he grasped his gray head in his hands and cried out insanely, "I can't think! I can't think!"

Thus it was that under the cool gaze of Lazarus, the man miraculously raised from the dead, all that serves to arm life, its sense and its joys, perished. And people began to say it was dangerous to allow him to see the Emperor; that it would be better to kill him and bury him secretly, and swear he had disappeared. Swords were sharpened, and youths devoted to the welfare of the people announced their readiness to become assassins, when Augustus upset the cruel plans by demanding that Lazarus appear before him.

Even though Lazarus could not be kept away, it

was felt that the heavy impression conveyed by his face might be somewhat softened. With that end in view, expert painters, barbers and artists were secured, and they worked on Lazarus' head the whole night. His beard was trimmed and curled. The disagreeable and deadly bluishness of his hands and face was covered up with paint; his hands were whitened, his cheeks rouged. The disgusting wrinkles of suffering that ridged his old face were patched up and painted, and on the smooth surface, wrinkles of good nature and laughter, and of pleasant, good-humored cheeriness, were laid on artistically with fine brushes.

Lazarus submitted indifferently to all they did with him, and soon was transformed into a stout, nice-looking old man, for all the world a quiet and good-humored grandfather of numerous grandchildren. He looked as though the smile with which he told funny stories had not left his lips, as though a quiet tenderness still lay hidden in the corner of his eyes. But the wedding dress they did not dare to take off; and they could not change his eyes— the dark, terrible eyes from out of which stared the incomprehensible *There*.

VI

Lazarus was untouched by the magnificence of the imperial apartments. He remained stolidly indifferent, as though he saw no contrast between his ruined house at the edge of the desert and the solid, beautiful palace of stone. Under his feet the hard marble of the floor took on the semblance of the moving sands of the desert, and to his eyes the throngs of gaily dressed, haughty men were as unreal as the emptiness of the air. They looked not into his face as he passed by, fearing to come under the awful bane of his eyes; but when the sound of his heavy steps announced that he had passed, heads were lifted, and eyes examined with timid curiosity the figure of the corpulent, tall, slightly stooping old man, as he slowly passed into the heart of the imperial palace. If death itself had appeared, men would not have feared it so much; for hitherto death had been known to the dead only, and life to the living only, and between these two there had been no bridge. But this strange being knew death, and that knowledge of his was felt to be mysterious and cursed. "He will kill our great, divine Augustus," men cried with horror, and they hurled curses after him. Slowly and stolidly he passed by them, penetrating even deeper into the palace.

Cæsar knew already who Lazarus was, and was prepared to meet him. He was a courageous man; he felt his power was invincible, and in the fateful encounter with the man "wonderfully raised from the dead" he refused to lean on other men's weak help. Man to man, face to face, he met Lazarus.

"Do not fix your gaze on me, Lazarus," he commanded. "I have heard that your head is like the head of Medusa, and turns into stone all upon whom you look. But I should like to have a close look at you, and to talk to you before I turn into stone," he added in a spirit of playfulness that concealed his real misgivings.

Approaching him, he examined closely Lazarus' face and his strange festive clothes. Though his eyes were sharp and keen, he was deceived by the skillful counterfeit.

"Well, your appearance is not terrible, venerable sir. But all the worse for men, when the terrible takes on such a venerable and pleasant appearance. Now let us talk."

Augustus sat down, and as much by glance as by words

began the discussion. "Why did you not salute me when you entered?"

Lazarus answered indifferently, "I did not know it was necessary."

"You are a Christian?"

"No."

Augustus nodded approvingly. "That is good. I do not like the Christians. They shake the tree of life, forbidding it to bear fruit, and they scatter to the wind its fragrant blossoms. But who are you?"

With some effort Lazarus answered, "I was dead."

"I heard about that. But who are you now?"

Lazarus' answer came slowly. Finally he said again, listlessly and indistinctly, "I was dead."

"Listen to me, stranger," said the Emperor sharply, giving expression to what had been in his mind before. "My empire is an empire of the living; my people are a people of the living and not of the dead. You are super-fluous here. I do not know who you are, I do not know what you have seen There, but if you lie, I hate your lies, and if you tell the truth, I hate your truth. In my heart I feel the pulse of life; in my hands I feel power, and my proud thoughts, like eagles, fly through space. Behind my back, under the protection of my authority, under the shadow of the laws I have created, men live and labor and rejoice. Do you hear this divine harmony of life? Do you hear the war cry that men hurl into the face of the future, challenging it to strife?"

Augustus extended his arms reverently and solemnly cried out, "Blessed art thou, Great Divine Life!"

But Lazarus was silent, and the Emperor continued more severely: "You are not wanted here. Pitiful rem-nant, half devoured of death, you fill men with distress and aversion to life. Like a caterpillar on the fields, you are gnawing away at the full seed of joy, exuding the slime of despair and sorrow. Your truth is like a rusted sword in the hands of a night assassin, and I shall condemn you to death as an assassin. But first I want to look into your eyes. Mayhap only cowards fear them, and brave men are spurred on to struggle and victory. Then will you merit not death but a reward. Look at me, Lazarus."

At first it seemed to divine Augustus as if a friend were looking at him, so soft, so alluringly, so gently fascinating was the gaze of Lazarus. It promised not horror but quiet rest, and the Infinite dwelt there as a fond mistress, a compassionate sister, a mother. And ever stronger grew its gentle embrace, until he felt, as it were, the breath of a mouth hungry for kisses. . . . Then it seemed as if iron bones protruded in a ravenous grip and closed upon him in an iron band; and cold nails touched his heart, and slowly, slowly sank into it.

"It pains me," said divine Augustus, growing pale; "but look, Lazarus, look!"

Ponderous gates, shutting off eternity, appeared to be slowly swinging open, and through the growing aperture poured in, coldly and calmly, the awful horror of the Infinite. Boundless Emptiness and Boundless Gloom entered like two shadows, extinguishing the sun, removing the ground from under the feet and the cover from over the head. And the pain in his icy heart ceased.

"Look at me, look at me, Lazarus!" commanded Augustus, staggering. . . .

Time ceased and the beginning of things came perilously near to the end. The throne of Augustus, so recently erected, fell to pieces, and emptiness took the place of the throne and of Augustus. Rome fell silently into ruins. A new city rose in its place, and it too was erased by emptiness. Like phantom giants, cities, kingdoms and countries swiftly fell and disappeared into emptiness—swallowed up in the black maw of the Infinite. . . .

"Cease," commanded the Emperor. Already the accent of indifference was in his voice. His arms hung powerless and his eagle eyes flashed and were dimmed again, struggling against overwhelming darkness. "You have killed me, Lazarus," he said drowsily.

These words of despair saved him. He thought of the people, whose shield he was destined to be, and a sharp, redeeming pang pierced his dull heart. He thought of them doomed to perish, and he was filled with anguish. First they seemed bright shadows in the gloom of the Infinite. How terrible! Then they appeared as fragile vessels with life-agitated blood, and hearts that knew both sorrow and great joy. And he thought of them with tenderness.

And so thinking and feeling, inclining the scales now to the side of life, now to the side of death, he slowly returned to life, to find in its suffering and joy a refuge from the gloom, emptiness and fear of the Infinite.

"No, you did not kill me, Lazarus," he said firmly. "But I will kill you. Go!"

Evening came, and divine Augustus partook of food and drink with great joy. But there were moments when his raised arm would remain suspended in the air, and the light of his shining, eager eyes was dimmed. It seemed as if an icy wave of horror washed against his feet. He was vanquished but not killed, and coldly awaited his doom, like a black shadow. His nights were haunted by horror, but the bright days still brought him the joys, as well as the sorrows, of life.

Next day, by order of the Emperor, they burned out Lazarus' eyes with hot irons and sent him home. Even Augustus dared not kill him.

Lazarus returned to the desert, and the desert received him with the breath of the hissing wind and the ardor of the glowing sun. Again, with matted beard uplifted, he sat on the stone; and two black holes, where the eyes had once been, looked dull and horrible at the sky. In the distance the Holy City surged and roared restlessly, but near him all was deserted and still. No one approached the place where Lazarus, miraculously raised from the dead, passed his last days, for his neighbors had long since abandoned their homes. His cursed knowledge, driven by the hot irons from his eyes deep into the brain, lay there in ambush; as if from ambush it might spring out upon men with a thousand unseen eyes. No one dared to look at Lazarus.

And in the evening, when the sun, swollen crimson and growing larger, bent its way towards the west, blind Lazarus slowly groped after it. He stumbled against stones and fell; corpulent and feeble, he rose heavily and walked on; and against the red curtain of sunset his dark form and outstretched arms gave him the semblance of a cross.

It happened once that he went and never returned. Thus ended the second life of Lazarus, who for three days had been in the mysterious thraldom of death and then was miraculously raised from the dead.

LAUGHTER

I

At six-thirty I was certain that she would come, and I was desperately happy. My coat was fastened only by the top button and fluttered in the cold wind; but I felt no cold. My head was proudly thrown back and my student's cap was cocked on the back of my head; my eyes with respect to the men they met were expressive of patronage and boldness, with respect to the women, of a seductive tenderness. Although she had been my only love for four whole days, I was so young, and my heart was so rich in love, that I could not remain perfectly indifferent to other women. My steps were quick, bold and free.

At six-forty-five my coat was fastened by two buttons, and I looked only at the women, no longer with a seductive tenderness, but rather with disgust. I only wanted *one*

woman—the others might go to the Devil; they only confused me, and, with their seeming resemblance to Her,
gave to my movements an uncertain and jerky indecision.

At six-fifty-five I felt warm.

At six-fifty-eight I felt cold.

As it struck seven I was convinced that she would not
come.

By eight-thirty I presented the appearance of the most
pitiful creature in the world. My coat was fastened with all
its buttons, collar turned up, cap tilted over my nose,
which was blue with cold; my hair was over my forehead,
my mustache and eyelashes were whitening with rime,
and my teeth gently chattered. From my shambling gait
and bowed back, I might have been taken for a fairly hale
old man returning from a party at the almshouse.

And She was the cause of all this—She! Oh, the Dev—!
No, I won't. Perhaps She couldn't get away, or She's ill,
or dead. She's dead!—and I swore.

II

"Eugenia Nikolaevna will be there tonight," one of my
companions, a student, remarked to me, without the slightest *arrière pensée*. He could not know that I had waited
for her in the frost from seven to half-past eight.

"Indeed," I replied, as if in deep thought, but within
my soul there leapt out, Oh, the Dev—! "There" meant
at the Polozovs' evening party. Now the Polozovs were
people with whom I was not upon visiting terms. But this
evening I would be there.

"You fellows!" I shouted cheerfully. "Today is Christ-
mas Day, when everybody enjoys himself. Let's do so too."

"But how?" one of them mournfully replied.

"And, where?" continued another.

"We'll dress up and go around to all the evening parties," I decided.

And these insensate individuals actually became cheerful. They shouted, leapt, and sang. They thanked me for my suggestion, and counted up the amount of "the ready" available. In the course of half an hour we had collected all the lonely, disconsolate students in town; and when we had recruited a cheerful dozen or so of leaping devils, we repaired to a hairdresser's—he was also a costumier—and let in there the cold, and youth, and laughter.

I wanted something somber and handsome, with a shade of elegant sadness; so I requested, "Give me the dress of a Spanish grandee."

Apparently this grandee had been very tall, for I was altogether swallowed up in his dress, and felt as absolutely alone as though I had been in a wide, empty hall. Getting out of this costume, I asked for something else.

"Would you like to be a clown? Motley with bells?"

"A clown, indeed!" I exclaimed with contempt.

"Well, then, a bandit. Such a hat and dagger!"

Oh! dagger! Yes, that would suit my purpose. But unfortunately the bandit whose clothes they gave me had scarcely grown to full stature. Most probably he had been a corrupt youth of eight years. His little hat would not cover the back of my head, and I had to be dragged out of his velvet breeches as out of a trap. A page's dress would not do: it was all spotted like the pard. The monk's cowl was all in holes.

"Look sharp; it's late," said my companions, who were already dressed, trying to hurry me up.

There was but one costume left—that of a distinguished Chinese man. "Give me the Chinese man's," I said with a wave of my hand. And they gave it to me. It was the Devil knows what! I am not speaking of the costume itself. I pass over in silence those idiotic, flowered boots, which were too short for me, and reached only half-way to my knees; but in the remaining, by far the most essential part stuck out like two incomprehensible adjuncts on either side of my feet. I say nothing of the pink rag which covered my head like a wig, and was tied by threads to my ears, so that they protruded and stood up like a bat's. But the mask!

It was, if one may use the expression, a face *in the abstract*. It had nose, eyes, and mouth all right enough, and all in the proper places; but there was nothing human about it. A human being could not look so placid—even in his coffin. It was expressive neither of sorrow, nor cheerfulness, nor surprise—it expressed absolutely nothing! It looked at you squarely, and placidly—and an uncontrollable laughter overwhelmed you. My companions rolled about on the sofas, sank impotently down on the chairs, and gesticulated.

"It will be the most original mask of the evening," they declared.

I was ready to weep; but no sooner did I glance in the mirror than I too was convulsed with laughter. Yes, it will be a most original mask!

"In no circumstances are we to take off our masks," said my companions on the way. "We'll give our word."

"Honor bright!"

III

Positively it was the most original mask. People followed me in crowds, turned me about, jostled me, pinched me. But when, harried, I turned on my persecutors in anger— uncontrollable laughter seized them. Wherever I went, a roaring cloud of laughter encompassed and pressed on me;

it moved together with me, and I could not escape from this circle of mad mirth. Sometimes it seized even myself, and I shouted, sang, and danced till everything seemed to go around before me, as if I was drunk. But how remote everything was from me! And how solitary I was under that mask! At last they left me in peace. With anger and fear, with malice and tenderness intermingling, I looked at her.

"It's I."

Her long eyelashes were lifted slowly in surprise, and a whole sheaf of black rays flashed upon me, and a laugh, resonant, joyous, bright as the spring sunshine—a laugh answered me.

"Yes, it's I; I, I say," I insisted with a smile. "Why didn't you come this evening?"

But she only laughed, laughed joyously.

"I suffered so much; I felt so hurt," I said, imploring an answer.

But she only laughed. The black sheen of her eyes was extinguished, and still more brightly her smile lit up. It was the sun indeed, but burning, pitiless, cruel.

"What's the matter with you?"

"Is it really you?" she said, restraining herself. "How comical you are!"

My shoulders were bowed, and my head hung down—such despair was there in my pose. And while she, with the expiring afterglow of the smile upon her face, looked at the happy, young couples that hurried by us, I said, "It's not nice to laugh. Don't you feel that there's a living, suffering face behind my ridiculous mask—and can't you see that it was only for the opportunity it gave me of seeing you that I put it on? You gave me reason to hope for your love, and then so quickly, so cruelly deprived me of it. Why didn't you come?"

With a protest on her tender, smiling lips, she turned sharply to me, and a cruel laugh utterly overwhelmed her. Choking, almost weeping, covering her face with a fragrant lace handkerchief, she brought out with difficulty, "Look at yourself in the mirror behind you. Oh, how droll you are!"

Contracting my brows, clenching my teeth with pain, with a face grown cold, from which all the blood had fled, I looked at the mirror. There gazed back at me an idiotically placid, stolidly complacent, inhumanly immovable face. And I burst into an uncontrollable fit of laughter. And with the laughter not yet subsided, but already with the trembling of rising anger, with the madness of despair, I said—no, almost shouted, "You shouldn't laugh!"

And when she was quiet again, I went on speaking in a whisper of my love. I had never spoken so well, for I had never loved so strongly. I spoke of the tortures of expectation, of the venomous tears of mad jealousy and grief, of my own soul, which was all love. And I saw how her drooping eyelashes cast thick, dark shadows over her blanched cheeks. I saw how across their dull pallor the fire, bursting into flame, threw a red reflection, and how her whole pliant body involuntarily bent towards me.

She was dressed as the Goddess of Night, and was all mysterious, clad in a black, mist-like face, which twinkled with stars of brilliants. She was as beautiful as a forgotten dream of far-off childhood. As I spoke, my eyes filled with tears, and my heart beat with gladness. And I perceived, I perceived at last, how a tender, piteous smile parted her lips, and her eyelashes were lifted all a-tremble. Slowly, timorously, but with infinite confidence, she turned her head towards me, and . . .

And such a shriek of laughter I had never heard!

"No, no, I can't," she almost groaned, and throwing

back her head, she burst into a resonant cascade of laughter.

Oh, if but for a moment I could have had a human face! I bit my lips, tears rolled over my heated face; but it—that idiotic mask, on which everything was in its right place, nose, eyes, and lips—looked with a complacency stolidly horrible in its absurdity. And when I went out, swaying on my flowered feet, it was a long time before I got out of reach of that ringing laugh. It was as though a silvery stream of water were falling from an immense height, and breaking in cheerful song upon the hard rock.

IV

Scattered over the whole sleeping street, and rousing the stillness of the night with our lusty, excited voices, we walked home.

A companion said to me, "You've had a colossal success. I never saw people laugh so— Hey! what are you up to? Why are you tearing your mask? I say, you fellows, he's gone mad! Look, he's tearing his costume to pieces! **By God! he's actually crying.**"

BEN TOBIT

On the dread day of that monstrous injustice, when Jesus
Christ was crucified among the thieves on Golgotha—on
that day, Ben Tobit, a merchant in Jerusalem, had been
suffering from an unbearable toothache since the early
hours of the morning. It had started the night before; his
right jaw had begun to hurt, and one tooth, the one in
front of the wisdom tooth, seemed to have risen a little
and it hurt when he touched his tongue to it. But after
supper the pain disappeared, and Ben Tobit promptly forgot all about it. In fact, he had that very day traded his
old donkey advantageously for a young, strong one, and
so he was in rather high spirits and totally unconcerned
about the ominous symptom.

That night he slept very well and very soundly, but just
before dawn something began to bother him, as if someone were calling him on matters of great importance, and

when Ben Tobit awakened with annoyance, he found that the toothache had returned, a direct and racking one that assailed him with the full force of sharp, stabbing pain. But now he could not tell whether it was the same tooth that had hurt him the night before, or whether other teeth were involved as well; his mouth and his head were filled with excruciating pain, as if he were being forced to chew a thousand sharp, red-hot nails. He filled his mouth with cool water from an earthen jug, and the fury of the pain subsided for a moment; his mouth began to twitch and throb, and this sensation was almost pleasant compared to the previous one. Ben Tobit lay back on his bed. He thought about his new donkey and he thought of how fortunate he would be if it were not for his teeth.

He tried to fall asleep again, but the water became warm, and in five minutes the pain was back, more savage than before. Ben Tobit sat up in his bed, and soon his body swayed back and forth like a pendulum. His whole face was pulled together and puckered about a big nose, and on that nose, turned white with agony, a drop of cold sweat gathered. Thus it was that, swaying back and forth and moaning in pain, he beheld the first rays of the sun that was destined to see Golgotha with its three crosses and to grow dim with horror and sorrow.

Ben Tobit was a kind and good man who disliked injustice, but when his wife awakened, he had barely opened his mouth before he began to say a great many unpleasant things to her, complaining repeatedly that he was left alone, like a jackal, to howl and to writhe in agony. His wife listened patiently to the undeserved reproaches, for she knew it was not a mean heart that made him say such things, and she brought him many fine remedies: cleansed dung of rats to be applied to the cheek, a strong tincture obtained from a scorpion, and an authentic sliver of the stone tablets that had been smashed to bits by Moses. The rat dung helped a little, but not for long, as did also the tincture and the sliver, but each respite was followed by a violent onslaught of even greater pain. During the brief periods of relief, Ben Tobit comforted himself by thinking of his little donkey and daydreaming about him; but when he felt worse, he moaned, scolded his wife, and threatened to dash his head against a rock if the pain did not subside. And he kept pacing all the time from one corner of the flat roof of his house to the other, ashamed to get too close to its outer edge because the kerchief he had tied around his head made him look like a woman.

Several times children came running to him to tell him hastily about Jesus of Nazareth. Ben Tobit would stop for a moment to listen to them; then he would contract his face and, stamping his foot angrily, would send them on their way. He was a kind man and fond of children, but now it irritated him to be pestered with all sorts of silly things.

He was also irritated because many people in the street and on neighboring roofs seemed to have nothing better to do than to stare in curiosity at him with his head wrapped in a kerchief like a woman's. He was just about to go downstairs when his wife called to him:

"Look, there are the thieves! This might interest you!"

"Leave me alone, please. Don't you see how I'm suffering?" Ben Tobit answered angrily.

But his wife's words gave him a slight feeling that his toothache might be lessening. So he reluctantly went to the edge of the roof. With his head tilted to one side, one eye closed, his cheek in the palm of a hand, his face peevish and tearful, he looked down.

A huge, turbulently milling crowd, shrouded in dust, incessantly shouting, was moving up the steep, narrow street. Surrounded by the crowd, the criminals moved along with bodies bent low under the heavy burdens of the crosses, the whips of the Roman soldiers writhing like black snakes above them. One of them—the one who had long, fair hair and who was wearing a torn, blood-stained robe—stumbled on a stone someone had thrown at his feet and fell. The shouting grew louder and the crowd, like a many-colored sea, seemed to close over the fallen man. Ben Tobit suddenly winced with pain, as if someone had stabbed a red-hot needle into his tooth and twisted it there. He moaned, "Oh—oh—oh," and walked away from the edge of the roof, petulantly preoccupied and full of resentment.

"How they yell!" he said enviously, visualizing wide-open mouths with strong, never-aching teeth and thinking how he himself would be shouting if he were well. This mental image brought on another savage attack of pain. He kept shaking his kerchief-wrapped head, lowing, "M—moo—oo . . ."

"They say he healed the blind," said his wife, who had remained at the edge of the roof and had thrown a small stone at the place where Jesus, brought to his feet by the whips, moved along slowly.

"Yes, of course! Let him heal my toothache!" Ben Tobit retorted mockingly. "What a dust they kick up! Like a herd! They ought to be dispersed with a cane!" he added peevishly, in bitterness. "Help me down, Sarah!"

His wife was right; the spectacle did somewhat divert Ben Tobit, or perhaps it was the rat dung that helped him at last, and he managed to fall asleep. When he awakened, the pain was almost gone; there was only a small swelling on his right jaw, so small it was hardly noticeable. His wife said it was completely unnoticeable, but Ben Tobit smiled knowingly: he knew well what a good wife he had and how much she loved to say pleasant things. His neighbor Samuel, the tanner, came to visit, and Ben Tobit took him to see his little donkey; he listened with pride while Samuel praised him and the animal enthusiastically.

Then, to satisfy Sarah's insistent curiosity, the three of them went to see the men crucified on Golgotha. On the way, Ben Tobit told Samuel the whole story from the beginning, how he had felt an ache in his right jaw the previous evening and how he was wakened by an excruciating pain during the night. For greater effect, he put on the air of a martyr, closed his eyes, shook his head and groaned, while the gray-bearded Samuel nodded sympathetically and said, "Oh, oh, oh—how painful!"

Ben Tobit enjoyed the sympathy and repeated the story, going back to the remote past when he had first had a tooth go bad, down on the left side. So it was, in animated conversation, that they came to Golgotha. The sun that was destined to shine upon the world on this dread day had already set behind the far hills, and in the West a crimson strip like a bloody mark, stretched across the sky. Against this background the crosses stood dark and indistinct, while white-clad figures knelt at the foot of the middle cross.

The crowd had dispersed long before; it was growing cold, and, with a brief glance at the crucified men, Ben Tobit took Samuel's arm and gently turned him homeward. He felt particularly eloquent; he wanted to say more about the toothache. And so they walked away, Ben Tobit resuming the air of a martyr, shaking his head and groaning artfully, while Samuel nodded and exclaimed sympathetically. Black night was rising from the dark, deep gorges and from the distant, burned plains—as though it were trying to hide the enormous misdeed of the earth from the eyes of heaven.

THE MARSEILLAISE

He was an utter zero of a man. He had the timorous spirit of a rabbit and the prideless patience of a beast of burden. When fate, with malicious irony, threw him into our dark, dejected company, we roared with insane laughter that so absurd a mistake could actually happen.

He—well, he cried. I have never in my life seen a man who could cry so profusely. Tears seemed to pour from his eyes, his nose, his mouth, almost like a soaking sponge being squeezed dry. I have seen men in our ranks weep, but their tears were like an angry fire from which even savage animals would flee in terror. Such manly tears, even if they aged their faces, gave new youth and strength to their eyes. Like lava cast up from the fiery core of the earth, their tears left permanent traces, burying beneath them whole worlds of trivial wants and trivial cares. But this man, when he wept, succeeded only in acquiring a red nose and a soaking handkerchief. He must surely have had to hang his handkerchiefs on a line to dry, for how could he otherwise have had a large enough supply?

During the entire time of his exile he appealed to every possible official, to those who had real authority and to those who he mistakenly thought had authority. He bowed, he wept, he declared his innocence, he begged them to have pity upon his youth, he promised he would never again say anything except in prayer and gratitude. But they all laughed at him—as we did too—and called him a miserable pig.

They would summon him—"Hey, little pig, come here!" —and he would promptly come running to them, hoping each time for news that he was to be returned to his native land. But they were only taunting him. They knew well— as we did—that he was innocent, but they used his suffering to intimidate the other little pigs, as though they were not cowardly enough already.

Sometimes, driven by the sheer animal fear of being alone, he would come to stay among us. But he could find no way to break through our stern silence. Desperately he called us his dear comrades, his dear friends, but we would shake our heads and warn him: "Watch out, someone might hear you!" and he, the wretched little pig, would look with alarm to the door. Could we possibly, under the circumstance, keep from laughing? So we laughed, we who had almost forgotten laughter. And he, reassured and encouraged by our laughter, would sit down among us and tell us, through streaming tears, about his treasured books left upon his table and about his mother and his brothers, of whom he had no news as to whether they were still alive or had died in terror and agony. Toward the end we refused to have anything to do with him and would just chase him away.

When we started our hunger strike, he was overcome with panic—panic of an indescribably comical nature. He was devoted to his stomach, little pig that he indeed was, and yet he was afraid both of his dear comrades and of the prison officials. He wandered around completely distraught, constantly mopping his brow with a handkerchief soggy with perspiration—or was it tears?

He asked me anxiously, "How long will you starve?"

"For a long time," I told him resolutely.

"And you won't eat anything on the sly?"

"Our mothers will send us *pirozhki*,"* I assured him. He looked uncertainly at me, shook his head, and with a sigh walked away.

The next day, green as a parrot with fear, he announced, "Dear comrades, I will starve with you."

We answered as though with a single voice, "You can starve by yourself."

And starve he did. We did not actually believe it, even as you may not believe it. We suspected that he ate something when no one could see, and the guards thought so too. When toward the end of our hunger strike he became ill with typhus brought on by starvation, we simply shrugged our shoulders and said, "The poor little pig."

One of us—one who never laughed—said grimly, "He is our comrade. We should go to him."

Fever had made him delirious, and his incoherent talk was as pitiful as the whole of his life. He talked of his dear books . . . of his mother and his brothers . . . he asked for *pirozhki* . . . he swore to his innocence and begged for pardon. He cried out for his native country, for his dear France, and—curse the softness of man's heart!—he tugged at our compassion with his cries of "dear France."

* A small meat pie or the like.—Trans.

We were all in his cell as he lay there dying. For a few moments before his death he regained consciousness. Small and feeble, he lay there, and we, his comrades, stood silently at his side. Then he broke the silence, and we all heard him say, "When I am dead, sing the *Marseillaise* over me."

"What are you saying?" we exclaimed in surprise, with mingled amusement and anger.

He said it again: "When I am dead, sing the *Marseillaise* over me."

And now for the first time it happened; his eyes were dry, and we, every one of us, wept. And our tears were now like the fire from which savage animals flee in terror.

He died, and we sang the *Marseillaise* over him. With strong youthful voices we sang that great hymn of freedom, and the ocean, sternly echoing our song, bore back on the crests of its waves to his beloved France the ashen hue of fear and the crimson hue of hope.

He became forever after a symbol to us—that utter zero of a man with the body of a rabbit and a beast of burden but with the vast soul of man. To your knees before this man, comrades and friends!

We were singing. The barrels of the rifles were leveled straight at us, the bolts clicked ominously, the sharp bayonets pointed threateningly at our hearts. And yet, while his black coffin swayed gently in the tender hands of fighting men, that brave song of freedom rang out ever louder, ever more exultingly.

We were singing the *Marseillaise*.

THE RED LAUGH

PART I

Horror and madness.

I felt it for the first time as we were marching along the road—marching incessantly for ten hours without stopping, never diminishing our step, never waiting to pick up those who had fallen, but leaving them to the enemy, that was moving behind us in a compact mass only three or four hours later, effacing the marks of our feet by their own.

It was very sultry. I do not know how many degrees there were—120°, 140°, or more—I only know that the heat was incessant, hopelessly even and profound. The sun was so enormous, so fiery and terrible, that it seemed as if the earth had drawn nearer to it and would soon be burnt up altogether in its merciless rays. Our eyes had ceased to look. The small, shrunk pupil, as small as a poppy seed, sought in vain for darkness under the closed eyelid; the sun pierced the thin covering and penetrated into the tortured brain in a blood-red glow. But, nevertheless, it was better so: with closed eyelids, and for a long time, perhaps for several hours, I walked along with my eyes shut, hearing the multitude moving around me: the heavy, uneven tread of many feet, men's and horses'; the grinding of iron wheels crushing the small stones; somebody's deep, strained breathing and the dry smacking of parched lips. But I heard no word. All were silent, as if an army of dumb people were moving, and when anyone fell down, he fell in silence; others stumbled against his body, fell down and rose mutely, and, without turning their heads, marched on, as though these dumb men were also blind and deaf. I stumbled and fell several times and then involuntarily opened my eyes, and all that I saw seemed a wild fiction, the terrible raving of a mad world. The air vibrated at a white-hot temperature, the stones seemed to be trembling silently, ready to flow, and in the distance, at a curve of the road, the files of men, guns and horses seemed detached from the earth, and trembled like a mass of jelly in their onward progress, and it seemed to me that they were not living people that I saw before me, but an army of incorporate shadows.

The enormous, near, terrible sun lit up thousands of tiny blinding suns on every gun barrel and metal plate, and these suns, as fiery white and sharp as the white-hot points of the bayonets, crept into your eyes from every side. And the consuming, burning heat penetrated into your body—into your very bones and brain—and at times it seemed to me that it was not a head that swayed upon my shoulders, but a strange and extraordinary globe, heavy and light, belonging to somebody else, and horrible.

And then—then I suddenly remembered my home: a corner of my room, a scrap of light blue wallpaper, and a dusty, untouched water bottle on my table—on my table, which has one leg shorter than the others, and had a small piece of paper folded under it. While in the next room— and I cannot see them—are my wife and little son. If I had had the power to cry out, I would have done so—so wonderful was this simple and peaceful picture—the scrap of light blue wallpaper and dusty, untouched water bottle. I know that I stood still and lifted up my arms, but some- body gave me a push from behind, and I quickly moved on, thrusting the crowd aside, and hastening where I knew not, but feeling now neither heat nor fatigue. And I marched on thus for a long time through the endless mute files, past red sunburnt necks, almost touching the help- lessly lowered hot bayonets, when suddenly the thought of what I was doing, where I was hastening, stopped me. I turned aside in the same hasty way, forced my way in to the open, clambered across a gulley, and sat down on a stone in a preoccupied manner, as if that rough hot stone were the aim of all my strivings.

And then I felt it for the first time. I clearly perceived that all these people, marching silently on in the glaring sun, torpid from fatigue and heat, swaying and falling— were mad. They did not know where they were going, they did not know what that sun was for, they did not know anything. It was not heads that they had on their shoulders, but strange and terrible globes. There—I saw a man in the same plight as I, pushing his way hurriedly through the rows and falling down; there—another, and a third. Suddenly a horse's head appeared above the throng, with bloodshot and senseless eyes and a wide-open grin- ning mouth, that only hinted at a terrible, unearthly cry; this head appeared, fell down, and for an instant the crowd stopped, growing denser in that spot; I could hear hoarse, hollow voices, then a shot, and again the silent, endless march continued.

An hour passed as I sat on that stone, but the multitude still moved on past me, and the air and earth and the distant phantom-like ranks trembled as before. And again the burning heat pierced my body, and I forgot what for an instant I had pictured to myself; and the multitudes moved on past me, but I did not know who they were. An hour ago I was alone on the stone, but now I was surrounded by a group of gray people; some lying motionless, perhaps dead; others were sitting up and staring vacantly at those passing by. Some had guns and resembled soldiers; others were stripped almost naked, and the skin on their bodies was so livid, that one did not dare to look at it.

Not far from me someone was lying with his bared back upturned. One could see by the unconcerned manner in which he had buried his face in the sharp, burning sand, by the whiteness of the palm of his upturned hand, that he was dead, but his back was as red as if he were alive, and only a slight yellowish tinge, such as one sees on smoked meat, spoke of death. I wanted to move away from him, but I had not the strength, and, tottering from weakness, I continued looking at the endless phantom-like swaying files of men. By the condition of my head I knew that I should soon have a sunstroke too, but I awaited it calmly, as in a dream, where death seems only a stage on the path of wonderful and confused visions.

And I saw a soldier part from the crowd and direct his steps in a decided manner towards us. For an instant I lost sight of him in a ditch, but when he reappeared and moved on towards us, his gait was unsteady, and in his endeavors to control his restlessly tossing body, one felt he was using his last strength. He was coming so straight upon me that I grew frightened and, breaking through the heavy torpor that enveloped my brain, I asked, "What do you want?"

He stopped short, as if it were only a word that he was waiting for, and stood before me, enormous, bearded, in a torn shirt. He had no gun, his trousers hung only by one button, and through a slit in them one could see his white body. He flung his arms and legs about and he was visibly trying to control them, but could not; the instant he brought his arms together, they fell apart again.

"What's the matter? You'd better sit down," I said.

But he continued standing, vainly trying to gather himself together, and stared at me in silence. Involuntarily I got up from the stone and, tottering, looked into his eyes—and saw an abyss of horror and insanity in them. Everybody's pupils were shrunk—but his had dilated and covered his whole eye: what a sea of fire he must have seen through those enormous black windows! Maybe I had only imagined it, maybe in his look there was only death—but, no, I was not mistaken—in those black, bottomless pupils, surrounded by a narrow orange-colored rim, like a bird's eye, there was more than death, more than the horror of death. "Go away!" I cried, falling back. "Go away!" And as if he were only waiting for a word, enormous, disorderly and mute as before, he suddenly fell down upon me, knocking me over. With a shudder I freed my legs from under him, jumped up and longed to run—somewhere away from men, into the sunlit, unpeopled and quivering distance, when suddenly, on the left-hand side, a cannon boomed forth from a hilltop, and directly after it two others, like an echo. And somewhere above our heads a shell flew past with a gladsome, many-voiced scr—e—e—ch and howl.

We were outflanked.

The murderous heat, fear and fatigue disappeared instantly. My thoughts cleared, my mind grew clear and sharp, and when I ran up, out of breath, to the files of men drawing up, I saw serene, almost joyous faces, heard hoarse, but loud voices, orders, jokes. The sun seemed to have drawn itself up higher, so as not to be in the way, and had grown dim and still—and again a shell, like a witch, cut the air with a gladsome scr—e—e—ch.

I came up . . . .

FRAGMENT II

. . . . Nearly all the horses and men. The same in the eighth battery. In our twelfth battery, towards the end of the third day, there remained only three guns—all the others being disabled—six men and one officer, myself. We had neither slept nor eaten for twenty hours; for three days and nights a Satanic roar and howl enveloped us in a cloud of insanity, isolated us from the earth, the sky and ourselves—and we, the living, wandered about like lunatics. The dead—they lay still, while we moved about doing our duty, talking and laughing, and we were—like lunatics. All our movements were quick and certain, our orders clear, the execution of them precise, but if you had suddenly asked any one of us who we were, undoubtedly we would not have been able to find an answer in our troubled brains. As in a dream, all faces seemed familiar, and all that was going on seemed quite familiar and natural—as if it had happened before; but when I looked closely at any face or gun, or began listening to the din, I was struck by the novelty and endless mystery of everything. Night approached imperceptibly, and before we had time to notice it and wonder where it had come from, the sun was again burning above our heads. And only from those who came to our battery did we learn that it was the third day of the battle that was dawning, and instantly forgot it again: to us it appeared as one endless day without any beginning, sometimes dark, sometimes bright, but always incomprehensible and blind. And nobody was afraid of death, for nobody understood what death was.

On the third or fourth night—I do not remember which —I lay down for a minute behind the breastwork, and, as soon as I shut my eyes, the same familiar and extraordinary picture stood before them: the scrap of light blue wallpaper and the dusty, untouched water bottle on my table. While in the next room—and I could not see them —were my wife and little son. But this time a lamp with a green shade was burning on the table, so it must have been evening or night. The picture stood motionless, and I contemplated it very calmly and attentively for a long time, letting my eyes rest on the light reflected in the crystal of the water bottle, and on the wallpaper, and wondered why my son was not asleep, for it was night and time for him to go to bed. Then I again began examining the wallpaper—every spiral, silvery flower, square and line—and never imagined that I knew my room so well. Now and then I opened my eyes and saw the black sky with beautiful, fiery stripes upon it, then shut them again and saw once more the wallpaper, the bright water bottle, and wondered why my son was not asleep, for it was night and time for him to go to bed. Once a shell burst not far from me, making my legs give a jerk, and somebody cried out loudly, louder than the bursting of the shell, and I said to myself, "Somebody is killed," but I did not get up and did not tear my eyes away from the light blue wallpaper and the water bottle.

Afterwards I got up, moved about, gave orders, looked

at the men's faces, trained the guns, and kept on wondering why my son was not asleep. Once I asked the sergeant, and he explained it to me at length with great detail, and we kept nodding our heads. And he laughed, and his left eyebrow kept twitching, while his eye winked cunningly at somebody behind us. Behind us were somebody's feet—and nothing more.

By this time it was quite light, when suddenly there fell a drop of rain. Rain—just the same as at home, the most ordinary little drops of rain. But it was so sudden and out of place, and we were so afraid of getting wet, that we left our guns, stopped firing, and tried to find shelter anywhere we could.

The sergeant with whom I had only just been speaking got under the gun carriage and dozed off, although he might have been crushed any minute; the stout artilleryman, for some reason or other, began undressing a corpse, while I began running about the battery in search of something—a cloak or an umbrella. And the same instant, over the whole enormous area, where the rain cloud had burst, a wonderful stillness fell. A belated shrapnel shot shrieked and burst, and everything grew still—so still that one could hear the stout artilleryman panting, and the drops of rain splashing upon the stones and guns. And this soft and continuous sound, that reminded one of autumn—the smell of the moist earth and the stillness—seemed to tear the bloody, savage nightmare asunder for an instant; and when I glanced at the wet, glistening gun, it unexpectedly reminded me of something dear and peaceful—my childhood, or perhaps my first love. But in the distance a gun boomed forth particularly loud, and the spell of the momentary lull disappeared; the men began coming out of their hiding places as suddenly as they had hid themselves; a gun roared, then another, and once again the weary brain was enveloped by bloody, indissoluble gloom. And nobody noticed when the rain stopped. I only remember seeing the water rolling off the fat, sunken, yellow face of the killed artilleryman; so I supposed it rained for rather a long time . . . .

. . . . Before me stood a young volunteer, holding his hand to his cap and reporting to me that the general wanted us to retain our position for only two hours more, when we should be relieved. I was wondering why my son was not in bed, and answered that I could hold on as much as he wished. But suddenly I became interested in the young man's face, probably because of its unusual and striking pallor. I never saw anything whiter than that face: even the dead have more color than that young, beardless face had. I suppose he became terrified on his way to us, and could not recover himself; and in holding his hands to his cap, he was only making an effort to drive away his mad fear by a simple and habitual gesture.

"Are you afraid?" I asked, touching his elbow. But his elbow seemed as if made of wood, and he only smiled and remained silent. Better to say, his lips alone were twitching into a smile, while his eyes were full of youth and terror only—nothing more.

"Are you afraid?" I repeated kindly. His lips twitched, trying to frame a word, and the same instant there happened something incomprehensible, monstrous and supernatural. I felt a draught of warm air upon my right cheek, that made me sway—that is all—while before my eyes, in place of the white face, there was something short, blunt and red, and out of it the blood was gushing as out of an uncorked bottle, such as is drawn on badly executed sign-boards. And that short red and flowing "something" still seemed to be smiling a sort of smile, a toothless laugh—a red laugh.

I recognized it—that red laugh. I had been searching for it and I had found it—that red laugh. Now I understood what there was in all those mutilated, torn, strange bodies. It was a red laugh. It was in the sky, it was in the sun, and soon it was going to overspread the whole earth—that red laugh!

While they, with precision and calmness, like lunatics . . . .

FRAGMENT III

They say there are a great number of madmen in our army, as well as in the enemy's. Four lunatic wards have been opened. When I was on the staff, our adjutant showed me . . . .

FRAGMENT IV

. . . . Coiled round like snakes. He saw the wire, chopped through at one end, cut the air and coil itself around three soldiers. The barbs tore their uniforms and stuck into their bodies, and, shrieking, the soldiers spun round in frenzy, two of them dragging the third, who was already dead, after them. Then only one remained alive, and he tried to push the two that were dead away from him; but they trailed after him, whirling and rolling over each other and over him; and suddenly all three became motionless.

He told me that no less than two thousand men were lost at that one wire entanglement. While they were hacking at the wire and getting entangled in its serpentine coils, they were pelted by an incessant rain of balls and grape-shot. He assured me it was very terrifying, and if only they had known in which direction to run, that attack would have ended in a panic flight. But ten or twelve continuous lines of wire and the struggle with it, a whole labyrinth of pitfalls with stakes driven in at the bottom, had muddled them so, that they were quite incapable of defining the direction of escape.

Some, like men blind, fell into the funnel-shaped pits, and hung upon the sharp stakes, pierced through the stomach, twitching convulsively and dancing like toy clowns; they were crushed down by fresh bodies, and soon the whole pit filled to the edges, and presented a writhing mass of bleeding bodies, dead and living. Hands thrust themselves out of it in all directions, the fingers working convulsively, catching at everything; and those who once got caught in that trap could not get back again: hundreds of fingers, strong and blind, like the claws of a lobster, gripped them firmly by the legs, caught at their clothes, threw them down upon themselves, gouged out their eyes and throttled them. Many seemed as if they were intoxicated, and ran straight at the wire, got caught in it, and remained shrieking, until a bullet finished them.

Generally speaking, they all seemed like people intoxicated: some swore dreadfully, others laughed when the wire caught them by the arm or leg, and died there and then. He himself, although he had had nothing to eat or drink since the morning, felt very queer. His head swam, and there were moments when the feeling of terror in him changed to wild rapture, and from rapture again to terror. When somebody struck up a song at his side, he caught up the tune, and soon a whole unanimous chorus broke forth. He did not remember what they sang, only that it was lively in a dancing strain. Yes, they sang, while all

around them was red with blood. The very sky seemed to
be red, and one might have thought that a catastrophe
had overwhelmed the universe—a strange disappearance
of colors: the light blue and green and other habitual
peaceful colors had disappeared, while the sun blazed
forth in a red flare light.

"The red laugh," I said.

But he did not understand.

"Yes, and they laughed, as I told you before, like people intoxicated. Perhaps they even danced. There was
something of the sort. At least the movements of those
three resembled dancing."

He remembers distinctly, when he was shot through the
chest and fell, his legs twitched for some time until he lost
consciousness, as if he were dancing to music. And at the
present moment, when he thinks of that attack, a strange
feeling comes over him: partly fear and partly the desire
to experience it all over again.

"And get another ball in your chest?" I asked.

"There now, why should I get a ball each time? But it
wouldn't be half so bad, old boy, to get a medal for brav-
ery."

He was lying on his back, with a waxen face, sharp
nose, prominent cheekbones and sunken eyes. He was lying looking like a corpse and dreaming of a medal! Morti-
fication had already set in: he had a high temperature,
and in three days' time he was to be thrown into the grave
to join the dead; nevertheless, he lay smiling dreamily
and talking about a medal.

"Have you telegraphed your mother?" I asked.

He glanced at me with terror, animosity and anger, and
did not answer. I was silent, and then the groans and rav-
ings of the wounded became audible. But when I rose to
go, he caught my hand in his hot, but still strong one, and

fixed his sunken, burning eyes upon me in a lost and distressed way.

"What does it all mean, eh? What does it all mean?" he asked in a frightened and persistent manner, pulling at my hand.

"What?"

"Everything—in general. Now, she's waiting for me. But I can't. My country—is it possible to make her understand, what my country means?"

"The red laugh," I answered.

"Ah! you're always joking, but I'm serious. It's indispensable to explain it; but is it possible to make her understand? If you only knew what she says in her letters— what she writes! And you know her words—are grayhaired. And you . . ." he looked curiously at my head, pointed his finger, and suddenly breaking into a laugh, said, "Why, you've grown bald. Have you noticed it?"

"There are no looking glasses here."

"Many have grown bald and gray. Look here, give me a looking glass. Give me one! I feel white hair growing out of my head. Give me a looking glass!" He became delirious, crying and shouting out, and I left the hospital.

That same evening we got up an entertainment—a sad and strange entertainment, at which, amongst the guests, the shadows of the dead assisted. We decided to gather in the evening and have tea, as if we were at home, at a picnic. We got a samovar, we even got a lemon and glasses, and established ourselves under a tree, as if we were at home, at a picnic. Our companions arrived noisily in twos and threes, talking, joking and full of gleeful expectation—but soon grew silent, and avoided looking at each other, for there was something fearful in this meeting of spared men. In tatters, dirty, itching, as if we were covered by a dreadful ringworm, with hair neglected, thin and worn, having lost all familiar and habitual aspect, we seemed to see each other for the first time as we gathered around the samovar, and, seeing each other, we grew terrified. In vain I looked for a familiar face in this group of disconcerted men—I could not find one. These men, restless, hasty and jerky in their movements, starting at every sound, constantly looking for something behind their backs, trying to fill up that mysterious void into which they were too terrified to look, by superfluous gesticulations—were new, strange men, whom I did not know. And their voices sounded different, articulating the words with difficulty in jerks, easily passing into angry shouts or senseless irrepressible laughter at the slightest provocation. And everything around us was strange to us. The tree was strange, and the sunset strange, and the water strange, with a peculiar taste and smell, as if we had left the earth and entered into a new world together with the dead—a world of mysterious phenomena and ominous somber shadows. The sunset was yellow and cold; black, unillumined, motionless clouds hung heavily over it, while the earth under it was black, and our faces in that ill-omened light seemed yellow, like the faces of the dead. We all sat watching the samovar, but it went out, its sides reflecting the yellowishness and menace of the sunset, and it seemed also an unfamiliar, dead and incomprehensible object.

"Where are we?" somebody asked, and uneasiness and fear sounded in his voice. Somebody sighed; somebody convulsively cracked his fingers; somebody laughed; somebody jumped up and began walking quickly around the table. These last days one could often meet with such men, who were always walking hastily, almost running, at times strangely silent, at times mumbling something in an uncanny way.

"At the war," answered he who had laughed, and again

he burst into a hollow, lingering laugh, as if something was choking him.

"What's he laughing at?" somebody asked indignantly. "Look here, stop it!"

The other choked once more, gave a titter and stopped obediently.

It was growing dark, the cloud seemed to be settling down on the earth, and we could with difficulty distinguish each other's yellow phantom-like faces.

Somebody asked, "And where's Fatty-legs?" ("Fatty-legs" we called a fellow officer, who, being short, wore enormous water-tight boots.)

"He was here just now. Fatty-legs, where are you?"

"Fatty-legs, don't hide. We can smell your boots."

Everybody laughed, but their laugh was interrupted by a rough, indignant voice, that sounded out of the darkness:

"Stop that! Aren't you ashamed? Fatty-legs was killed this morning, reconnoitering."

"He was here just now. It must be a mistake."

"You imagined it. Hey! you there, behind the samovar, cut me a slice of lemon."

"And me!"

"And me!"

"The lemon's finished."

"How is that, boys?" sounded a gentle, hurt voice, full of distress and almost crying; "why, I only came for the sake of the lemon."

The other again burst into a hollow and lingering laugh, and nobody checked him. But he soon stopped. He gave a snigger, and was silent. Somebody said:

"Tomorrow we begin the advance on the enemy."

But several voices cried out angrily:

"Nonsense, advance on the enemy, indeed!"

"But you know yourself——"

"Shut up. As if we can't talk of something else."

The sunset faded. The cloud lifted, and it seemed to grow lighter; the faces became more familiar, and he, who kept circling round us, grew calmer and sat down.

"I wonder what it's like at home now?" he asked vaguely, and in his voice there sounded a guilty smile.

And once again all became terrible, incomprehensible and strange—so intensely so, that we were filled with horror, almost to the verge of losing consciousness. And we all began talking and shouting at the same time, bustling about, moving our glasses, touching each other's shoulders, hands, knees—and all at once became silent, giving way before the incomprehensible.

"At home?" somebody cried out of the darkness. His voice was hoarse and quivering with emotion, fear and hatred. And some of the words would not come out, as if he had forgotten how to say them.

"At home? What home? Why, is there home anywhere? Don't interrupt me or else I'll fire. At home I used to take a bath every day—can you understand?—a bath with water—water up to the very edges. While now—I don't even wash my face every day. My head is covered with scurf, and my whole body itches and over it crawl, crawl . . . I'm going mad from dirt, while you talk of—home! I'm like an animal, I despise myself, I can't recognize myself, and death is not at all terrifying. You tear my brain with your shrapnel shots. Aim at what you will, all hit my brain—and you can speak of—home. What home? Streets, windows, people, but I wouldn't go into the street now for anything. I should be ashamed to. You brought a samovar here, but I was ashamed to look at it."

The other laughed again. Somebody called out:

"Damn it all! I *shall* go home."

"Home?"

"You don't understand what duty is!"

"Home? Listen! He wants to go home!"

There was a burst of laughter and of painful shouts—
and again all became silent—giving way before the incomprehensible. And then not only I, but every one of
us, felt *that*. It was coming towards us out of those dark,
mysterious and strange fields; it was rising from out of
those obscure, dark ravines, where, maybe, the forgotten
and lost among the stones were still dying; it was flowing
from the strange, unfamiliar sky. We stood in silence
around the dying-out samovar, losing consciousness from
horror, while an enormous, shapeless shadow, that had
arisen above the world, looked down upon us from the
sky, with a steady and silent gaze. Suddenly, quite close
to us, probably at the Commander's house, music burst
forth, and the frenzied, joyous, loud sounds seemed to
flash out into the night and stillness. The band played
with frenzied mirth and defiance, hurriedly, discordantly,
too loudly, and too joyously, and one could feel that those
who were playing and those who were listening, saw, as
we did, that same enormous, shapeless shadow, risen
above the world. And it was clear that the player on the
trumpet carried in himself, in his very brain and ears,
that same enormous, dumb shadow. The abrupt and
broken sound tossed about, jumping and running away
from the others, quivering with horror and insanity in its
lonesomeness. And the other sounds seemed to be looking
round at it, so clumsily they ran, stumbling, falling, and
again rising in a disorderly crowd—too loud, too joyous,
too close to the black ravines, where most probably the
forgotten and lost among the boulders were still dying.

And we stood for a long time around the cold samovar
and were silent.

FRAGMENT V

. . . . I was already asleep when the doctor roused me by pushing me cautiously. I woke, and jumping up, cried out, as we all did when anybody wakened us, and rushed to the entrance of our tent. But the doctor held me firmly by the arm, excusing himself:

"I frightened you, forgive me. I know you want to sleep . . . ."

"Five days and nights . . ." I muttered, dozing off. I fell asleep and slept, as it seemed to me, for a long time, when the doctor again began speaking, poking me cautiously in the ribs and legs.

"But it's very urgent. Dear fellow, please—it's so pressing. I keep thinking . . . I can't . . . I keep thinking, that some of the wounded were left . . ."

"What wounded? Why, you were bringing them in the whole day long. Leave me in peace. It's not fair—I haven't slept for five days!"

"Dear boy, don't be angry," muttered the doctor, awkwardly putting my cap on my head; "everybody's asleep, it's impossible to rouse anybody. I've got hold of an engine and seven carriages, but we're in want of men. I understand. . . . Dear fellow, I implore you. Everybody's asleep and everybody refuses. I'm afraid of falling asleep myself. I don't remember when I slept last. I believe I'm beginning to have hallucinations. There's a dear fellow, put down your feet, just one—there—there . . . ."

The doctor was pale and tottering, and one could see that if he were only to lie down for an instant he would fall asleep and remain so without waking for several days running. My legs sank under me, and I am certain I fell asleep as I walked—suddenly and unexpectedly a row of black outlines appeared before us—the engine and carriages. Near them, scarcely distinguishable in the darkness, some men were wandering about slowly and silently. There was not a single light either on the engine or carriages, and only the shut ash box threw a dim, reddish light onto the rails.

"What is this?" I asked, stepping back.

"Why, we're going in the train. Have you forgotten? We're going in the train," muttered the doctor.

The night was chilly, and he was trembling from cold, and as I looked at him I felt the same rapid, tickling shiver all over my body.

"Damn you!" I cried loudly. "Just as if you couldn't have taken somebody else."

"Hush! Please, hush!" and the doctor caught me by the arm.

Somebody out of the darkness said:

"If you were to fire a volley from all the guns, nobody would stir. They're all asleep. One could go up and bind them all. Just now I passed quite close to the sentry. He looked at me and didn't say a word, never stirred. I suppose he was asleep too. It's a wonder he doesn't fall down."

He who spoke yawned, and his clothes rustled; evidently he was stretching himself. I leaned against the side of the carriage, intending to climb up—and was instantly overcome by sleep. Somebody lifted me up from behind and laid me down, while I began pushing him away with my feet, without knowing why, and again I fell asleep, hearing, as in a dream, fragments of a conversation:

"At the seventh verst."

"Have you forgotten the lanterns?"

"No, he won't go."

"Give them here. Back a little. That's it."

The carriages were jerking backwards and forwards,

something was rattling. And gradually, because of all these sounds, even though I was lying comfortably and quietly, sleep deserted me. But the doctor was sound asleep, and when I took him by the hand, it was like the hand of a corpse, heavy and limp. The train was now moving slowly and cautiously, shaking slightly, as if groping its way.

The student acting as hospital orderly lighted the candle in the lantern, lighting up the walls and the black aperture of the entrance, and said angrily:

"Damn it! Much they need us by this time. But you'd better wake him, before he falls into a sound sleep, for then you won't be able to do anything with him. I know by myself."

We roused the doctor, and he sat up, rolling his eyes vacantly. He tried to lie down again, but we did not let him.

"It would be good to have a drop of vodka now," the student said.

We drank a mouthful of brandy, and all sleepiness disappeared entirely. The big black square of the door began to grow pink, then red—somewhere from behind the hills appeared an enormous mute flare of a conflagration, as if the sun were rising in the middle of the night.

"It's far away. About twenty versts."

"I feel cold," the doctor said, snapping his teeth.

The student looked out of the door and beckoned me to come up to him. I looked out: at different points of the horizon motionless flares of similar conflagration stood out in a mute row, as if dozens of suns were rising simultaneously. And now the darkness was not so great. The distant hills were growing more densely black, sharply outlined in a broken and wavy contour against the sky, while in the foreground all was flooded with a red, soft glow, silent and motionless. I glanced at the student; his face was tinged by the same red fantastic color of blood, which had changed itself into air and light.

"Are there many wounded?" I asked.

He waved his hand. "A great many madmen. More so than wounded."

"Real madmen?"

"What others can there be?"

He was looking at me, and his eyes wore the same fixed, wild expression, full of cold horror, as that of the soldier who had died of sunstroke.

"Stop that," I said, turning away.

"The doctor is mad also. Just look at him."

The doctor had not heard. He was sitting cross-legged, like a Turk, swaying to and fro, soundlessly moving his lips and fingertips. And in his gaze there was the same fixed, stupefied, blunt, stricken expression.

"I feel cold," he said, and smiled.

"Hang you all!" I cried, moving away into a corner of the carriage. "What did you call me up for?"

Nobody answered. The student stood gazing out at the mute spreading glow, and the back of his head with its curly hair was youthful; and when I looked at him, I do not know why, but I kept picturing to myself a delicate woman's hand passing through that hair. And this image was so unpleasant, that a feeling of hatred sprang up in my breast, and I could not look at him without a feeling of loathing.

"How old are you?" I asked, but he did not turn his head and did not answer.

The doctor kept on rocking himself.

"I feel cold."

"When I think," said the student, without turning around, "when I think that there are streets, houses, a university . . ."

He broke off, as if he had said all, and was silent. Suddenly the train stopped almost instantaneously, making me knock myself against the wall, and voices were to be heard. We jumped out. In front of the very engine, upon the rails lay something, a not very large lump, out of which a leg was projecting.

"Wounded?"

"No, dead. The head's torn off. Say what you will, but I'll light the headlight. Otherwise we'll be crushing somebody."

The lump with the protruding leg was thrown aside; for an instant the leg lifted itself up, as if it wanted to run through the air, and all disappeared in a black ditch. The headlight was lit and the engine instantly grew black.

"Listen!" somebody whispered, full of silent terror.

How was it that we had not heard it before? From everywhere—the exact place could not be defined—a groan, unbroken and scraping, wonderfully calm in its breadth, and even indifferent, as it seemed, was borne upon us. We had heard many cries and groans, but this resembled none of those heard before. On the dim, reddish surface our eyes could perceive nothing, and therefore the very earth and sky, lit up by a never-rising sun, seemed to be groaning.

"The fifth verst," said the engine driver.

"That's where it comes from," and the doctor pointed forwards. The student shuddered and slowly turned towards us.

"What is it? It's terrible to listen to!"

"Let's move on."

We walked along in front of the engine, throwing a dense shadow upon the rails—not black but of a dim red color, lit up by the soft, motionless flares that stood out mutely at the different points of the black sky. And with each step we made, that wild unearthly groan, that had no visible source, grew ominously, as if it were the red air, the very earth and sky, that were groaning. In its ceaselessness and strange indifference it recalled at times the noise of grasshoppers in a meadow—the ceaseless noise of grasshoppers in a meadow on a warm summer day. And we came upon dead bodies oftener and oftener. We examined them rapidly and threw them off the rails—those indifferent, calm, limp bodies, that left dark, oily stains where the blood had soaked into the earth where they had lain. At first we counted them, but soon got muddled, and ceased. They were many—too many for that ominous night, that breathed cold and groans from each fibre of its being.

"What does it mean?" cried the doctor, and threatened somebody with his fist. "Just listen . . ."

We were nearing the sixth verst, and the groans were growing distinct and sharp, and we could almost feel the distorted mouths, from which those terrible sounds were issuing.

We looked anxiously into the rosy gloom, so deceitful in its fantastic light, when suddenly, almost at our feet, beside the rails, somebody gave a loud, calling, crying groan. We found him instantly, that wounded man, whose face seemed to consist only of two eyes, so big they appeared, when the light of the lantern fell on his face. He stopped groaning, and rested his eyes on each of us and our lanterns in turn, and in his glance there was a mad joy at seeing men and lights—and a mad fear that all would disappear like a vision. Perhaps he had seen men with lanterns bending over him many times, but they had always disappeared in a bloody, confused nightmare.

We moved on and almost instantly stumbled against two more wounded, one lying on the rails, the other groaning in a ditch. As we were picking them up, the doctor, trembling with anger, said to me, "Well?" and turned away. Several steps farther on we met a man wounded slightly, who was walking alone, supporting one arm with the other. He was walking with his head thrown back, straight towards us, but seemed not to notice us when we drew aside to let him pass. I believe he did not see us. He stopped for an instant near the engine, turned aside, and went past the train.

"You had better get in!" cried the doctor, but he did not answer.

These were the first that we found, and they horrified us. But later on we came upon them oftener and oftener along the rails or near them, and the whole field, lit up by the motionless, red flare of the conflagrations, began stirring as if it were alive, breaking out into loud cries, wails, curses and groans. All those dark mounds stirred and crawled about like half-dead lobsters let out of a basket, with outspread legs, scarcely resembling men in their broken, unconscious movements and ponderous immobility. Some were mute and obedient, others groaned, wailed, swore and showed such a passionate hate towards us who were saving them, as if *we* had brought about that bloody, indifferent night, and been the cause of all those terrible wounds and their loneliness amidst the night and dead bodies.

The train was full, and our clothes were saturated with blood, as if we had stood for a long time under a rain of blood, while the wounded were still being brought in, and the field, come to life, was stirring wildly as before.

Some of the wounded themselves crawled up, some walked up, tottering and falling. One soldier almost ran up to us. His face was smashed, and only one eye remained, burning wildly and terribly, and he was almost naked, as if he had come from the bathroom. Pushing me aside, he caught sight of the doctor, and with his left hand rapidly seized him by the chest.

"I'll smash your snout!" he cried, shaking the doctor, and added slowly and mordantly a coarse oath: "I'll smash your snouts, you rabble!"

The doctor broke away from the soldier, and advancing towards him, cried chokingly:

"I'll have you court-martialed, you scoundrel! To prison with you! You're hindering my work! Scoundrel! Brute!"

We pulled them apart, but the soldier kept on crying out for a long time: "Rabble! I'll smash your snout!"

I was beginning to get exhausted, and went a little way off to have a smoke and rest a bit. The blood, dried to my hands, covered them like a pair of black gloves, making it difficult for me to bend my fingers, so that I kept dropping my cigarettes and matches. And when I succeeded in lighting my cigarette, the tobacco smoke struck me as novel and strange, with quite a peculiar taste, the like of which I never experienced before or after. Just then the ambulance student with whom I had traveled came up to me, and it seemed to me as if I had met with him several years back, but where, I could not remember. His tread was firm, as if he were marching, and he was staring through me at something farther on and higher up.

"And they're sleeping," he said, as it seemed, quite calmly.

I flew into a rage, as if the reproach were addressed to me.

"You forget that they fought like lions for ten days."

"And they're sleeping," he repeated, looking through me and higher up. Then he stooped down to me and, shaking his finger, continued in the same dry and calm way: "I'll tell you—I'll tell you . . ."

"What?"

He stooped still lower towards me, shaking his finger meaningly, and kept repeating the words as if they expressed a completed idea:

"I'll tell you—I'll tell you. Tell them . . ." And still looking at me in the same severe way, he shook his finger once more, then took out his revolver and shot himself in the temple. And this did not surprise or terrify me in the least. Putting my cigarette in the left hand, I felt his wound with my fingers, and went back to the train.

"The student has shot himself. I believe he's still alive," I said to the doctor. The latter caught hold of his head and groaned.

"Damn him! . . . There's no room. There, that one will go and shoot himself, too, soon. And I give you my word of honor," he cried angrily and menacingly, "I'll do the same! Yes! And let me beg you—just walk back. There's no room. You can lodge a complaint against me if you like."

And he turned away, still shouting, while I went up to the other who was about to commit suicide. He was an ambulance man, and also, I believe, a student. He stood, pressing his forehead against the wall of the carriage, and his shoulders shook with sobs.

"Stop!" I said, touching his quivering shoulder. But he did not turn around or answer, and continued crying. And the back of his head was youthful, like the other student's, and as terrifying, and he stood in an absurd manner with his legs spread out like a person drunk, who is sick; and his neck was covered with blood; probably he had clutched it with his own hands.

"Well?" I said impatiently.

He pushed himself away from the carriage, and stooping like an old man, with his head bent down, he went away into the darkness away from all of us. I do not know why, but I followed him, and we walked along for a long time away from the carriages. I believe he was crying, and a feeling of distress stole over me, and I wanted to cry too.

"Stop!" I cried, standing still.

But he walked on, moving his feet ponderously, bent down, looking like an old man with his narrow shoulders and shuffling gait. And soon he disappeared in the reddish haze, that resembled light and yet lit nothing. And I remained alone. To the left of me a row of dim lights floated past—it was the train. I was alone—amidst the dead and dying. How many more remained? Near me all was still and dead, but farther on the field was stirring, as if it were alive—or so it seemed to me in my loneliness. But the moan did not grow less. It spread along the earth—high-pitched, hopeless, like the cry of a child or the yelping of thousands of cast-away puppies, starving and cold. Like a sharp, endless, icy needle it pierced your brain and slowly moved backwards and forwards—backwards and forwards. . . .

FRAGMENT VI

. . . They were our own men. During the strange confusion of all movements that reigned in both armies, our own and the enemy's, during the last month, frustrating all orders and plans, we were sure it was the enemy that was approaching us, namely, the 4th corps. And everything was ready for an attack, when somebody clearly discerned our uniforms, and ten minutes later our guess had become a calm and happy certainty: they were our own men. They apparently had recognized us too: they advanced quite calmly, and that calm motion seemed to express the same happy smile of an unexpected meeting.

And when they began firing, we did not understand for some time what it meant, and still continued smiling—under a hail of shrapnel and bullets, that poured down upon us, snatching away at one stroke hundreds of men. Somebody cried out by mistake and—I clearly remember—we all saw that it was the enemy, that it was his uniform and not ours, and instantly answered the fire. About fifteen minutes after the beginning of that strange engagement both my legs were torn off, and I recovered consciousness in the hospital after the amputation.

I asked how the battle had ended, and received an evasive, reassuring answer, by which I could understand that we had been beaten; and afterwards, legless as I was, I was overcome by joy at the thought that now I would be sent home, that I was alive—alive for a long time to come, alive forever. And only a week later I learned some particulars, that once more filled me with doubts and a new, unexperienced feeling of terror. Yes, I believe they were our own men after all—and it was with one of our shells, fired out of one of our guns by one of our men, that my legs had been torn off. And nobody could explain how it had happened. Something occurred, something darkened our vision, and two regiments, belonging to the same army, facing each other at a distance of one verst, had been destroying each other for a whole hour in the full conviction that it was the enemy they had before them. Later on, the incident was remembered and spoken of reluctantly in half-words and—what is most surprising of all—one could feel that many of the speakers did not admit the mistake even then. That is to say, they admitted it, but thought that it had occurred later on, that in the beginning they really had the enemy before them, but that he disappeared somewhere during the general fray, leaving us in the range of our own shells. Some spoke of it openly, giving precise explanations, which seemed to them plausible and clear. Up to this very minute I cannot say for certain how the strange blunder began, as I saw with equal clearness first our red uniforms and then their orange-colored ones. And somehow very soon everybody forgot about the incident, forgot about it to such an extent that it was spoken of as a real battle and in that sense many accounts were written and sent to the papers in all good faith; I read them when I was back home. At first the public's attitude towards us, the wounded in that engagement, was rather strange—we seemed to be less pitied than those wounded in other battles, but soon even that disappeared too. And only new facts, similar to the one just described, and a case in the enemy's army, when two detachments actually destroyed each other almost entirely, having come to a hand-to-hand fight during the night—gives me the right to think that a mistake did occur.

Our doctor, the one that did the amputation, a lean, bony old man, tainted with tobacco smoke and carbolic acid, everlastingly smiling at something through his yellowish-gray thin mustache, said to me, winking his eye:

"You're in luck to be going home. There's something wrong here."

"What is it?"

"Something's going wrong. In our time it was simpler."

He had taken part in the last European war almost a quarter of a century back and often referred to it with pleasure. But this war he did not understand, and, as I noticed, feared it.

"Yes, there's something wrong," he sighed, and frowned, disappearing in a cloud of tobacco smoke. "I would leave too, if I could."

And, bending over me, he whispered through his yellow, smoked mustache:

"A time will come when nobody will be able to go away from here. Yes, neither I nor anybody."

And in his old eyes, so close to me, I saw the same fixed, dull, stricken expression. And something terrible, unbearable, resembling the fall of thousands of buildings, darted through my head, and, growing cold from terror, I whispered:

"The red laugh."

And he was the first to understand me. He hastily nodded his head and repeated:

"Yes. The red laugh."

He sat down quite close to me and looking around began whispering rapidly, in a senile way, wagging his sharp, gray little beard.

"You're leaving soon, and I'll tell you. Did you ever see a fight in an asylum? No? Well, I saw one. And they fought like sane people. You understand—like sane people." He significantly repeated the last phrase several times.

"Well, and what of that?" I asked, also in a whisper, full of terror.

"Nothing. Like sane people."

"The red laugh," I said.

"They were separated by water being poured over them."

I remembered the rain that had frightened us so, and got angry.

"You're mad, doctor!"

"Not more than you. Not more than you in any case."

He hugged his sharp old knees and chuckled; and, looking at me over his shoulder and still with the echo of that unexpected painful laugh on his parched lips, he winked at me slyly several times, as if we two knew something very funny, that nobody else knew. Then, with the solemnity of a professor of black magic giving a conjuring performance, he lifted his arm and, lowering it slowly, carefully touched with two fingers that part of the blanket under which my legs would have been, if they had not been cut off.

"And do you understand this?" he asked mysteriously.

Then, in the same solemn and significant manner, he waved his hand towards the row of beds on which the wounded were lying, and repeated:

"And can you explain this?"

"The wounded?" I said. "The wounded?"

"The wounded," he repeated like an echo. "The wounded. Legless and armless, with pierced sides, smashed-in chests and torn-out eyes. You understand it? I'm very glad. So I suppose you'll understand this also?"

With an agility quite unexpected for his age, he flung himself down and stood on his hands, balancing his legs in the air. His white working clothes turned down, his face grew purple and, looking at me fixedly with a strange up-turned gaze, with difficulty he threw a few broken words at me:

"And this . . . do you . . . also . . . understand?"

"Stop!" I whispered in terror, "or else I'll cry out."

He turned over into a natural position, sat down again near my bed and, taking breath, remarked instinctively:

"And nobody can understand it."

"Yesterday they were firing again."

"Yes, they were firing yesterday and the day before," he said, nodding his head affirmatively.

"I want to go home!" I said in distress. "Doctor, dear fellow, I want to go home. I can't remain here any longer. At times I can't bring myself to believe that I have a home, where it's so good."

He was thinking of something and did not answer, and I began to cry.

"My God, I have no legs. I used to love my bicycle so, to walk and run, and now I have no legs. I used to dance my boy on the right foot and he laughed, and now . . . Curse you all! What shall I go home for? I'm only thirty . . . Curse you all!"

And I sobbed and sobbed as I thought of my dear legs, my fleet, strong legs. Who took them away from me, who dared to take them away!

"Listen," said the doctor, looking aside. "Yesterday I saw a mad soldier that came to us. An enemy's soldier. He was stripped almost naked, beaten and scratched and hungry as an animal, his hair was unkempt, as ours is, and he resembled a savage, primitive man or monkey. He waved his arms about, made grimaces, sang and shouted and wanted to fight. He was fed and driven out again— into the open country. Where could we have kept him? Days and nights they wander about the hills, backwards and forwards in all directions, keeping to no path, having no aim or resting place, all in tatters, like ominous phantoms. They wave their arms, laugh, shout and sing, and when they come across anybody they begin to fight. or maybe, without noticing each other, pass by. What do

they eat? Probably nothing, or, maybe, they feed on the
dead bodies together with the beasts, together with those
fat wild dogs that fight in the hills and yelp the whole
night long. At night they gather about the fires like monstrous moths or birds awakened by a storm, and you need
only light a fire to have in less than half-an-hour a dozen
noisy, tattered, wild shapes resembling chilled monkeys,
gathering around it. Sometimes they're fired at by mistake,
sometimes on purpose, for they make you lose all patience
with their unintelligible, terrifying cries. . . ."

"I want to go home!" I cried, shutting my ears.

But new terrible words, sounding hollow and phantom-
like, as if they were passing through a layer of wadding,
kept hammering at my brain.

"They are many. They die by hundreds in the prec-
ipices and pitfalls, that are made for sound and clever
men, in the remnants of the barbed wire and on the stakes
they take part in the regular battles and fight like heroes
—always in the foremost ranks, always undaunted, but
often turn against their own men. I like them. At present
I'm only beginning to go mad, and that's why I'm sitting
and talking to you, but when my senses leave me entirely, I'll go out into the open country—I'll go out into
the open country, and I'll give a call—I'll give a call, I'll
gather those grave ones, those knights-errant, around me,
and declare war to the whole world. We'll enter the towns
and villages in a joyous crowd, with music and songs,
leaving in our wake a trail of red, in which everything
will whirl and dance like fire. Those that remain alive will
join us, and our brave army will grow like an avalanche,
and will cleanse the whole world. Who said that one must
not kill, burn or rob? . . ."

He was shouting now, that mad doctor, and seemed to
have awakened by his cries the slumbering pain of all

those around him with their ripped-open chests and sides, torn-out eyes and cut-off legs. The ward filled with a broad, rasping, crying groan, and from all sides pale, yellow, exhausted faces, some eyeless, some so monstrously mutilated that it seemed as if they had returned from hell, turned towards us. And they groaned and listened, and a black, shapeless shadow, risen up from the earth, peeped in cautiously through the open door, while the mad doctor went on shouting, stretching out his arms:

"Who said one must not kill, burn, or rob? We'll kill and burn and rob. We, a joyous careless band of braves, we'll destroy all; their buildings, universities and museums, and merry as children, full of fiery laughter, we'll dance on the ruins. I'll proclaim the madhouse our fatherland; all those that have not gone mad—our enemies and madmen; and when I, great, unconquerable and joyous, will begin to reign over the whole world, its sole lord and master, what a glad laugh will ring over the whole universe."

"The red laugh!" I cried, interrupting him. "Help! Again I hear the red laugh!"

"Friends!" continued the doctor, addressing himself to the groaning, mutilated shadows. "Friends! we shall have a red moon and a red sun, and the animals will have a merry red coat, and we'll skin all those that are too white —that are too white. . . . You haven't tasted blood? It's slightly sticky and slightly warm, but it's red, and has such a merry red laugh! . . ."

FRAGMENT VII

. . . . It was godless and unlawful. The Red Cross is respected by the whole world, as a thing sacred, and they saw that it was a train full of harmless wounded and not soldiers, and they ought to have warned us of the mine. The poor fellows, they were dreaming of home . . . .

FRAGMENT VIII

. . . . Around a samovar, around a real samovar, out of which the steam was rising as out of an engine—even the glass on the lamp had grown dim, there was so much steam. And the cups were the same, blue outside and white inside, very pretty little cups, a wedding present. My wife's sister gave them—she is a very kind and good woman.

"Is it possible they are all whole?" I asked incredulously, mixing the sugar in my glass with a clean silver spoon.

"One was broken," my wife said absently; she was holding the tap open just then, and the water was running out easily and prettily.

I laughed.

"What's it about?" my brother asked.

"Oh, nothing. Wheel me into the study just once more. You may as well trouble yourself for the sake of a hero. You idled away your time while I was away, but now that it's over, I'll bring you to order." And I began singing, as a joke, of course: "My friends, we're bravely hurrying towards the foe . . ."

They understood the joke and smiled, only my wife did not lift up her face; she was wiping the cups with a clean embroidered cloth. And in the study I saw once again the light blue wallpaper, a lamp with a green shade and a table with a water bottle upon it. And it was a little dusty.

"Pour me some water out of this," I ordered merrily.

"But you've just had tea."

"That doesn't matter, pour me out some. And you," I said to my wife, "take our son, and go into the next room for a minute. Please."

And I drank the water with delight in small sips, while my wife and son were in the next room, and I could not see them.

"That's all right. Now come here. But why isn't he in bed by this time?"

"He's so glad you've come home. Darling, go to your father."

But the child began to cry, and hid himself at his mother's feet.

"Why is he crying?" I asked, in perplexity, and looked around. "Why are you all so pale and silent, following me like shadows?"

My brother burst into a loud laugh and said, "We're not silent."

And my sister said, "We're talking the whole time."

"I'll go and see about the supper," my mother said, and hurriedly left the room.

"Yes, you are silent," I repeated, with sudden conviction. "Since morning I haven't heard a word from you; I'm the only one who chats, laughs, and makes merry. Aren't you glad to see me then? And why do you all avoid looking at me? Have I changed so? Yes, I'm changed. But I don't see any looking glasses about. Have you put them all away? Give me a looking glass."

"I'll bring you one directly," my wife answered, and did not come back for a long time, and the looking glass was brought by the maid. I looked into it, and—I had seen myself before in the train, at the station—it was the same face, grown older a little, but the most ordinary face. They, I believe, expected me to cry out and faint—so glad were they when I asked calmly:

"What is there so unusual in me?"

Laughing louder and louder, my sister left the room hurriedly, and my brother said with calm assurance, "Yes, you haven't changed much, only grown slightly bald."

"You can be thankful that my head isn't broken," I answered unconcernedly. "But where do they all disappear? First one, then another. Wheel me about the rooms, please. What a comfortable armchair, it doesn't make the slightest sound. How much did it cost? You bet I won't spare the money; I'll buy myself such a pair of legs, better . . . My bicycle!"

It was hanging on the wall, quite new, only the tires were limp for want of pumping. A tiny bit of mud had dried to the tire of the back wheel—the last time I had ridden it. My brother was silent and did not move my chair, and I understood his silence and irresoluteness.

"Only four officers remained alive in our regiment," I said, surlily. "I'm very lucky. You can take it for yourself—take it away tomorrow."

"All right, I'll take it," my brother agreed submissively. "Yes, you are lucky. Half of the town is in mourning. While legs—that's really—"

"Of course, I'm not a postman."

My brother stopped suddenly and asked, "But why does your head shake?"

"That's nothing. The doctor said it will pass."

"And your hands too?"

"Yes, yes. And my hands too. It will all pass. Wheel me on, please. I'm tired of remaining still."

They upset me, those discontented people, but my gladness returned to me when they began making my bed; a real bed, a handsome bed, that I had bought just before our wedding four years ago. They spread a clean sheet, then they shook the pillows and turned down the blanket;

while I watched the solemn proceedings, my eyes were full of tears from laughing.

"And now undress me and put me to bed," I said to my wife. "How good it is!"

"This minute, dear."

"Quicker!"

"This minute, dear."

"Why; what are you doing?"

"This minute, dear."

She was standing behind my back, near the toilet table, and I vainly tried to turn my head so as to see her. And suddenly she gave a cry, such a cry as one hears only at the war:

"What does it all mean?"

She rushed towards me, put her arms around me, and fell down, hiding her head near the stumps of my cut-off legs, from which she turned away with horror, and again pressed herself against them, kissing them, and crying:

"What have you become? Why, you're only thirty years old. You were young and handsome. What does it all mean? How cruel men are. What is it for? For whom is it necessary? You, my gentle, poor darling, darling . . . ."

At her cry they all ran up—my mother, sister, nurse—and they all began crying and saying something or other, and fell at my feet wailing. While on the threshold stood my brother, pale, terribly pale, with a trembling jaw, and cried out in a high-pitched voice:

"I shall go mad with you all. I shall go mad!" while my mother groveled at my chair and had not the strength to cry, but only gasped, beating her head against the wheels. And there stood the clean bed with the well-shaken pillows and turned-down blanket, the same bed that I bought just before our wedding four years ago . . . .

FRAGMENT IX

. . . . I was sitting in a warm bath, while my brother was pacing up and down the small room in a troubled manner, sitting down, getting up again, catching hold of the soap and towel, bringing them close up to his short-sighted eyes and again putting them back in their places. At last he stood up with his face to the wall and picking at the plaster with his finger, continued hotly:

"Judge for yourself: one cannot teach people mercy, sense, logic—teach them to act consciously for tens and hundreds of years running with impunity. And, in particular, to act consciously. One can become merciless, lose all sensitiveness, get accustomed to blood and tears and pain —for instance butchers, and some doctors and officers do, but how can one renounce truth, after one has learnt to know it? In my opinion it is impossible. I was taught from infancy not to torture animals and be compassionate; all the books that I've read told me the same, and I'm painfully sorry for all those that suffer at your cursed war. But time passes, and I'm beginning to get accustomed to all those deaths, sufferings and all this blood; I feel that I'm getting less sensitive, less responsive in my everyday life and respond only to great stimulants, but I can't get accustomed to *war;* my brain refuses to understand and explain a thing that's senseless in its basis. Millions of people gather at one place and, giving their actions order and regularity, kill each other, and it hurts everybody equally, and all are unhappy—what is it if not madness?" My brother turned round and looked at me inquiringly with his short-sighted, artless eyes.

"The red laugh," I said merrily, splashing about.

"I'll tell you the truth," and my brother put his cold

hand trustingly on my shoulder, but quickly pulled it back, as if he were frightened at its being naked and wet. "I'll tell you the truth; I'm very much afraid of going mad. I can't understand what's happening. I can't understand it, and it's dreadful. If only anybody could explain it to me, but nobody can. You were at the front, you saw it all—explain it to me."

"Deuce take you," I answered jokingly, splashing about.

"There, and you too," my brother said sadly. "Nobody is capable of helping me. It's dreadful. And I'm beginning to lose all understanding of what is permissible and what is not, what has sense and what is senseless. If I were to seize you suddenly by the throat, at first gently, as if caressing you, and then firmly, and strangle you, what would that be?"

"You're talking nonsense. Nobody does such things."

My brother rubbed his cold hands, smiled softly, and continued:

"When you were away, there were nights when I didn't sleep, couldn't sleep, and strange ideas entered my head—to take a hatchet, for instance, and go and kill everybody—mother, sister, the servants, our dog. Of course they were only fancies, and I would never do so."

"I should hope not," I smiled, splashing about.

"Then again, I'm afraid of knives, of all that's sharp and shining; it seems to me that if I were to take up a knife I should certainly kill somebody with it. Now, isn't it true—why shouldn't I plunge it into somebody, if it were sharp enough?"

"The argument is sufficient. What a queer fellow you are, brother! Just open the hot-water tap."

My brother opened the tap, let in some hot water, and continued:

"Then again, I'm afraid of crowds—of men, when many

of them gather together. When of an evening I hear a noise in the street—a loud shout, for instance—I start and believe that a massacre has begun. When several men stand together, and I can't hear what they're talking about, it seems to me that they'll suddenly cry out, fall upon each other, and blood will flow. And you know"— he bent mysteriously towards my ear—"the papers are full of murders—strange murders. It's all nonsense that there are as many brains as there are men; mankind has only one intellect, and it's beginning to get muddled. Just feel my head, how hot it is. It's on fire. And sometimes it gets cold, and everything freezes in it, grows benumbed, and changes into a terrible deadlike piece of ice. I must go mad; don't laugh, brother. I must go mad. A quarter of an hour has passed, it's time for you to get out of your bath."

"A little bit more. Just a minute."

It was so good to be sitting again in that bath and listening to the well-known voice, without reflecting upon the words, and to see all the familiar, simple and ordinary things around me: the brass, slightly green tap, the walls, with the familiar pattern, and all the photographic outfit laid out in order upon the shelves. I would take up photography again, take simple, peaceful landscapes and portraits of my son walking, laughing and playing. One could do that without legs. And I would take up my writing again—about clever books, the progress of human thought, beauty, and peace.

"Ho, ho, ho!" I roared, splashing about.

"What's the matter with you?" my brother asked, growing pale and full of fear.

"Nothing. I'm glad to be home."

He smiled at me as one smiles at a child or at one younger than oneself, although I was three years older than he, and grew thoughtful, like a grown-up person or an old man who has great, burdensome old thoughts.

"Where can one fly to?" he asked, shrugging his shoulders. "Every day, at about the same hour, the papers close the circuit, and all mankind gets a shock. This simultaneousness of feelings, tears, thoughts, sufferings and horror deprives me of all stay, and I'm like a chip of wood tossing about on the waves, or a bit of dust in a whirlwind. I'm forcibly torn away from all that's habitual, and there's one terrible moment every morning, when I seem to hang in the air over the black abyss of insanity. And I shall fall into it, I must fall into it. You don't know all, brother. You don't read the papers, and much is held back from you— you don't know all, brother."

I took all his words for rather a gloomy joke—the usual attitude towards all those who, being touched by insanity, have an inkling of the insanity of war, and gave us a warning. I considered it as a joke, as if I had forgotten for the moment, while I was splashing about in the hot water, all that I had seen over there. "Well, let them hold things back from me, but I must get out of the bath, anyway," I said lightly, and my brother smiled and called my man, and together they lifted me out of my bath and dressed me. Afterwards I had some fragrant tea, which I drank out of my cutglass tumbler, and said to myself that life was worth living even without a pair of legs; and then they wheeled me into the study up to my table and I prepared for work.

Before the war I was on the staff of a journal reviewing foreign literature, and now, disposed within my reach, lay a heap of those dear, sweet books in yellow, blue and brown covers. My joy was so great, my delight so profound, that I could not make up my mind to begin reading them, and I merely fingered the books, passing my hand caressingly over them. I felt a smile spread over my face, most probably a very silly smile, but I could not keep it back, as I contemplated admiringly the type, the vignettes, the severe, beautiful simplicity of the drawings. How much thought and sense of beauty there was in them all! How many people had to work and search, how much talent and taste were needed to bring forth that letter, for instance, so simple and elegant, so clever, harmonious and eloquent in its interlaced lines.

"And now I must set to work," I said seriously, full of respect for work.

And I took up my pen to write the heading and, like a frog tied to a string, my hand began plunging about the paper. The pen stuck into the paper, scratched it, jerked about, slipped irresistibly aside, and brought forth hideous lines, broken, crooked, devoid of all sense. And I did not cry out or move, I grew cold and still as the approaching terrible truth dawned upon me; while my hand danced over the brightly illuminated paper, and each finger shook in such hopeless, living, insane horror, as if they, those fingers, were still at the front and saw the conflagrations and blood, and heard the groans and cries of indescribable pain. They had detached themselves from me, those madly quivering fingers, they were alive, they had become ears and eyes; and, growing cold from horror, without the strength to move or cry out, I watched their wild dance over the clean, bright white page.

And all was quiet. They thought I was working, and had shut all the doors so as not to interrupt me by any sound—and I was alone in the room, deprived of the power of moving, obediently watching my shaking hands.

"It's nothing," I said aloud, and in the stillness and loneliness of the study my voice sounded hollow and nasty, like the voice of a madman. "It's nothing. I'll dictate. Why, Milton was blind when he wrote his *Paradise Regained*. I can think, and that's the chief thing, in fact it's all."

And I began inventing a long, clever phrase about the blind Milton, but the words got confused, fell away as out of a rotten printing frame, and when I came to the end of the phrase, I had forgotten the beginning. Then I tried to remember what made me begin, and why I was inventing that strange, senseless phrase about Milton, and could not.

"Paradise Regained, Paradise Regained," I repeated, and could not understand what it meant.

And then I saw that I often forgot very many things, that I had become strangely absent-minded, and confused familiar faces; that I forgot words even in a simple conversation, and sometimes, remembering a word, I could not understand its meaning. And I clearly pictured to myself my daily existence. A strange, short day, cut off like my legs, with empty mysterious spaces, long hours of unconsciousness or apathy, about which I could remember nothing.

I wanted to call my wife, but could not remember her name—and this did not surprise or frighten me. Softly I whispered:

"Wife!"

The incoherent, unusual word sounded softly and died away without bringing any response. And all was quiet. They were afraid of disturbing me at my work by any careless sound, and all was quiet—a perfect study for a savant—cosy, quiet, disposing one to meditation and creative energy. "Dear ones, how solicitous they are of me!" I thought tenderly.

And inspiration, sacred inspiration, came to me. The sun burst forth in my head, and its burning, creative rays darted over the whole world, dropping flowers and songs

—flowers and songs. And I wrote on through the whole night, feeling no exhaustion, but soaring freely on the wings of mighty, sacred inspiration. I was writing something great—something immortal—flowers and songs—flowers and songs. . . .

PART II

FRAGMENT X

. . . Happily he died last week on Friday. I say "happily," and repeat that my brother's death was a great blessing to him. A cripple with no legs, palsied, with a smitten soul, he was terrible and piteous in his senseless creative ecstasy. Ever since that night, he wrote for two months, without leaving his chair, refusing all food, weeping and scolding whenever we wheeled him away from his table even for a short time. He moved his dry pen over the paper with wonderful rapidity, throwing aside page after page, and kept on writing and writing. Sleep deserted him, and only twice did we succeed in putting him to bed for a few hours, thanks to a strong narcotic; but, later, even a narcotic was powerless to conquer his senseless creative ecstasy. At his order the curtains were kept drawn over all the windows the whole day long and the lamp was allowed to burn, giving the illusion of night, while he wrote on, smoking one cigarette after another. Apparently he was happy, and I never happened to meet any healthy person with such an inspired face—the face of a prophet or of a great poet. He became extremely emaciated, with the waxen transparency of a corpse or of an ascetic, and his hair grew quite gray; he began his senseless work a comparatively young man, but finished it an old one. Sometimes he hurried on his work, writing more than usual, and his pen would stick into the pages and break, but he never noticed it; at such times one dared not touch him, for at the slightest contact he was overtaken by fits of tears and laughter; but sometimes, very rarely, he rested blissfully from his work and talked to me affably, each time asking the same questions: Who was I, what was my name, and since when had I taken up literature.

And then he would condescendingly tell, always using the same words, what an absurd fright he had had at the thought that he had lost his memory and was incapable of work, and how splendidly he had refuted the insane supposition there and then by beginning his great immortal work about the flowers and songs.

"Of course I do not count upon being recognized by my contemporaries," he would say proudly and unassumingly at the same time, putting his trembling hand on the heap of empty sheets, "but the future—the future—will understand my idea."

He never once remembered the war or his wife and son; the mirage of his endless work engrossed his attention so undividedly that it is doubtful whether he was conscious of anything else. One could walk and talk in his presence—he noticed nothing, and not for an instant did his face lose its expression of terrible tension and inspiration. In the stillness of the night, when everybody was asleep and he alone wove untiringly the endless thread of insanity, he seemed terrible, and only his mother and I ventured to approach him. Once I tried to give him a pencil instead of his dry pen, thinking that perhaps he really wrote something, but on the paper there remained only hideous lines, broken, crooked, devoid of any sense. And he died in the night at his work. I knew my brother well, and his insanity did not come as a surprise to me;

the passionate dream of work that filled all his letters from the war and was the stay of his life after his return, had to come into inevitable collision with the impotence of his exhausted, tortured brain, and bring about the catastrophe. And I believe that I have succeeded in reconstructing with sufficient accuracy the successive feelings that brought him to the end during that fatal night. Generally speaking, all that I have written down concerning the war is founded upon the words of my dead brother, often so confused and incoherent; only a few separate episodes were burned into his brain so deeply and indelibly that I could cite the very words that he used in telling me them. I loved him, and his death weighs upon me like a stone, oppressing my brain by its senselessness. It has added one more loop to the incomprehensible that envelops my head like a web, and has drawn it tight. The whole family has left for the country on a visit to some relatives, and I am alone in the house—the house that my brother loved so. The servants have been paid off, and only the porter from the house next door comes every morning to light the fires; the rest of the time I am alone, and resemble a fly caught between two window frames,* plunging about and knocking myself against a transparent but insurmountable obstacle. And I feel, I know, that I shall never leave the house. Now, when I am alone, the war possesses me wholly and stands before me like an inscrutable mystery, like a terrible spirit, to which I can give no form. I give it all sorts of shapes—of a headless skeleton on horseback, of a shapeless shadow, born in a black thundercloud mutely enveloping the earth—but not one of them can give me an answer and extinguish the cold, constant, blunt horror that possesses me.

* In Russia the windows have double panes during the winter for the purpose of keeping out the cold.—Trans.

I do not understand war, and I must go mad, like my brother, like the hundreds of men that are sent back from there. And this does not terrify me. The loss of reason seems to me honorable, like the death of a sentry at his post. By the expectancy, the slow and infallible approach of madness, the instantaneous feeling of something enormous falling into an abyss, the unbearable pain of tortured thought, my heart has grown benumbed, it is dead, and there is no new life for it, but thought is still alive—still struggling, once mighty as Samson, but now helpless and weak as a child—and I am sorry for my poor thought. There are moments when I cannot endure the torture of those iron clasps that are compressing my brain; I feel an irrepressible longing to run out into the street, into the market place, where there are people, and cry out:

"Stop the war this instant—or else . . ."

But what "else" is there? Are there any words that can make them come to their senses? Words, in answer to which one cannot find just such other loud and lying words? Or must I fall upon my knees before them and burst into tears? But then, hundreds of thousands are making the earth resound with their weeping, but does that change anything? Or, perhaps, kill myself before them all? Kill myself! Thousands are dying every day, but does that change anything?

And when I feel my impotence, I am seized with rage —the rage of war, which I hate. Like the doctor, I long to burn down their houses with all their treasures, their wives and children; to poison the water which they drink; to raise all the killed from their graves and throw the corpses into their unclean houses onto their beds. Let them sleep with them as with their wives or mistresses!

Oh, if only I were the Devil! I would transplant all the horrors that hell exhales onto their earth. I would become the lord of all their dreams, and, when they cross their children with a smile before falling asleep, I would rise up before them a black vision. Yes, I must go mad—only let it come quicker—let it come quicker. . . .

FRAGMENT XI

. . . Prisoners, a group of trembling, terrified men. When they were led out of the train, the crowd gave a roar—the roar of an enormous, savage dog, whose chain is too short and not strong enough. The crowd gave a roar and was silent, breathing deeply, while they advanced in a compact group with their hands in their pockets, smiling with their white lips as if currying favor, and stepping out as if somebody were just about to strike them with a long stick under their knees from behind. But one of them walked at a short distance from the others, calm, serious, without a smile, and when my eyes met his black ones I saw bare, open hatred in them. I saw clearly that he despised me and thought me capable of anything; if I were to begin killing him, unarmed as he was, he would not have cried out or tried to defend or right himself—he considered me capable of anything.

I ran along together with the crowd, to meet his gaze once more, and only succeeded as they were entering a house. He went in last, letting his companions pass before him, and glanced at me once more. And then I saw such pain, such an abyss of horror and insanity in his big black eyes, as if I had looked into the most wretched soul on earth.

"Who is that with the eyes?" I asked of a soldier of the escort.

"An officer—a madman. There are many such."

"What's his name?"

"He doesn't say. And his countrymen don't know him.

A stranger they picked up. He's been saved from hanging himself once already, but what is there to be done!" And the soldier made a vague gesture and disappeared inside the doorway.

And now, this evening, I am thinking of him. He is alone amidst the enemy, who, in his opinion, are capable of doing anything with him, and his own people do not know him. He keeps silence and waits patiently for the moment when he will be able to go out of this world altogether. I do not believe that he is mad, and he is no coward; he was the only one who held himself with dignity in that group of trembling, terrified men, whom apparently he does not regard as his own people. What is he thinking about? What a depth of despair must be in the soul of that man, who, dying, does not wish to name himself. Why give his name? He has done with life and men, he has grasped their real value and notices none around him, either his own people or strangers, shout, rage and threaten though they might. I made inquiries about him. He was taken in the last terrible battle during which several tens of thousands of men lost their lives and he showed no resistance when he was being taken prisoner: he was unarmed for some reason or other, and, when the soldier, not having noticed it, struck him with his sword, he did not get up or try to act in self-defense. But the wound, unhappily for him, was a slight one.

But, maybe, he is really mad? The soldier said there were many such. . . .

FRAGMENT XII

. . . It is beginning. When I entered my brother's study yesterday evening, he was sitting in his armchair at his table heaped with books. The hallucination disappeared the moment I lighted a candle, but for a long time I could not bring myself to sit down in the armchair that he had occupied. At first it was terrifying—the empty rooms in which one was constantly hearing rustlings and crackings were the cause of this dread, but afterwards I even liked it—better he than somebody else. Nevertheless, I did not leave the armchair the whole evening; it seemed to me that if I were to get up, he would instantly sit down in my place. And I left the room very quickly without looking around. The lamps ought to have been lit in all the rooms, but was it worth while? It would have been perhaps worse if I had seen anything by lamplight—as it was, there was still room for doubt.

Today I entered with a candle, and there was nobody in the armchair. Evidently it must have been only a shadow. Again I went to the station—I go there every morning now—and saw a whole carriage full of our mad soldiers. It was not opened, but shunted onto another line, and I had time to see several faces through the windows. They were terrible, especially one. Fearfully drawn, the color of a lemon, with an open, black mouth and fixed eyes, it was so like a mask of horror that I could not tear my eyes away from it. And it stared at me, the whole of it, and was motionless, and glided past together with the moving carriage, just as motionless, without the slightest change, never transferring its gaze for an instant. If it were to appear before me this minute in that dark door, I do not believe I should be able to hold out. I made inquiries: there were twenty-two men. The infection is spreading. The papers are hushing up something, and, I believe, there is something wrong in our town too. Black, closely shut carriages have made their appearance—I counted six during one day in different parts of the town. I suppose I shall also go off in one of them one of these days.

And the papers clamor for fresh troops and more blood every day, and I am beginning to understand less and less what it all means. Yesterday I read an article full of suspicion, stating that there were many spies and traitors amongst the people, warning us to be cautious and mindful, and that the wrath of the people would not fail to find out the guilty. What guilty, and guilty of what? As I was returning from the station in the tram, I heard a strange conversation, I suppose in reference to the same article.

"They all ought to be hung without any trial," one said, looking scrutinizingly at me and all the passengers. "Traitors ought to be hung, yes."

"Without any mercy," confirmed the other. "They've been shown mercy enough!"

I jumped out of the tram. The war was making everybody shed tears, and they were crying too—why, what did it mean? A bloody mist seemed to have enveloped the earth, hiding it from our gaze, and I was beginning to think that the moment of the universal catastrophe was approaching. The red laugh that my brother saw. The madness was coming from over there, from those bloody burned-out fields, and I felt its cold breath in the air. I am a strong man and have none of those illnesses that corrupt the body, bringing in their train the corruption of the brain also, but I see the infection catching me, and half of my thoughts belong to me no longer. It is worse than the plague and its horrors. One can hide from the plague, take measures, but how can one hide from all-penetrating thought, that knows neither distances nor obstacles?

In the daytime I can still fight against it, but during the night I become, as everybody else does, the slave of my dreams—and my dreams are terrible and full of madness. . . .

FRAGMENT XIII

. . . Universal mob fights, senseless and sanguinary. The slightest provocation gives rise to the most savage club law, knives, stones, logs of wood coming into action, and it is all the same who is being killed—red blood asks to be let loose, and flows willingly and plentifully.

There were six of them, all peasants, and they were being led by three soldiers with loaded guns. In their quaint peasant's dress, simple and primitive like a savage's, with their quaint countenances, that seemed as if made of clay and adorned with felted wool instead of hair, in the streets of a rich town, under the escort of disciplined soldiers— they resembled slaves of the antique world. They were being led off to the war, and they moved along in obedience to the bayonets, as innocent and dull as cattle led to the slaughterhouse. In front walked a youth, tall, beardless, with a long goose neck, at the end of which was a motionless, little head. His whole body was bent forward like a switch, and he stared at the ground under his feet as fixedly as if his gaze penetrated into the very depths of the earth. The last in the group was a man of small stature, bearded and middle-aged; he had no desire to resist, and there was no thought in his eyes, but the earth attracted his feet, gripped them tightly, not letting them loose, and he advanced with his body thrown back, as if struggling against a strong wind. And at each step, the soldier gave him a push with the butt end of his rifle, and one leg, tearing itself from the earth, convulsively thrust itself forwards, while the other still stuck tightly. The faces of the soldiers were weary and angry, and evidently they had been marching thus for a long time; one felt they were tired and indifferent as to how they carried their guns and how they marched, keeping no step, with their feet turned in like countrymen. The senseless, lingering and silent resistance of the peasants seemed to have dimmed their disciplined brains, and they had ceased to understand where they were going and what their goal was.

"Where are you leading them to?" I asked of one of the soldiers. He started, glanced at me, and in the keen flash of his eyes I felt the bayonet as distinctly as if it were already at my breast.

"Go away!" said the soldier; "go away, or else . . ."

The middle-aged man took advantage of the moment and ran away; he ran with a light trot up to the iron railings of the boulevard and sat down on his heels, as if he were hiding. No animal would have acted to stupidly, so senselessly. But the soldier became savage. I saw him go close up to him, stoop down, and, thrusting his gun into the left hand, strike something soft and flat with the right one. And then again. A crowd was gathering. Laughter and shouts were heard. . . .

FRAGMENT XIV

. . . . In the eleventh row of stalls. Somebody's arms were pressing closely against me on my right and left-hand side, while far around me in the semidarkness motionless heads stuck out, tinged with red from the lights upon the stage. And gradually the mass of people, confined in that narrow space, filled me with horror. Everybody was silent, listening to what was being said on the stage or, perhaps, thinking out his own thoughts, but since they were many they were more audible, for all their silence, than the loud voices of the actors. They were coughing, blowing their noses, making a noise with their feet and clothes, and I could distinctly hear their deep, uneven breathing, that was heating the air. They were terrible, for each of them could become a corpse, and they all had senseless brains. In the calmness of those well-brushed heads, resting upon white, stiff collars, I felt a hurricane of madness ready to burst every second.

My hands grew cold as I thought how many and how terrible they were, and how far away I was from the entrance. They were calm, but what if I were to cry out "Fire!" And full of terror, I experienced a painfully passionate desire, of which I cannot think without my hands growing cold and moist. Who could hinder me from crying out—yes, standing up, turning around and crying out: "Fire! Save yourselves—fire!"

A convulsive wave of madness would overwhelm their still limbs. They would jump up, yelling and howling like animals; they would forget that they had wives, sisters, mothers, and would begin casting themselves about like men stricken with sudden blindness, in their madness throttling each other with their white fingers fragrant with scent. The light would be turned on, and somebody with an ashen face would appear upon the stage, shouting that all was in order and that there was no fire, and the music, trembling and halting, would begin playing something wildly merry—but they would be deaf to everything— they would be throttling, trampling, and beating the heads of the women, demolishing their ingenious, cunning head-dresses. They would tear at each other's ears, bite off each other's noses, and tear the very clothes off each other's bodies, feeling no shame, for they would be mad. Their sensitive, delicate, beautiful, adorable women would scream and writhe helplessly at their feet, clasping their knees, still believing in their generosity—while they would beat them viciously upon their beautiful, upturned faces, trying to force their way towards the entrance. For men are always murderers, and their calmness and generosity is the calmness of a well-fed animal, that knows itself out of danger.

And when, having made corpses of half their number, they would gather at the entrance in a trembling, tattered group of shamefaced animals, with a false smile upon their lips, I would go on the stage and say with a laugh:

"It has all happened because you killed my brother." Yes, I would say with a laugh: "It has all happened because you killed my brother."

I must have whispered something aloud, for my neighbor on the right-hand side moved angrily in his chair and said:

"Hush! You're interrupting."

I felt merry and wanted to play a joke. Assuming a warning, severe expression, I stooped towards him.

"What is it?" he asked suspiciously. "Why do you look at me so?"

"Hush, I implore you," I whispered with my lips. "Don't you perceive a smell of burning? There's a fire in the theatre."

He had enough power of will and good sense not to cry out. His face grew pale, his eyes starting out of their sockets and almost protruding over his cheeks, enormous as bladders, but he did not cry out. He rose quietly, and without even thanking me, walked totteringly towards the entrance, convulsively keeping back his steps. He was afraid of the others guessing about the fire and preventing him from getting away—him, the only one worthy of being saved.

I felt disgusted and left the theatre also; besides, I did not want to make known my *incognito* too soon. In the street I looked towards that part of the sky where the war was raging; everything was calm, and the night clouds, yellow from the lights of the town, were slowly and calmly drifting past.

"Perhaps it's only a dream, and there is no war?" I thought, deceived by the stillness of the sky and town.

But a boy, crying joyously, sprang out from behind a corner:

"A terrible battle. Enormous losses. Buy a list of telegrams—night telegrams!"

I read it by the light of the street lamp. Four thousand dead. In the theatre, I should say, there were not more than one thousand. And the whole way home I kept repeating: "Four thousand dead."

Now I am afraid of returning to my empty house. When I put my key into the lock and look at the dumb, flat door, I can feel all its dark, empty rooms behind it, which, however, the next minute, a man in a hat would pass through, looking furtively around him. I know the way well, but on the stairs I begin lighting match after match, until I find a candle. I never enter my brother's study, and it is locked with all that it contains. And I sleep in the dining room, where I have shifted altogether; there I feel calmer, for the air seems to have still retained the traces of talking and laughing and the merry clang of dishes. Sometimes I distinctly hear the scraping of a dry pen— and when I lie down on my bed . . .

FRAGMENT XV

. . . That absurd and terrible dream. It seemed as if the skull had been taken off my brain and, bared and unprotected, it submissively and greedily imbibed all the horrors of those bloody and senseless days. I was lying curled up, occupying only five feet of space, while my thought embraced the whole world. I saw with the eyes of all mankind, and listened with its ears; I died with the killed, sorrowed and wept with all that were wounded and left behind, and, when blood flowed out of anybody's body, I felt the pain of the wound and suffered. Even all that had not happened and was far away I saw as clearly as if it had happened and was close by, and there was no end to the sufferings of my bared brain.

Those children, those innocent little children. I saw them in the street, playing at war and chasing each other, and one of them was already crying in a high-pitched, childish voice—and something shrank within me from horror and disgust. And I went home; night came on—and in fiery dreams, resembling midnight conflagration, those innocent little children changed into a band of child murderers.

Something was ominously burning in a broad, red glare, and in the smoke there swarmed monstrous, misshapen children, with heads of grown-up murderers. They were jumping lightly and nimbly, like young goats at play, and were breathing with difficulty, like sick people. Their mouths, resembling the jaws of toads or frogs, opened widely and convulsively; behind the transparent skin of their naked bodies the red blood was coursing angrily— and they were killing each other at play. They were the most terrible of all that I had seen, for they were little and could penetrate everywhere.

I was looking out of the window and one of the little ones noticed me, smiled, and with his eyes asked me to let him in. "I want to go to you," he said.

"You'll kill me."

"I want to go to you," he said, growing suddenly pale, and began scrambling up the white wall like a rat—just like a hungry rat. He kept losing his footing, and squealed and darted about the wall with such rapidity that I could not follow his impetuous, sudden movements.

"He can crawl in under the door," I said to myself with horror, and as if he had guessed my thoughts, he grew thin and long, and waving the end of his tail rapidly, he crawled into the dark crack under the front door. But I had time to hide myself under the blanket, and heard him searching for me in the dark rooms, cautiously stepping along with his tiny, bare feet. He approached my room very slowly, stopping now and then, and at last entered it; but I did not hear any sound, either rustle or movement, for a long time, as if there was nobody near my bed. And then somebody's little hand began lifting up the edge of the coverlet, and I could feel the cold air of the room upon my face and chest. I held the blanket tightly, but it persisted in lifting itself up on all sides; and all of a sudden my feet became so cold, as if I had dipped them into water. Now they were lying unprotected in the chill darkness of the room, and he was looking at them.

In the yard, behind the house, a dog barked and was silent, and I heard the trail of the chain as the dog went into its kennel. But he still watched my naked feet and kept silence; I knew he was there by the unendurable horror that was binding me like death with a stony, sepulchral immobility. If I could have cried out, I would have awakened the whole town, the whole world, but my voice was dead within me, and I lay submissive and motionless, feeling the little cold hands moving over my body and nearing my throat.

"I can't!" I groaned. Gasping and waking up for an instant, I saw the vigilant darkness of the night, mysterious and living, and again I believe I fell asleep. . . .

"Don't fear," said my brother, sitting down upon my

bed, and the bed creaked, so heavy was he—dead. "Never fear, you see it's a dream. You only imagine that you were being strangled, while in reality you're asleep in the dark rooms, where there isn't a soul, and I'm in my study, writing. Nobody understood what I wrote about, and you derided me as one insane, but now I'll tell you the truth. I'm writing about the red laugh. Do you see it?"

Something enormous, red and bloody, was standing before me, laughing a toothless laugh.

"That's the red laugh. When the earth goes mad, it begins to laugh like that. You know, the earth has gone mad. There are no more flowers or songs on it; it's become round, smooth and red like a scalped head. Do you see it?"

"Yes, I see it. It's laughing."

"Look what its brain is like. It's red, like bloody porridge, and is muddled."

"It's crying out."

"It's in pain. It has no flowers or songs. And now—let me lie down upon you."

"You're heavy and I'm afraid."

"We, the dead, lie down on the living. Do you feel warm?"

"Yes."

"Are you comfortable?"

"I'm dying."

"Awake and cry out. Awake and cry out. I'm going away. . . ."

FRAGMENT XVI

. . . Today is the eighth day of the battle. It began last Friday, and Saturday, Sunday, Monday, Tuesday, Wednesday and Thursday have passed—and Friday has come again and is gone—and it is still going on. Both armies, hundreds of thousands of men, are standing in front of each other, never flinching, sending explosive, crashing projectiles without stopping, and every instant living men are turned into corpses. The roar and incessant vibration of the air has made the very sky shudder and gather black thunderclouds above their heads—while they continue to stand in front of each other, never flinching and still killing each other. If a man does not sleep for three nights, he becomes ill and loses his memory, but they have not slept for a whole week, and are all mad. That is why they feel no pain, do not retreat, and go on fighting until they have killed all to the last man. They say that some of the detachments came to the end of their ammunition, but still they fought on, using their fists and stones, and biting each other like dogs. If the remnants of those regiments return home, they will have canine teeth like wolves—but they will not return, they have gone mad and die, every man of them. They have gone mad. Everything is muddled in their heads, and they cease to understand anything! If they were to be turned around suddenly and sharply, they would begin firing at their own men, thinking that they were firing at the enemy.

Strange rumors—strange rumors that are told in a whisper, those repeating them turning white from horror and dreadful forebodings. Brother, brother, listen what is being told of the red laugh! They say phantom regiments have appeared, large bands of shadows, the exact copy of living men. At night, when the men forget themselves for an instant in sleep, or in the thick of the day's fight, when the bright day itself seems a phantom, they suddenly appear, firing out of phantom guns, filling the air with phantom noises; and men, living but insane men, astounded by the suddenness of the attack, fight to the death against the phantom enemy, go mad from horror, become gray in an instant and die. The phantoms disappear as suddenly as they appear, and all becomes still, while the earth is strewn with fresh mutilated bodies. Who killed them? You know, brother, who killed them. When there is a lull between two battles and the enemy is far off, suddenly in the darkness of the night there resounds a solitary, frightened shot. And all jump up and begin firing into the darkness, into the silent dumb darkness, for a long time, for whole hours. Whom do they see there? Whose terrible, silent shape, full of horror and madness appears before them? You know, brother, and I know, but men do not know yet, but they have a foreboding and ask, turning pale: "Why are there so many madmen? Before there never used to be so many."

"Before there never used to be so many madmen," they say, turning pale, trying to believe that now it is as before, and that the universal violence done to the brains of humanity would have no effect upon their weak little intellects.

"Why, men fought before and always have fought, and nothing of the sort happened. Strife is a law of nature," they say with conviction and calmness, growing pale, nevertheless, seeking for the doctor with their eyes, and calling out hurriedly: "Water, quick, a glass of water!"

They would willingly become idiots, those people, only not to feel their intellect reeling and their reason succumbing in the hopeless combat with insanity.

In those days, when men over there were constantly being turned into corpses, I could find no peace, and sought the society of my fellow men; and I heard many conversations and saw many false, smiling faces, that asserted that the war was far off and in no way concerned them. But much oftener I met naked, frank horror, hopeless, bitter tears and frenzied cries of despair, when the great Mind itself cried out of man its last prayer, its last curse, with all the intensity of its power:

"Whenever will the senseless carnage end?"

At the home of some friends, whom I had not seen for a long time, perhaps several years, I unexpectedly met a mad officer, invalided from the war. He was a school fellow of mine, but I did not recognize him: if he had lain for a year in his grave, he would have returned more like himself than he was then. His hair was gray and his face quite white, his features were but little changed—but he was always silent, and seemed to be listening to something, and this stamped upon his face a look of such formidable remoteness, such indifference to all around him, that it was fearful to talk to him. His relatives were told he went mad in the following circumstances: they were in the reserve, while the neighboring regiment was ordered to make a bayonet charge. The men rushed shouting "Hurrah" so loudly as almost to drown the noise of the cannon —and suddenly the guns ceased firing, the "Hurrah" ceased also, and a sepulchral stillness ensued: they had run up to the enemy and were charging him with their bayonets. And his reason succumbed to that stillness.

Now he is calm when people make a noise around him, talk and shout: he listens and waits; but if only there is a moment's silence, he catches hold of his head, rushes up to the wall or against the furniture, and falls down in a fit resembling epilepsy. He has many relations, and they take turns and surround him with sound, but there remain the nights, long solitary nights—but here his father, a gray-haired old man, slightly wandering in his mind too, helped. He hung the walls of his son's room with loudly ticking clocks, that constantly struck the hour at different times, and at present he is arranging a wheel resembling an in-

cessantly going rattle. None of them lose hope that he will
recover, as he is only twenty-seven, and their house is even
gay. He is dressed very cleanly—not in his uniform—great
care is taken of his appearance, and he is even handsome
with his white hair, young, thoughtful face and well-bred,
slow, tired movements.

When I was told all, I went up and kissed his hand, his
white, languid hand, which will never more be lifted for a
blow—and this did not seem to surprise anybody very
much. Only his young sister smiled at me with her eyes,
and afterwards showed me such attention that it seemed
as if I were her betrothed and she loved me more than anybody in the world. She showed me such attention that I
very nearly told her about my dark, empty rooms, in
which I was worse than alone—miserable heart, that never
loses hope. . . . And she managed it so that we remained
alone.

"How pale you are and what dark rings you have under
your eyes," she said kindly. "Are you ill? Are you grieving for your brother?"

"I'm grieving for everybody. And I don't feel well."

"I know why you kissed my brother's hand. They didn't
understand. Because he's mad, yes?"

"Yes, because he's mad."

She grew thoughtful and looked very much like her
brother, only younger.

"And will you . . ." she stopped and blushed, but did
not lower her eyes, "will you let me kiss your hand?"

I kneeled before her and said, "Bless me."

She paled slightly, drew back and whispered:

"I don't believe."

"And I also."

For an instant her hand touched my head, and the instant was gone.

"Do you know," she said, "I'm leaving for the war?"

"Go! But you won't be able to bear it."

"I don't know. But they need help, the same as you or my brother. It's not their fault. Will you remember me?"

"Yes. And you?"

"And I'll remember you too. Good-bye!"

"Good-bye for ever!"

And I grew calm and felt happier, as if I had passed through the most terrible that there is in death and madness. And yesterday, for the first time, I entered my house calmly without any fear, and opened my brother's study and sat for a long time at his table. And when in the night I suddenly awoke as if from a push, and heard the scraping of the dry pen upon the paper, I was not frightened, but thought to myself, almost with a smile:

"Work on, brother, work on! Your pen is not dry, it is steeped in living human blood. Let your paper seem empty —in its ominous emptiness it is more eloquent of war and reason than all that is written by the most clever men. Work on, brother, work on!"

And this morning I read that the battle is still raging, and again I was possessed with a dread fear and a feeling of something falling upon my brain. It is coming, it is here; it is already standing upon the threshold of these empty, light rooms. Remember, remember me, dear girl; I am going mad. Thirty thousand dead, thirty thousand dead! . . .

FRAGMENT XVII

. . . A fight is going on in the town. There are dark and dreadful rumors. . . .

FRAGMENT XVIII

This morning, looking in the newspaper through the endless list of killed, I saw a familiar name; my sister's af-
fianced husband, an officer called for military service at
the same time as my dead brother, was killed. And, an
hour later, the postman handed me a letter addressed to
my brother, and I recognized the handwriting of the de-
ceased on the envelope: the dead was writing to the dead.
But still it was better so than the dead writing to the living.
Pointed out to me was a mother who kept receiving letters
from her son for a whole month after she had read of his
terrible death in the papers: he had been torn to pieces by
a shell. He was a fond son, and each letter was full of en-
dearing and encouraging words and youthful, naïve hopes
of happiness. He was dead, but wrote of life with a fearful
accuracy every day, and the mother ceased to believe in
his death; and when a day passed without any letter, then
a second and third, and the endless silence of death ensued, she took in both hands a large old-fashioned revolver
belonging to her son, and shot herself in the breast. I believe she survived, but I am not sure; I never heard.

I looked at the envelope for a long time, and thought:
He held it in his hands, he bought it somewhere, he gave
the money to pay for it, and his servant went to fetch it
from some shop; he sealed and perhaps posted it himself.
Then the wheel of the complex machine called "post"
came into action, and the letter glided past forests, fields
and towns, passing from hand to hand, but rushing infalli-
bly towards its destination. He put on his boots that last
morning, while it went gliding on; he was killed, but it
glided on; he was thrown into a pit and covered up with
dead bodies and earth, while it still glided on past forests,

fields and towns, a living phantom in a gray, stamped envelope. And now I was holding it in my hands.

Here are the contents of the letter. It was written with a pencil on scraps of paper, and was not finished: something interfered.

> . . . *Only now do I understand the great joy of war, the ancient, primitive delight of killing man—clever, scheming, artful man, immeasurably more interesting than the most ravenous animal. To be ever taking life is as good as playing at lawn tennis with planets and stars. Poor friend, what a pity you are not with us, but are constrained to weary away your time amidst an unleavened daily existence! In the atmosphere of death you would have found all that your restless, noble heart yearned for. A bloody feast—what truth there is in this somewhat hackneyed comparison! We go about up to our knees in blood, and this red wine, as my jolly men call it in jest, makes our heads swim. To drink the blood of one's enemy is not at all such a stupid custom as we think: they knew what they were doing. . . .*

> . . . *The crows are cawing. Do you hear, the crows are cawing. From where have they all gathered? The sky is black with them; they settle down beside us, having lost all fear, and follow us everywhere; and we are always underneath them, like under a black lace sunshade or a moving tree with black leaves. One of them approached quite close to my face and wanted to peck at it: he thought, most probably, that I was dead. The crows are cawing, and this troubles me a little. From where have they all gathered? . . .*

> . . . *Yesterday we stabbed them all while they were sleeping. We approached stealthily, scarcely touching*

the ground with our feet, as if we were stalking wild ducks. We stole up to them so skilfully and cautiously that we did not touch a corpse and did not scare one single crow. We stole up like shadows, and the night hid us. I killed the sentry myself—knocked him down and strangled him with my hands, so as not to let him cry out. You understand: the slightest sound, and all would have been lost. But he did not cry out; he had no time, I believe, even to guess that he was being killed.

They were all sleeping around the smouldering fires —sleeping peacefully, as if they were at home in their beds. We hacked about us for more than an hour, and only a few had time to awake before they received their death blow. They howled and of course begged for mercy. They used their teeth. One bit off a finger on my left hand, with which I was incautiously holding his head. He bit off my finger, but I twisted his head clean off. How they did not all wake up I cannot imagine. One could hear their bones crackling and their bodies being hacked. Afterwards we stripped all naked and divided their clothes amongst ourselves. My friend, don't get angry over a joke. With your susceptibility you will say this savors of marauding, but then we are almost naked ourselves; our clothes are quite worn out. I have been wearing a woman's jacket for a long time, and re-semble more a whore than an officer of a victorious army. By the bye, you are, I believe, married, and it is not quite right for you to read such things. But . . . you understand? Women. Damn it, I am young, and thirst for love! Stop a minute: I believe it was you who was engaged to be married? It was you, was it not, who showed me the portrait of a young girl and told me she was your promised bride? . . . And there was some-thing sad, something very sad and mournful underneath

*it. And you cried. That was a long time ago, and I re-
member it but confusedly; there is no time for softness
at war. And you cried. What did you cry about? What
was there written that was as sad and mournful as a
drooping flower? And you kept crying and crying. Were
you not ashamed, an officer, to cry?*

*. . . The crows are cawing. Do you hear, friend, the
crows are cawing. What do they want?*

Further on, the pencil-written lines were effaced, and it
was impossible to decipher the signature. And strange to
say, the dead man called forth no compassion in me. I distinctly pictured to myself his face, in which all was soft and
delicate as a woman's: the color of his cheeks, the clearness and morning freshness of the eyes, the beard so bushy
and soft, that a woman could almost have adorned herself
with it. He liked books, flowers and music, feared all that
was coarse, and wrote poetry—my brother, as a critic, declared that he wrote very good poetry. And I could not
connect all that I knew and remembered of him with the
cawing crows, bloody carnage and death.

. . . The crows are cawing. . . .

And suddenly for one mad, unutterably happy instant,
I clearly saw that all was a lie and that there was no war.

There were no killed, no corpses, there was no anguish
of reeling, helpless thought. I was sleeping on my back
and seeing a dream, as I used to in my childhood: the silent, dread rooms, devastated by death and terror, and myself with a wild letter in my hand. My brother was living,
and they were all sitting at the tea table, and I could hear
the noise of the crockery.

. . . The crows are cawing. . . .

No, but it is true. Unhappy earth, it is true. The crows
are cawing. It is not the invention of an idle scribbler,

aiming at cheap effects, or of a madman, who has lost his senses. The crows are cawing. Where is my brother? He was noble-hearted and gentle and wished no one evil. Where is he? I am asking you, you cursed murderers. I am asking you, you cursed murderers, crows sitting on carrion, wretched, imbecile animals, before the whole world. For you are animals. What did you kill my brother for? If you had a face, I would give you a blow upon it, but you have no face, you have only the snout of a wild beast. You pretend that you are men, but I see claws under your gloves and the flat skull of an animal under your hat; I hear insanity rattling its rusty chains hidden beneath your clever conversation. And with all the power of my grief, my anguish and dishonored thought, I curse you, you wretched, imbecile animals!

FRAGMENT THE LAST

". . . We look to you for the regeneration of human life!" So shouted a speaker, holding on with difficulty to a small pillar, balancing himself with his arms, and waving a flag with a large inscription half hidden in its folds: "Down with the war!"

"You, who are young, you, whose lives are only just beginning, save yourselves and the future generations from this horror, from this madness. It is unbearable, our eyes are drowned with blood. The sky is falling upon us, the earth is giving way under our feet. Kind people . . ."

The crowd was buzzing enigmatically, and the voice of the speaker was drowned at times in the living, threatening noise.

". . . Suppose I'm mad, but I'm speaking the truth. My father and brother are rotting over there like carrion. Make bonfires, dig pits and destroy, bury all your arms.

Demolish all the barracks, and strip all the men of their bright clothes of madness, tear them off. One can't bear it. . . . Men are dying. . . ."

Somebody very tall gave him a blow and knocked him off the pillar; the flag rose once again and fell. I had no time to see the face of the man who struck him, as instantly everything turned into a nightmare. Everything became commotion, became agitated and howled; stones and logs of wood went flying through the air, fists, which were beating somebody, appeared above the heads. The crowd, like a living, roaring wave, lifted me up, carried me along several steps and threw me violently against a fence, then carried me back and away somewhere, and at last pressed me against a high pile of wood, that inclined forwards, threatening to fall down upon somebody's head. Something crackled and rattled against the beams in rapid, dry succession; an instant's stillness—and again a roar burst forth, enormous, open-mouthed, terrible in its overwhelming power. And then the dry, rapid crackling was heard again and somebody fell down near me, with the blood flowing out of a red hole where his eye had been. And a heavy log of wood came whirling through the air and struck me in the face, and I fell down and began crawling, I knew not where, amidst the trampling feet, and came to an open space. Then I climbed over some fences, breaking all my nails, clambered up piles of wood; one pile fell to pieces under me and I fell amidst a cataract of thumping logs; at last I succeeded with difficulty in getting out of a closed-in space—while behind me all crashed, roared, howled and crackled, trying to overtake me. A bell was ringing somewhere; something fell with a thunderous crash, as if it were a five-story house. The twilight seemed to have stopped still, keeping back the night, and the roar of shots, as if steeped in red, had driven away the darkness. Jumping over the last fence, I found myself in a narrow, crooked lane resembling a corridor, between two obscure walls, and began running. I ran for a long time, but the lane seemed to have no outlet; it was terminated by a wall, behind which piles of wood and scaffolding rose up black against the sky. And again I climbed over the mobile, shifting piles, falling into pits, where all was still and smelled of damp wood, getting out of them again into the open, not daring to look back, for I knew quite well what was happening by the dull, reddish color that tinged the black beams and made them look like murdered giants. My smashed face had stopped bleeding and felt numbed and strange, like a mask of plaster; and the pain had almost quite disappeared. I believe I fainted and lost consciousness in one of the black holes into which I had fallen, but I am not certain whether I only imagined it or it was really so, as I can remember myself only running.

I rushed about the unfamiliar streets, which had no lamps, past the black death-like houses for a long time, unable to find my way out of the dumb labyrinth. I ought to have stopped and looked around me to define the necessary direction, but it was impossible to do so: the still distant din and howl was following at my heels and gradually overtaking me; sometimes, at a sudden turning, red and enveloped in clouds of livid, curling smoke, it struck me in the face and then I turned back and rushed on until it was at my back once more. At one corner I saw a strip of light, that disappeared at my approach: it was a shop that was being hastily closed. Through a wide chink I caught a glimpse of the counter and a barrel, but suddenly all became enveloped in a silent, crouching gloom. Not far from the shop I met a man, who was running towards me, and we almost collided in the darkness, stopping short at the distance of two steps from each other. I do not know who he was: I only saw the dark blue alert outline.

"Are you coming from over there?" he asked.

"Yes."

"And where are you running to?"

"Home."

"Ah! Home?"

He was silent for an instant and suddenly flung himself upon me, trying to bring me to the ground, and his cold fingers searched hungrily for my throat, but got entangled in my clothes. I bit his hand, loosened myself from his grip, and set off running through the deserted streets, with him after me, stamping loudly with his boots, for a long time. Then he stopped—I suppose the bite hurt him.

I do not know how I hit upon my street. It had no lamps either, and the houses had not a single light, as though they were dead, and I would have run past without recognizing it, if I had not by chance lifted my eyes and seen my house. But I hesitated for some time: the house in which I had lived for so many years seemed to me unfamiliar in that strange, dead street, in which my loud breathing awakened an extraordinary and mournful echo. Then I was seized with a sudden, wild terror at the thought that I had lost my key when I had fallen, and I found it with difficulty, although it was there all the time in the pocket of my coat. And when I turned the lock, the echo repeated the sound loudly and extraordinarily, as if all the doors of those dead houses in the whole street had opened simultaneously.

At first I hid myself in the cellar, but it was terrible and dull down there, and something began darting before my eyes, so I quietly stole into the rooms. Groping my way in the dark, I locked all the doors and, after a short meditation, decided to barricade them with the furniture, but the sound of the furniture being moved was terribly loud in the empty rooms and terrified me. "I shall await death thus. It's all the same," I decided. There was some water, very warm water, in the water jug, and I washed my face in the dark and wiped it with a sheet. The parts that were smashed galled and smarted much, and I felt a desire to look at myself in the looking glass. I lit a match, and in its uneven, faint light there glanced at me from out of the darkness something so hideous and terrible that I hastily threw the match upon the floor. I believe my nose was broken. "It makes no difference now," I said to myself. "Nobody will mind."

And I felt gay. With strange grimaces and contortions of the body, as if I were impersonating a thief on the stage, I went into the larder and began searching for food. I clearly saw the unsuitableness of all my grimaces, but it pleased me so. And I ate with the same contortions, pretending that I was very hungry.

But the darkness and quiet frightened me. I opened the window into the yard and began listening. At first, probably as the traffic had ceased, all seemed to me to be quite still. And I heard no shots. But soon I clearly distinguished a distant din of voices: shouts, the crash of something falling, a laugh. The sounds grew louder perceptibly. I looked at the sky; it was livid and sweeping past rapidly. And the coach house opposite me, and the paving of the streets, and the dog's kennel, all were tinged with the same reddish glare. I called the dog softly: "Neptune!"

But nothing stirred in the kennel, and near it I distinguished in the livid light a shining piece of broken chain. The distant cries and noise of something falling kept on growing, and I shut the window.

"They're coming here!" I said to myself, and began looking for some place to hide myself. I opened the stoves, fumbled at the grate, opened the cupboards, but they would not do. I made the round of all the rooms, excepting the study, into which I did not want to look. I knew he was sitting in his armchair at his table, heaped with books, and this was unpleasant to me at that moment.

Gradually it began to appear that I was not alone: around me people were silently moving about in the darkness. They almost touched me, and once somebody's breath sent a cold thrill through the back of my head.

"Who's there?" I asked in a whisper, but nobody answered.

And when I moved on, they followed me, silent and terrible. I knew that it was only a hallucination because I was ill and apparently feverish, but I could not conquer my fear, from which I was trembling all over as if I had the ague. I felt my head: it was hot as if on fire.

"I'd better go there," I said to myself. "He's one of my own people after all."

He was sitting in his armchair at the table, heaped with books, and did not disappear as he did the last time, but remained seated. The reddish light was making its way through the red drawn curtains into the room, but did not light up anything, and he was scarcely visible. I sat down on the couch at a distance from him and waited. All was still in the room, while from outside the even, buzzing noise, the crash of something falling and disjointed cries were borne in upon us. And they were nearing us. The livid light became brighter and brighter, and I could distinguish him in his armchair—his black, iron-like profile, outlined by a narrow stripe of red.

"Brother!" I said.

But he kept silence, immobile and black, like a monument. A board cracked in the next room and suddenly everything became extraordinarily still, as it does where there are many dead. All the sounds died away and the livid light itself assumed a scarcely perceptible shade of deathliness and stillness and became motionless and a little dim. I thought the stillness was coming from my brother and told him so.

"No, it's not from me," he answered. "Look out of the window."

I pulled the curtains aside and staggered back.

"So that's what it is!" I said.

"Call my wife; she hasn't seen that yet," my brother ordered.

She was sitting in the dining room, sewing something and, seeing my face, rose obediently, stuck her needle into her work and followed me. I pulled back the curtains from all the windows, and the livid light flowed in unhindered through the broad openings, but somehow did not make the room any lighter: it was just as dark and only the big red squares of the windows burned brightly.

We went up to the window. In front of the house there stretched an even, fiery red sky, without a single cloud, star or sun, and ended at the horizon, while below it lay just such an even, dark red field, and it was covered with dead bodies. All the corpses were naked and lay with their legs towards us, so that we could see only their feet and triangular heads. And all was still; apparently they were all dead, and there were no wounded left behind in that endless field.

"Their number is growing," my brother said.

He was standing at the window also, and all were there: my mother, sister and everybody that lived in the house. I could not distinguish their faces, and could recognize them only by their voices.

"It only seems so," my sister said.

"No, it's true. Just look."

And, truly, there seemed to be more bodies. We looked attentively for the reason and found it: at the side of a corpse, where there was a free space, a fresh corpse suddenly appeared; apparently the earth was throwing them up. And all the unoccupied spaces filled rapidly, and the earth grew lighter from the light pink bodies, which were lying side by side with their feet towards us. And the room grew lighter, filled with a pale pink dead light.

"Look, there's not enough room for them," my brother said.

And my mother answered:

"There's one here already."

We looked around: behind us on the floor lay a naked, light pink body with its head thrown back. And instantly at its side there appeared a second, and a third. And the earth threw them up one after the other, and soon the orderly rows of light pink dead bodies filled all the rooms.

"They're in the nursery, too," the nurse said. "I saw them."

"We must go away," my sister said.

"But we can't pass," my brother said.

"Look!"

And sure enough, they were lying close together, arm to arm, and their naked feet were touching us. And suddenly they stirred and swayed and rose up in the same orderly rows: the earth was throwing up new bodies, and they were lifting the first ones upwards.

"They'll smother us!" I said. "Let's save ourselves through the window."

"We can't!" cried my brother. "We can't! Look what's there!"

Behind the window, in a livid, motionless light stood the Red Laugh.

A SELECT LIST OF
VINTAGE RUSSIAN LIBRARY